THE BLOOD DIVIDE

A. A. Dhand

PENGUIN BOOKS

TRANSWORLD PUBLISHERS
Penguin Random House, One Embassy Gardens,
8 Viaduct Gardens, London SW11 7BW
www.penguin.co.uk

Transworld is part of the Penguin Random House group of companies
whose addresses can be found at global.penguinrandomhouse.com

Penguin
Random House
UK

First published in Great Britain in 2021 by Bantam Press
an imprint of Transworld Publishers
Penguin paperback edition published 2022

A CIP catalogue record for this book
is available from the British Library.

ISBN 9780552176545

Typeset in Aldus by Jouve (UK), Milton Keynes.
Printed and bound in Great Britain by Clays Ltd, Elcograf S.p.A.

The authorized representative in the EEA is Penguin Random House Ireland,
Morrison Chambers, 32 Nassau Street, Dublin D02 YH68.

Penguin Random House is committed to a sustainable future
for our business, our readers and our planet. This book is made
from Forest Stewardship Council® certified paper.

In loving memory of my mother, Veena Dhand

PROLOGUE

1947, Punjab, India

'HURRY!' WHISPERED RANI, PULLING at Amrita's arm. 'They're coming!'

Amrita was shaking, terrified that the moment they had all been dreading had arrived. Rani kept her hand clasped firmly around her best friend's wrist, taking care not to drop Sandeep, her six-month-old baby cradled in her other arm.

The crowd of women around them moved quickly, some glancing over their shoulders, their eyes wide with terror. Rani heard more urgent whispers.

'They're coming!'

Amrita began to sob but Rani had no words to console her, to dispel her deepest fears. Sandeep caught on to the feverish atmosphere and began to cry. Usually he only cried when he was hungry. Now it was because he could sense the danger.

They needed to get to the village hall to have the best chance of surviving the night.

The sun was setting now but the thick heat was taking its toll. Two women in front of Rani collapsed from dehydration. None of them had been given any warning – no time to prepare or make an escape.

Sweat dripped from Rani's temple on to Sandeep's face. She'd latched him quickly to her nipple and as he sucked what little energy she had, she wiped the perspiration from his cheeks and tried not to break down. Her little man. So beautiful. So perfect. She wished her husband was here. She looked up to the heavens.

'Protect us,' she whispered.

Her feet dragged along the dusty footpath, baked hard and unforgiving by the blistering sun. The local wells had dried up weeks ago. Water was rationed.

Once inside the hall she kept her arm firmly around Amrita, to make sure they weren't separated. The hall was swollen with women. It had reached capacity some time ago, yet still they crammed inside. Amrita was only eighteen, a year younger than Rani; they had their whole lives ahead of them.

Women fanned the hot air, trying desperately to cool their young and stop themselves from passing out. Losing the battle, Amrita slumped to the ground. Rani could only watch, helpless, fighting to stay upright herself. She looked around for some water but there was none.

With the doors sealed behind them, the hundred or so women of the village sat roasting in the dark and airless room. Nervous, terrified chatter broke out.

'They are coming! They are here!'

A pungent smell of sweat suffocated the room. Sandeep lay still in Rani's arms. She wasn't sure if he was sleeping or—

She pushed the thought from her mind. She was terrified he wouldn't last the night boxed in this heat. But none of them were certain of survival.

And there were things far worse than the heat.

2

Rani glanced at the exit doors. A woman had stood up and was fighting to escape, to take her chances outside where the men of the village were preparing to defend their land.

The two men at the doors pushed her to the floor. She stood to come at them again. This time they drew their swords and the woman backed away, slumping her shoulders in defeat.

Tanveer Singh, the eldest leader of the village and her father-in-law, appeared on stage at the front of the hall. A babble of distress swept the room. Rani stared at him, searching his face for a truth she didn't want to accept.

Tanveer beckoned his daughter to join him on stage. She was only eleven. A small, meek girl with long black hair. Her grey Punjabi suit was too big and the hems of the trousers trailed along the floor as she shuffled towards her father. He muttered something in her ear and she fell to her knees, head bowed. He looked up, his face ashen.

'They are here,' he said.

The women began to cry. Softly though, as if they knew their fate had been decided when the doors had been sealed. This blind acceptance of what was about to happen upset Rani the most. She looked down at her little man, innocent and beautiful, lost in his last dream.

At the front of the hall, Tanveer removed his *kirpan*, the sword he carried as a devout Sikh, from his waist. He raised it high above his daughter's head. Few women had the courage to watch.

Most kept their eyes rooted to the floor.

Seconds later, the screaming began.

PART ONE

ONE

Bradford, August 2019

THE BLURRY VISION OF Jack Baxi's dead wife, Kirin, her face streaked with tears, loomed at him from the television screen. It wasn't an unusual sight. Jack passed out most evenings watching footage of his wedding day almost thirty years ago.

Kirin's father had ended his speech with a line Jack could never forget.

It was written this way. This union was forged in blood decades ago . . .

The footage always froze at this point. It was an apt place for the tape to end. It mirrored the last time he had seen his wife alive – crying.

He pointed at the television, a near-empty bottle of Chivas Regal in his hand.

'You should have bloody stayed with them,' he said.

He swigged the last drops of whisky from the bottle and tossed it aside.

The sound came again; the one that had roused him. A powerful banging from downstairs. *Was someone inside his corner shop?*

The phone started to ring. Who would be calling him at two in the morning? In fact, who the hell ever called Jack?

Unless it was about the cellar.

No. They wouldn't call him on the landline. Was it an emergency? The sobering thought stirred him into action. He picked up the cordless handset lying next to him.

'Yes?' he said.

'Jatinder Baxi?'

He was caught off-guard. It had been a long time since anyone had called him by his real name. Shit; his run-down corner shop had been servicing the local estate for twenty years now, and he bet none of them knew he was called 'Jatinder'. The sign outside stated 'Proprietor: J. Baxi'.

'Who wants to know?' he replied.

'This is Detective Constable Kuldeep Singh. I'm at your back door. Would you open it, please?'

'Police?'

'Yes. Mr Baxi, it's raining heavily out here so if you could come quickly, I would appreciate it.'

Click.

Jack stared at the receiver. His heart was pounding. The alcohol-induced fog swilling around his brain momentarily cleared.

Police. Not uniform, but CID.

The cellar must have been compromised.

He had always feared that this day would come.

You've got careless, Jack. You must have. They know. And now it's over.

Jack clambered to his feet. The living room came hazily into focus.

You're drunk. In no state to entertain the police. You've got to stall.

He crept over to the window and peered cautiously between the curtains on to the forecourt. There were no cars. Detective Singh must have parked around the back.

But what if he's not a detective? He had read many stories in the Bradford *Telegraph and Argus* about criminals knocking on corner-shopkeepers' doors late at night and pretending to be the police.

Shit. What to do?

Jack wasn't used to being frightened but his hands were shaking and it wasn't the alcohol.

If it's not the police, then it's someone who knows about the cellar. And if that's the case, this is going to get messy.

He needed to make a decision. Nervous, Jack ran his hands over his face, thick stubble grating against his fingertips.

'I'm not falling for this,' he whispered. 'CID my ass.'

The phone rang again.

Jack's heart started hammering in his chest.

Five rings. Eight.

He walked over to it and picked up.

'Yes?' he snapped.

'Mr Baxi, I'd sure appreciate you opening this door.'

'That is not going to happen.'

'Sir, I'm sorry to have to disturb you at this hour but—'

'How do I know you're a real police officer? I am not opening my door at two a.m. to a stranger. I don't care who you say you are.'

'I understand, sir. You are quite right. If you have a pen handy I can give you the number of the station and they will confirm my ID. That should put your mind at rest.'

Jack had little comeback. Beads of sweat trickled down his face.

'How do I know you're not giving me a false number and this is an elaborate plan to rob my store?'

'If you feel more comfortable you can dial 999 and ask to be put through to Bradford Central Despatch.'

'I'll do that,' replied Jack and hung up.

It was the police. No doubt about it. Jack didn't need to check. Singh's voice had carried an almost arrogant confidence.

But Jack had bought some time. To do what with, he wasn't yet sure.

Jack sat down on the ageing leather couch. He pulled on his shabby white trainers and turned off the television. The room was plunged into darkness. Jack found it comforting. He often drank alone in the dark, imagining how his life might have turned out if he hadn't gone to jail all those years before.

He trudged down the stairs and opened the door into his corner shop. The red glow from the Coca-Cola sign on the fridge provided sparse illumination.

Jack stood for a moment. Was this the end of Baxi Stores?

I won't go back to prison. Not after all this time.

He could run. He had been planning his getaway for years. But he'd never imagined it would end like this. Fleeing in the middle of the night; abandoning his shop. It might be small compared to what he'd once owned but it was all he had left. For almost twenty years he had laboured inside it, servicing – or 'fleecing', his punters might have said – the Elmswood estate of Bradford.

While the estate was notoriously popular with the police, Jack kept a low profile. The intimidating council tower-blocks surrounding his store were constantly visited by the authorities. Dawn raids, late-night busts, the odd murder: no one batted an eyelid in Elmswood. Jack had the estate's respect because he'd been there; he'd served his time. *He belonged.*

He made his way behind the counter and glanced at the clock above the cigarette rack: 02.32.

Thoughts of escaping from the side door where deliveries were unloaded flickered through his mind.

It had to be about the cellar.

Jack rested his hands on the counter, a place he stood behind for fourteen hours every day, and tried to think.

The phone rang again.

He glared at the handset and walked off into the storeroom to his left. Grabbing his trusted baseball bat, he placed it by the back door, out of sight. It had seen off more than its fair share of troublemakers.

Jack caught sight of himself in a mirror. Christ, he looked older than fifty – bloodshot eyes, greying hair. He coughed and sniffed the alcohol on his breath.

That wouldn't do.

He hurried back into his store, grabbed a bottle of cheap mouthwash, rinsed his mouth with it then swallowed.

Returning to the back door, Jack unlocked it and hit the switch to open the external shutter, the joints in the steel creaking noisily as it rattled upwards.

The phone stopped ringing.

Jack took several deep breaths then opened the door.

TWO

DETECTIVE KULDEEP SINGH SEEMED to fill the stockroom. He looked roughly the same age as Jack and was about the same height, six foot two, but the dark blue turban on his head made him appear taller. Singh was much stockier than Jack, though. He looked like he would have been right at home on a farm, throwing around bales of hay. He had a firm handshake and his hands were coarse like sandpaper. They'd definitely experienced more hard work than your regular CID suit.

'It really is very bad out there,' said Detective Singh, shaking water from his raincoat all over the floor. He propped his umbrella against the wall and a pool of water formed at its base. He had an accent Jack knew well. Like Jack, Detective Singh must have lived in England for years but he hadn't been born here. He over-enunciated his words. Jack imagined that when Detective Singh was speaking lazily, his 'V's came out as 'W's. It was a common flaw with Asians who hadn't spoken English as their primary language.

'Would you like to see my ID?'

'Naturally.'

Singh handed it to him. Jack gave it a once-over.

'What's this about?' said Jack, passing the card back. 'I'm a little pissed off at being woken up at two a.m. when I've got a store to open at five.'

Singh nodded. 'I can understand that, Mr Baxi.'

He pronounced Jack's surname authentically; it came from his lips as 'Baxshi'.

'It's Jack.'

Singh reached into his pocket and pulled out a pen and a note-pad. Jack saw the gleam of a thick gold *kara*, a bangle that identified one's affiliation to Sikhism.

Jack didn't wear his any more. His father had been a staunch advocate of religion but he had died during a vacation to India. Jack had barely been a teenager and quickly lost interest without his father's strict tutelage. He still wore a silver pendant of the *khanda* – the Sikh symbol of faith – round his neck. His father had given it to him before taking the ill-fated trip. It was the one piece of nostalgia he allowed himself.

Water continued to drip from Singh's raincoat on to the floor. The dim glow from the fluorescent tube in the ceiling was poor.

'What's this about?' Jack repeated, impatiently.

'Sir, I am—'

'I told you already; it's Jack.'

'These Goray always give us some form of nickname, no?'

Jack didn't reply. He had no desire to make small-talk with CID. The term 'Goray' was Indian slang for Westerners. Some of Jack's locals referred to themselves with it.

If you keep ripping us Goray off, Jack, we ain't gonna come to your store no more!

'Jack, I'm investigating a serious assault, maybe even the attempted murder of a sixty-seven-year-old man that took place late last night.'

'Attempted murder?'

Jack relaxed a little, which seemed strange considering the revelation, but the further this was from the subject of his cellar, the better. He knew nothing about any assault.

'Yes, the victim was found in Peel Park. I think you might know him. Benedict Cave?'

The name meant nothing to Jack. He shook his head.

'Never heard of him.'

Singh was staring at Jack, scrutinizing him. There was a silence of no more than ten seconds but it was uncomfortable enough for Jack to break it.

'Seriously, I don't know him,' he said slowly and rather more forcefully than he intended.

'Are you sure, Jack?'

'Yes. Could this really not have waited till morning?'

Singh continued to stare at him as he pulled an iPhone from his pocket.

'This is his picture.'

Jack ignored him.

'I told you I don't know anyone called Benedict Cave.'

'Just look at the picture,' said Singh, with the hint of arrogance that a CID suit brought.

Jack glanced at the screen. He saw the battered face of an old man, blood streaking his white hair.

'Like I said, I don't know him. Never seen him before.'

Singh put his phone, pen and notebook away but didn't move to leave.

'Is that all?'

Singh didn't respond.

Jack moved past him to get the door. Singh's powerful grip on his arm stopped him. Singh's breath was warm on his ear: 'Just another couple of questions and I'll be on my way.'

There was something sinister about his grip. Aggressive almost.

'The thing is, Jack, we found something on this man that connects you to him.'

'That's impossible.'

Singh pulled out a torn piece of paper from his pocket, and handed it over.

Looking at it, what little colour there was on Jack's face disappeared.

How could this be?

Singh looked triumphant. 'Why would a man you don't know have a piece of paper in his pocket with your name, address and telephone number on it?'

'I don't know.'

'There's more,' replied Singh. 'We found a mobile phone on this man and he called you today at two p.m.'

'That's impossible!' snapped Jack, feeling a conspiracy afoot. A thought suddenly needled him. The CID was holding evidence found on the victim of a heavy assault. Which now had his prints all over it. Was this normal protocol?

Singh's gaze raked over Jack's face.

'I . . . I . . . close my store from one till three and have a sleep. I never took that call.' Jack's voice wasn't helping. It was gift-wrapped in ambiguity.

Singh took out his phone again. He tapped a few buttons and then put it back in his pocket.

'Look, Detective, there must be some sort of mistake.'

'There is no mistake,' he replied. 'Tell me how you know Benedict Cave.'

'I don't. I promise you.'

Jack sounded like he was pleading and his ego didn't like it. He hated the police. Now they were here with ludicrous claims, trying to entrap him.

This had to be about the cellar.

There was a knock at the door.

'My colleagues,' said Singh and turned to open it before Jack could object.

Two Asian men in dark raincoats marched into the room, dragging with them a tiny-framed Asian woman in a dark head-scarf. Jack had never seen her before either. She'd been gagged and tears were streaming down her face. The men shoved her to the floor, where she let out an exhausted whimper.

'What the hell is going on?' shouted Jack.

Singh stepped forwards. Jack never saw the stun gun, just felt a sharp agonizing pulse in his neck.

He didn't even have time to scream.

THREE

WHEN JACK CAME ROUND, he was hunched on the floor in his storeroom, tape over his mouth and his hands bound behind his back.

The young woman sat slumped on the other side of the room. She must have been about twenty. Her face was marked with purple bruises, and her large oval-shaped green eyes looked exhausted. Or maybe drugged? Either way, her whole body was shaking.

The two thugs stood on either side of Jack. Both their faces were hidden in the shadows but Jack made out the silhouette of their turbans. Asian hit-squad, he thought. Detective Singh was standing behind the girl. The son of a bitch fixed Jack with the same piercing gaze he'd given him earlier before he tasered him. Jack tried to speak but could only grunt.

'Let me tell you how this is going to work,' said Singh calmly. 'I'm going to remove the tape. Make one sound, and my colleagues will silence you.'

Jack felt the barrel of a gun pressed against his temple.

'Do you understand?' asked Singh.

Jack nodded.

'I asked before how you knew Benedict Cave. I want an answer.'

The tape was ripped from Jack's mouth. He winced and spilled drool down his chin.

'I told you,' he said, panting, 'I don't know the guy – never seen him before in my life.'

There was a scuffle and his arms were grabbed from behind. He cried out at the unmistakable sound of a knife being unsheathed.

'No,' snapped Singh. 'We cannot mark him like that.'

Jack felt his bladder heavy and urgent. He'd encountered his fair share of dire situations but this was easily the worst. *It had to have something to do with his cellar. Had to.* But why hadn't they mentioned it yet?

'I don't believe you,' said Singh. He rested his hands on the girl's shoulders, massaging them gently. She recoiled from his touch.

Singh brought his lips to the girl's ear, his eyes burning with an anger Jack didn't understand. 'Let's find out what you both know,' he hissed.

The first time they dunked his head in the bathtub of water, Jack pissed himself. He'd been blindfolded and it amplified the panic. He wasn't sure how long he was under, but just as his lungs felt ready to collapse, his head was pulled free and he was flung savagely across the room. He banged his head against the wall so hard it cracked the tiles.

Air rushed into his lungs, but more slowly than he needed. He choked, too weak to yell for help. Jack tried desperately to find some connection to Benedict Cave. Anything to buy him some time. Feeling helpless and alone, he started to cry; deep racking sobs.

'Please,' he spat, 'I honestly don't know anything. I'm just a shopkeeper!'

They grabbed him roughly under the arms and forced him back to the tub. Jack faintly registered the sound of the girl screaming from another room before his head was pushed once more underwater.

Jack was lying on the bathroom floor, the blindfold discarded next to him. His mouth burned with the bitter taste of vomit. Voices were whispering outside the room. He moved his head weakly to the side and saw the girl lying next to him. Her headscarf had slipped from her hair and was dangling across her neck.

Was she dead?

Jack looked away. He didn't want to know. If she was dead, then he was next. His mouth was tightly gagged and he had little energy. He wondered what time it was and if the paper boys who did the early morning rounds might be arriving soon and could raise the alarm.

The bathroom doorway filled with Singh's frame. He stared blankly at Jack, arms folded. He sighed, then looked at the girl.

'I believe you,' he said. 'Both of you.'

Jack was relieved. Finally – the first bit of good news all night.

'But we cannot take any chances,' added Singh and disappeared from sight.

Any hope Jack had started to feel was extinguished. He raised his head off the floor, trying to hear the voices outside. He caught the odd word but nothing that made sense.

'Cigarettes.'

'Bed.'

'Natural.'

'I'm on duty till eight; I'll attend.'

Money – he had lots of money stashed away.

He tried to make some noise. His legs found strength at the

thought of bribing Singh and his men. He lifted them off the floor and kicked the door shut.

It was opened just as quickly and Singh came towards him, stun gun in hand. The last thing Jack remembered before the taser hit him was the smell of Singh's mint-flavoured chewing gum.

Smoke. Heat. And among those sensations, the feeling of drowning. A banging against his head.

Pain.

So much pain.

Another powerful bang against his scalp.

And a woman's voice. His wife's? Had he been dreaming it all?

'Please!' screamed the voice. 'Wake up!'

Jack tried to open his eyes but they were leaden as if they had been taped shut.

'What?' he mumbled. The next slap was so forceful his head rolled a full 90 degrees across the pillow.

Jack cursed, forcing his eyes open. The girl was on her knees in front of him, her headscarf wrapped around her nose and mouth. The air in the bedroom was thick with smoke wafting under the door. The heat of a fire raging through the building was unmistakable.

'Quick!' yelled the girl. 'You have to get up.'

Jack tried to raise his head from the pillow but an agonizing pain shot through his neck. He recalled the taser-gun and the water in the bathtub.

'Are they gone?' he asked, stifling a cough.

The girl nodded. 'Please!' she shouted, crying hysterically. 'I don't want to die.'

Jack gritted his teeth and, gripping the sides of the mattress, lifted his body off the bed. Smoke was filling the room with alarming speed. He blinked, and noticed the gag discarded next to him. He guessed Singh hadn't wanted it found in his mouth, in case it raised questions. He checked his pocket for his phone – still there.

The girl made for the window. Jack grabbed her before she got there.

'No,' he said, pulling her away.

She turned angrily towards him. 'What are you doing?'

'The windows have bars across them and they might be out there watching. We can't let them know we're trying to get free.' Jack hurried to the corner of the room, wrenched open his wardrobe and removed some towels.

There was a sink next to it. Jack started soaking the towels under the tap. He heard the girl coughing behind him.

'Stay low,' he said, 'there's more air.' He threw her a water-logged towel. 'Wring this out and wrap it around your head.'

He grabbed her hand, pulling her towards the door. He feared opening it in case there was a wall of flames behind it; it was their only way out but he didn't fancy death by incineration.

'When I open this, stay against this wall. If it's clear, we do not stop under any circumstances. Do you understand?'

She nodded.

'What's your name?'

'Aisha,' she shouted.

'I'm Jack. Don't let go of my hand. Whatever happens.'

'I won't,' she replied. 'But where are we going?'

'To the cellar,' replied Jack and opened the door.

FOUR

SINGH WALKED BRISKLY AWAY from the parade of shops, head down, hands in his pockets. The rain that had lashed the city for nine days had finally stopped and would be no saviour once Baxi's store ignited.

Although it was barely above freezing, Singh was sweating. It had been some years since the organization had called for his services. And what a task he had been landed with – Jatinder Baxi. Everyone had thought that particular situation was long ago settled.

Singh glanced around nervously as he approached his Range Rover. You didn't stray into this part of Bradford unless you had to – boarded-up houses and frequent sightings of police tape made sure only a particular type of clientele lived here. Singh worried the local drug dealers might have been awake at this hour but the Elmswood estate was deserted.

His men had cut across the football field behind Baxi's store; from there they would watch the back entrance. As soon as the shop was alight, Singh would leave.

The shop was an old relic with a dimly lit orange lamp over the sign reading *Baxi Stores*. The front had three large paned windows, behind which were internal shutters, meaning the fire would be well concealed. By the time the fire brigade arrived, there would be little evidence left. Singh had started the fire in the hallway using a bottle of lighter fluid he'd taken from the shop – a nice touch, he thought.

Spirals of smoke started to rise from the slate roof of the building, and the odd spark flared against the night sky. Singh breathed a sigh of relief. It wouldn't be long; the acceleration was always breath-taking.

'*Kismet,*' whispered Singh – the Indian word for fate.

Flames erupted through the roof at last.

There was an almighty crack as the shop windows exploded. Singh had been waiting for this – the off-licence section of the store had caught alight, a catalyst to the growing inferno.

Singh started the car and quickly pulled away without turning his headlights on. He dialled the last caller on his mobile phone and waited for the international dial tone.

'Yes?' said the familiar voice, quivering slightly with age.

'Sahib,' said Singh humbly, 'forgive me, did I wake you?'

'On a night like tonight, who will find sleep? Tell me, is it done?'

Flames exploding into the night sky in Singh's rear-view mirror lit up the horizon.

'Yes, Sahib, it is done.'

FIVE

THE BLAST OF HEAT that assaulted Jack when he opened the bedroom door was terrifying.

He sprang across the landing, clinging to Aisha's hand, and started down the stairs. Scalding flames licked wildly towards them and smoke stung his eyes like acid. The caustic heat was suffocating and he started to panic, realizing that no matter where he turned, there was no escape. Only a few paces down the staircase, he saw the bottom half had collapsed.

Quickly he turned round and pushed Aisha back up the steps. She resisted for a moment, uncertain of where to go. Jack moved past her and marched her through the living room towards the spare bedroom. It was the furthest part of the house from the blaze.

The heat seemed to chase them as though they were leaving a trail of petroleum.

There was a small alcove in the bedroom. Jack cursed at the pile of old suitcases sitting there. Beneath them lay a hatch that concealed a long-disused second staircase.

Jack hurled the suitcases across the room, working like a man possessed. As he threw the last one, he saw Aisha slump to the floor.

With the alcove clear, Jack grabbed the corner of the carpet. It took three frantic attempts to rip it back. At last, the hidden handle was revealed and he pulled the hatch open, spurred on at seeing the steps intact. They led down into the main stockroom from where they would be able to access the cellar.

Jack grabbed Aisha's shoulders. He shook her, gently at first, and, when she didn't respond, harder until she came round. Shining the torch from his phone down the steps, he yelled for her to get moving. Jack went immediately after her, pulling the hatch closed to seal off their escape route.

At the foot of the stairs, Aisha crumpled against a wall of beer crates that were stopping them from going any farther.

'Are you OK?' he said, irate at his own stupidity at blocking their escape route.

She coughed and said, 'I need a minute.'

With the light from his phone, Jack was relieved to see that the storeroom seemed unaffected so far. It had a sturdy fire door, the only one in the building. Jack pushed at the crates of beer – around twenty, he reckoned, but they didn't budge. There was a gap between the top one and the ceiling; enough for a small child to squeeze through.

Jack turned towards Aisha, praying she was up to what he needed her to do.

'Aisha, I need you to climb on top of these crates – through the gap. On the other side, there's a drop of about two metres. It's our only chance to get out of here.'

'I don't—'

'You'll need to jump but be careful. Once you're on the ground, start shifting these crates as fast as you can.'

'But how will I—'

'There's no time for questions. I promise you, do this and we'll get out of here. Or would you rather burn alive where we're standing?'

The fear and urgency in his voice spurred her into action. Still weak, she moved past him and groped her way to the top of the crates.

Jack helped her, knowing time was critical. The sound of his shop disintegrating behind them was unmistakable. Aisha disappeared from sight.

Aisha Iqbal was alive and she *would not* die in this place. After the first stack of crates there was a stepped drop. The second row wasn't as high. She clambered down to it and grimaced as she felt wooden splinters pierce the back of her legs.

Jack was right – it was a long way down to the floor. The glow from under the fire door to her left provided a glimmer of light, at least.

She would have to go head first and use her hands to break the fall.

Aisha was terrified. This whole night had happened to the wrong girl. She had never done anything wrong. How could she have got mixed up in whatever this was?

With her arms outstretched, Aisha tried to use the friction of the plastic covers on the crates of beer to crawl down them. It worked until halfway when her bodyweight sent her crashing to the floor. She took the fall on her hands, tucking her head down to do a forward roll but her body fell to the right as she toppled to the ground.

Jack's voice was immediate. 'Aisha? Are you all right?'

She got to her feet, her attention focused by the smoke filtering into the storeroom and the building collapsing around them.

Adrenaline seemed to give her strength and Aisha began lifting crates of beer from the stack and throwing them to one side.

She'd managed five when she felt Jack's hands on her shoulders. She flinched – tripping backwards over a crate and crashing into the wall.

Jack shuffled through the gap she'd created, dropping his phone in the process. It clattered to the floor and the torchlight went out. He pushed himself down the row of crates, landing heavily on the floor. He leapt up, taking Aisha's hand and pulling her towards him.

'Careful, there's beer all over the floor. Keep behind me.'

At the end of the room was another tiny storage space leading to what appeared to be an external door. Jack tried the light switch but it didn't work.

Aisha was coughing violently again. The fire door would not last much longer. Smoke was pouring in.

Jack fell to his knees. He felt as if his tank had drained to empty.

'Get on the floor. Keep your head low,' he said to her.

He felt around the floor for the break in the concrete, and then, like he did countless times each month, opened the tiny hatch to reveal a cast-iron ring. Jack pulled at it, raising a slab that gave them access to the cellar. He ushered Aisha towards it. She hesitated.

'It leads into the cellars. Ladder on the left. Hurry,' he whispered, fighting off the urge to just push her down it. She moved slowly.

Jack had planned for situations where he might be forced to escape into his cellar – a raid by the police or falling foul of the people he did business with.

He slipped down the ladder after her and pulled the slab closed behind him.

SIX

THE DARKNESS WAS ABSOLUTE, the only sound that of Aisha coughing. Jack wasn't so bad. He wondered whether a lifetime of smoking had afforded him some level of tolerance.

'Hey, kid, you OK?' he said, scrambling to his feet.

'I'm here,' she said weakly.

'Are you hurt?'

'I think I might be bleeding. A wound on my thigh.'

Jack edged his way towards her voice. 'Are you sure?'

'As sure as a medical student can be. I'm either bleeding or I've wet myself down one leg only.'

Aisha burst into another choking fit.

Jack felt around for her and helped her to her feet.

'It's pitch black here. Isn't there a light?'

'Not in this part, and my phone's knackered from the fall. It's not far to the cellars. This passageway runs the length of the shops on this parade. I own them all, so I'm the only one with access.'

'Can you get us there safely without being able to see any-thing?'

Jack turned his face away from her as a bout of coughing took his breath away.

'Yes. Just follow me. Don't let go of my hand,' he said, struggling to breathe.

The unmistakable sound of rats scurrying around them stopped her dead. 'Oh God,' she whispered.

Jack pulled her a little harder. 'Perspective,' he replied.

'It's pitch black and there are rats. My perspective is fine,' she hissed.

'The quicker you walk, the quicker you will be free of them. Standing like a statue will only bring them right to you.'

That got Aisha moving.

'Careful, there's a small step here,' said Jack, slowing down.

'Let's hope the light in your cellar works,' replied Aisha.

Jack stopped and felt along the wall to his left. 'Let go of my hand.'

'What? Why?' said Aisha, tightening her grip on him.

'I'm right here – I just need to feel for the door.'

Reluctantly, Aisha let go. 'Keep talking,' she said, her voice pleading.

'I own all of the shops above us. There's mine, which used to be two shops, which is why that second staircase was there. Never been so glad not to have taken it out completely.'

Where was the damn door? Jack kept tracing his hand along the wall.

'I sort of acquired the units over the years. I lease them out now but I kept the cellars for myself. It means only I have access down here. Decent storage,' he added, filling the silence as best he could. 'Ahhh – I found the door. OK, this is going to be a bit tricky. It's got three combination locks on it.'

Jack felt for the first one and slowly punched in the code.

'Jack?' whispered Aisha.

'I'm here, just punching in the code. C-X-Y-2001. That's the year I bought my shop. Two more to go.'

'Those men – who attacked us. Do you know them?'

Jack paused. 'No. You?'

'I've never seen them before.'

Jack opened the second lock.

'One more to go,' he said, feeling for it, two-thirds of the way down the sturdy wooden door. He punched in the code, relieved when the door opened. 'We're in. Take my hand.'

'Got it,' she said, finding it in the darkness and moving slowly towards him.

Jack found the light switch on the inner wall.

They shielded their eyes as hostile rays of bright yellow brought the room to life. Jack closed the door behind him as they shuffled inside.

Aisha's hand was splayed across her face, allowing her eyes to adjust to the light. She kept them focused on the floor, then slowly raised her gaze.

'Oh my God,' she whispered. 'What is this place?'

SEVEN

DETECTIVE SINGH WAS INSIDE the Guru Gobind Singh temple on Leeds Road. Dawn was yet to break and after leaving Baxi's shop he had returned home, showered and then arrived here, alone.

He was sitting on the floor, cross-legged, eyes closed, feeling uneasy. Singh had derived no pleasure from what had taken place. In fact, a deep anxiety was building within him. His stomach felt tight and he could hear his heart beating.

How was it that something put into place decades ago had now returned in the most dramatic of circumstances?

He wasn't used to feeling this kind of apprehension and it irritated him.

Baxi's death was just the beginning.

If they weren't able to break Benedict Cave and get the information they needed, what then? How would they ever resolve what had come to pass and ask forgiveness for getting it so, so wrong?

Singh opened his eyes and stared across the wide, expansive floor space. He thought back to his childhood when he had visited this temple every Sunday with Jatinder Baxi, not that the stupid man had remembered him. Singh had smelled the alcohol on his breath, forbidden in Sikhism – not that a selfish type like Baxi cared about that.

Singh thought back to the times he and Jatinder had spent in this very hall. He could remember their *kirpans*, their sacred swords, clashing as they trained in how to use them. Jatinder had always been the better fighter and Singh could vividly remember losing his cool on several occasions at being unable to match him.

How things had changed.

Unlike his rival, Singh had followed his destiny and risen to a senior position within their organization. A role that, at one point, had been highlighted for Jatinder.

Singh cast his mind back seventeen years.

He had been a rookie police detective and the job he had been called upon to do had filled him with dread.

Yet he was certain he had fulfilled it, so to be here now, in these circumstances, troubled him deeply. It felt like something higher was at work.

Singh had been here over an hour and still his inner torment raged.

Only one man could alleviate that.

Singh got to his feet, walked over to pay his respects to the Sikh holy book, the Guru Granth Sahib, asking for the strength to do what was necessary.

Then he left the temple, heading for the only man who could put this sorry episode to rest.

Benedict Cave.

EIGHT

'SIT DOWN OVER THERE,' said Jack, pointing Aisha in the direction of a wooden bench.

Aisha moved slowly, clearly stunned by what she saw. The room was meticulously organized, section by section, into illegal contraband, bags of marijuana, cocaine and finally rare, imported whiskies. Neatly arranged signs on the goods depicted which European country they came from.

Jack could sense she was alarmed. She'd told him she was a medical student so he knew she wasn't stupid. He wanted to get this part over with and move on to the more pressing issue of why they had been thrown together.

'I let a guy use my cellars. I don't ask him why.'

Aisha turned to face him. 'Outside you said that only you had access down here.'

Jack chewed his lip, irritated at the foolish slip. He decided not to push it any further. 'Sit down.'

Aisha shook her head. She pointed to a dark stain on her left thigh. 'I need to see to this injury. It's still bleeding. Can you step outside, please?'

'Christ, your eye, it looks like it's damaged – there's a black mark next to your pupil.'

'It's a coloboma – a small hole in my eye. I was born with it. It's nothing.'

Jack nodded and moved away. 'Do you need anything?'

Aisha glanced calmly around the room and pointed to a shelf. 'One of those bottles of water and some sort of cloth I can use as a bandage.'

Jack gathered the items and left them on the bench.

He became aware of the stench of piss from where he'd wet himself when being tortured earlier. Fortunately, he kept an emergency bag down here with a change of clothes, in case he needed to make a rapid getaway. Jack grabbed the bag, opened it, took out a torch and the clothes and headed for the door.

Aisha stopped him.

'Wait. Can you hand me one of those bottles of vodka as well, or whatever has the highest alcohol content?'

Jack looked puzzled. 'You need a drink?'

'No, you fool, to disinfect the wound.'

Aisha unbuttoned her jeans, inching them down slowly.

'Lordy,' she said, breathing heavily. She tried to look at the back of her legs but couldn't see anything suspect. Moving her hand to the area that was throbbing, Aisha felt a thick wooden splinter lodged in her flesh. She grabbed it and tried to pull it free but cried out in pain.

The door opened and Jack stuck his head through the gap. 'Are you OK?'

'I don't need your help with this. Close the door.'

Aisha had no desire to undress in front of a strange man. All she needed to do was pull the splinter free in one swift motion.

Gathering her courage, she grabbed hold of it and pulled. The pain was surprising and caught her off-guard. She screamed, lost her balance and went sprawling to the floor.

This time Jack didn't hesitate to enter the room. While he was desperate to get down to why they had been thrown together like this, the girl *had* saved his life and he was certain she wasn't a threat.

'Jack – leave me . . .'

He glared at her, but softened it at the pain on her face. 'Stop acting like a child. We don't have time for your ego.' He looked at the wound on the back of her thigh. 'It's messy. I need a closer look.'

Aisha was fighting back tears. Hesitantly, she rolled on to her side.

Jack wanted to crack a joke about her Winnie the Pooh underwear but thought better of it.

'I can't really see with all this blood. Looks like a deep gash.'

He uncapped the bottle of water, and poured it slowly over the wound. He felt Aisha's body tense.

'It's just water,' he said.

He grabbed the white cloth he had handed her earlier and used it to wipe blood from her skin. Aisha squealed with pain.

'It's not as bad as it looks. Probably won't even need stitches.'

'How big is the puncture wound?' said Aisha.

'About an inch. It's deeper than it is longer. I won't lie, this next part is going to hurt. If you want to scream – let it out.'

Jack unscrewed the cap from the vodka bottle and Aisha gritted her teeth.

'Ready?' he asked.

She nodded.

Jack doused the wound with vodka. Aisha clamped her hand over her mouth to stop from screaming. She suffered as long as she could before waving her other hand for Jack to stop.

With the wound cleansed, Jack wrapped the cloth around her thigh, tying it as tight as he dared.

'All done,' he said, reaching across her and patting her awkwardly on the back. 'I know that hurt.'

He waited while she pulled her jeans up then helped her to perch on the edge of the bench.

'I realize that as a Muslim you probably don't drink, but a few shots of this stuff will take the edge off.'

Aisha shook her head. She pointed across the room to a packet of sugar nestled next to some cups and a kettle. 'Can you bring the sugar to me? That will help.'

Jack walked across the room and grabbed the packet. 'Here.'

Aisha poured it into her mouth.

They sat in silence for several minutes while she got herself together.

'I'm OK now,' she whispered.

Jack nodded. 'We need to start at the beginning, Aisha. What the hell happened tonight?'

Aisha looked at him blankly. 'I have no idea.'

'How are you involved with those guys?'

Her tone was fierce and her face twisted into a scowl. 'I'm not. I've never seen them before in my life. I was on a university placement in Bradford A&E and finished my shift this evening at nine o'clock and that . . . that . . . Detective Singh was waiting for me. He told me my father had been in an accident.'

Jack scratched the stubble on his face, thinking. He was trying to place Aisha. There was something familiar about her, yet at the same time he was certain he'd never seen her before.

Aisha's voice shook as tears threatened. 'How could I have been such an idiot?'

'We're built to trust the police; it's not your fault.'

Aisha took a few shallow breaths and composed herself.

'I got in the back and Detective Singh got in the driver's side. He said my father had been taken to Leeds General Infirmary. I was putting my seat belt on when he turned to me and I felt a sharp pulse in my neck.'

'The taser,' Jack whispered, rubbing his own neck where Singh had hit him with several volts earlier.

Aisha nodded.

'And what happened when you woke up?' said Jack.

Aisha couldn't hold back any more and burst into tears, bringing her hands up to cover her face.

'They beat me. They kept asking me what Benedict Cave had told me.'

There was that name again. Benedict Cave.

'I told them I don't know anyone called Benedict Cave,' she said fiercely. 'But they didn't believe me. They used the water on me – like they did with you.'

Jack felt nauseous, and found it hard to breathe.

'I passed out at some point. The next thing I knew I was being marched into your shop.' Aisha wiped tears from her face. 'That's all I know.'

Jack needed some immediate facts.

'How old are you?' he asked.

'Twenty-one.'

'Where do you live?'

'Baildon.'

'What do your parents do?'

There was a slight pause, before she said, 'My father works in security and my stepmother is a housewife.'

'What are their names?'

'Habib and Sara Iqbal.'

The names meant nothing to Jack.

Above them, there was a sudden crack of what sounded like

his shop collapsing. They tensed and looked to the ceiling as if it might collapse too. Jack continued, his voice a little shaky. 'What about your birth-mum?'

'She died in childbirth.'

'I'm sorry,' said Jack. 'Do you have a boyfriend?'

'No.'

'Ex-boyfriend?'

'No.'

It gave Jack nothing to work with.

'I don't get it,' he said, sighing and walking away from her. 'Have you ever seen me before?'

'No.'

'Have you ever been to my shop before tonight?'

'I don't think so. I don't even know where we are.'

'The Elmswood estate.'

'God no,' said Aisha, shaking her head.

Jack wasn't surprised at her reaction. Elmswood had that kind of reputation.

'Aisha, there has to be *something* that links us,' he said coming back to her and crouching so they were at eye level.

'There is,' she replied quietly. 'Benedict Cave.'

NINE

'SO YOU *DO* KNOW him?' asked Jack.

Aisha shook her head.

'Singh and his men kept saying that Benedict Cave had visited me in A&E, and that I had spoken with him.'

'But you hadn't?'

'No.'

'And I never received a phone call from him, yet Detective Singh kept telling me I had,' said Jack.

They fell silent, trying to find a link.

'However we're involved in this, it's serious,' Jack said. 'Those guys, detectives or not, wanted us dead.'

'We need to go to the police,' said Aisha.

'No chance. They can't be trusted.'

'I mean the real police – that guy must have been a fake.'

'I don't think he was.' Jack explained the brazen way Detective Singh had tried to push him into verifying his identity.

'Did you call?' asked Aisha.

Jack shook his head. 'I don't like the police.'

'I can see why,' she said, looking around the room, one eyebrow raised.

'It's not what it looks like,' said Jack, knowing full well it was exactly what it looked like. He changed the subject. 'Do you have a safe place you can go to? Not home. They'll realize soon enough that we escaped from the building. We've got maybe twelve hours before Singh realizes there are no bodies.'

Aisha was silent. She looked to the floor. Jack saw her hesitation.

'Well?'

She nodded.

'Good. Where is it?'

'I've been living in student accommodation, but, well, I guess I can go back to my parents' house.'

The despondent way in which she said it made Jack think she was holding something back. It felt like some kind of family drama and he had no desire to get into any of that.

He moved to the desk in the centre of the room. 'Get yourself together, Aisha. We're out of here in fifteen minutes.'

Jack slung his rucksack over his shoulder. He was ready. He'd often thought about what might happen if he fell out with the people he did business with or got investigated by the police again and had to leave the country in a hurry. Two decades earlier, after his release from prison, he had sworn he'd never be put inside again.

To begin with, Jack had played it safe, but slowly he'd got back in the game, inching his way towards a fortune big enough to retire on. While he was broke compared to what he had once owned, Jack had gradually amassed enough dirty money to live the rest of his life abroad in relative luxury.

The rucksack he was carrying had been stored inside the large secure locker in the room. It contained his passport, driving licence, ten thousand pounds in cash, and four gold karas, totalling one kilo in weight, giving Jack assets of almost fifty thousand pounds.

He'd be leaving behind his properties, but had always known it might come to this. Over the years, he had re-mortgaged them constantly, spending the cash on items he could squirrel away – diamonds mostly. He had close to half a million pounds stashed in a secure location. In twenty-four hours, Jack Baxi would vanish.

Jack helped Aisha to her feet and checked she was strong enough to make the journey. He could see she was in pain.

'You're going to have to dig deep here, Aisha. Outside is the corridor we came in through. It stretches maybe a quarter of a mile and then we'll hit a steep metal ladder, on top of which is a manhole cover. We'll exit that way, then crawl over the embankment, slide down the other side and follow the disused railway track towards Thornbury.'

Aisha was looking at him, stunned. 'I'm not going anywhere. We need to wait down here until the *real* police can get to us.'

Jack turned away from her towards the door. 'Suit yourself. I'll make an anonymous call to the police when I'm able and let them know you're down here.'

'Wait,' said Aisha, her voice rising. 'You'd really leave me here? Like this?'

Jack faced her again. She looked forlorn, tired and vulnerable. But Jack couldn't wait around. 'I have no choice. People are trying to kill us. I'm not sticking around for that to happen.'

Aisha's demeanour changed. 'I'll come with you, but only if you get me back home to my father.'

'I'll put you in a taxi when we hit the centre of Bradford.'

'No, that's not good enough.'

Jack shrugged. 'It's the best offer you're getting.'

Aisha shuffled towards him, her top lip curling with the

effort. 'I saved your life tonight, Jack. You'd have died in your sleep or . . . or . . . stuck on those stairs if it hadn't been for me.'

Jack shifted his gaze away from her.

'You owe me at least this much.'

They were wasting precious time. Jack made a decision. 'I'll get you to your father, Aisha. So long as you don't quit on me, OK?'

'I won't.'

They made for the door. Jack opened it, waited until Aisha had stepped past him and paused. 'There's one last thing. Give me a moment.'

He fished inside his bag and handed her a robust-looking torch.

'You want me to wait out here alone?' she said anxiously.

Jack simply closed the door and returned to the safe.

The cellar had been his secret hiding place for decades but it was always going to end this way. The people he consorted with would never have let Jack go without a fight; he was a master in obtaining illegal goods. When he'd been jailed twenty years ago, it hadn't been his fault. His business partner at the time had been careless. Since then Jack had trusted no one.

He never would again.

Before he could leave, there was one piece of unfinished business. Jack took out the only thing left in the safe, a bottle of Dalmore whisky, a vintage 1964 collectors' item. It was worth thousands of pounds and he'd always intended to drink it when he retired.

Jack lifted the bottle from its handsome presentation case. His heart was racing as he opened it and tipped the contents all over the floor.

'To Baxi Stores. Rest in peace,' he whispered.

With the ritual complete, Jack took one last glance around the cellar and then at the ceiling, where, high above, his shop continued to burn. He closed his eyes and tried to push away the one memory that gnawed at him every day. There would never be any running away from what he had done to his wife. Leaving his store in ashes was a fitting finale for the horrors that had taken place seventeen years earlier.

Visions of his hands around his late wife's throat flashed across his mind.

Those same hands now punched at the light switch, plunging the room into darkness.

Jack opened the door and left the life he had led for almost two decades behind him.

TEN

JACK LED AISHA DOWN the narrow tunnel running parallel to the cellars. They each had a torch of their own but it didn't make their progress any easier. In the distance they could hear the sound of running water – the local sewer system. Several times, Jack had to pause while Aisha doubled over, retching.

'How's that wound?' asked Jack.

'Throbbing,' she replied.

Jack racked his brains over and over for some link – any link – with the girl next to him. His illegal goods businesses ensured that he dealt with a vast network of criminals. It wasn't just contraband: Jack could get his hands on passports, diamonds and even weapons, although he rarely got involved with that.

Could Aisha or Benedict Cave be connected to someone he had dealings with? He couldn't get to the bottom of it and it was driving him insane.

Jack stopped abruptly and turned to Aisha. 'I'm going to have to carry you.'

'You what?' she replied, a little taken back.

'There's a ditch here, full of water. It's too big to get across. No point both of us getting our feet wet.' He put his torch in his pocket and went to pick her up.

Aisha stepped back. 'I don't think you can,' she said.

'Relax, it's only for a few seconds. Unless you want a shoeful of crap.'

That changed her mind.

He moved to the side of her and scooped her into his arms.

'Careful,' she said instantly, her body rigid. Jack felt like he was holding a small lump of iron.

He took three large strides through the water and then put Aisha down. Just beyond her, a large steel ladder stretched from the ground all the way to a manhole at the top – fifty feet up, he reckoned.

'I'll go first and make sure it's clear. Switch your torch off as soon as I push up the cover.'

Jack climbed with cautious steps. At the top, he signalled for Aisha to turn off her torch, and then, bending his knees for extra force, he pushed up the heavy iron cover and peered through the gap. At the other end of the street he could see the fire consuming not only his shop but also the sandwich bar next door. Three fire engines had arrived, with flashing blue lights and there was a buzz of activity – firefighters, local busybodies and an ambulance. A quick scan of the area told him this was not the ideal moment for two figures to emerge from the sewer. It would be risky. And Singh and his men might well be on the lookout.

But there was no other choice.

Jack pulled the cover back in place and made his way back down to Aisha.

They'd have to make a dash for it. They only had to climb out and tip themselves over a shallow embankment wall. From there they'd scramble down into the cutting and make their way along the old railway line.

'OK, it's now or never. You ready?' said Jack.

Aisha nodded and rubbed her thigh.

Jack squeezed her shoulder. 'You've done well, Aisha. This ladder is going to be something else, though. You're going to need my help.'

'I know. You go first. I'll be close behind. When I put weight on my left leg I'm going to need you to take my hand and support me up to the next rung. It'll reduce the strain on my wound.'

'Got it,' said Jack. When he was three steps up the ladder, he turned and offered her his hand.

She was panting with the strain, but together they worked their way slowly up the rungs.

At the top, Jack turned off his torch and pushed the cover aside again.

The crowd of people were all intent on the fire. The embankment wall was only a few metres off to the right.

'When I go, follow me as fast as you can. You need to be right behind me, OK?'

Aisha gave a reluctant nod.

Jack waited for the right moment, shivering in the darkness, his teeth chattering. Staring into the night, he kept his eyes glued on the ever-expanding group of his regulars, who were no doubt worried that their local corner-shopkeeper had just been burned to a crisp.

There was an explosion and the front of Jack's store collapsed over the forecourt with a thunderous crash. The onlookers collided with one another as they leapt backwards to avoid flying bricks and dust. Jack saw his chance and leapt out from the manhole, hissing for Aisha to follow. They made a frantic dash for the embankment wall, Aisha hurling herself over it just after Jack. She lay panting on the grass beside him. Jack pointed to the drop below them.

'Slide down, no stopping,' he said. And with that, he was gone.

Aisha didn't hesitate. They slithered down the grassy slope, morning dew aiding their descent. When they were almost at the bottom, Jack scrambled to his feet and jumped the final few metres.

Aisha came careering into him, using his body as a barrier.

He didn't let her stop to rest.

'Come on,' he said, taking her by the hand. They headed south, away from Jack's shop and towards Thornbury, hugging the line of the embankment, keeping to the shadows.

Jack kept the pace brisk, ignoring Aisha's pleas for a break.

He was certain of one thing: soon enough, Singh and his men would realize that both Jack and Aisha were missing.

ELEVEN

'A BUS?' SAID AISHA. 'Are you serious?'

Jack nodded. 'No one will be looking for us yet. We're dead, remember? Just two people getting on a bus, that's all. Pull your scarf over your face, like this. How's the leg?'

'I can't feel a thing. Too cold.'

'Well, we've done the hard part. This bus will take us to the city centre. From there we can grab a taxi to your parents' place.'

There were three other people on the bus, all of them with their eyes closed, stealing forty winks. Jack led Aisha to the back seat and they sat in the corner.

It would take just under twenty minutes to get to the centre of Bradford. Jack knew the city well. He supplied black market goods to most of the corner shops, although always through an intermediary. Trafficking contraband was a complex task and since coming out of prison and going solo, Jack had been cautious. Jail had turned him into a colder, darker animal.

Cold enough that you caused your wife's death, Jack.

He tried to banish the image of his wife's bulging eyes as he started to strangle her.

That was an accident. I . . . I . . . lost control.

Jack looked at Aisha. She was dozing, head bobbing on her chest as the bus made its way through Thornbury. Jack wondered yet again how she had come to be mixed up in the night's events. It had to be a case of mistaken identity. A petite Asian girl wearing a headscarf was commonplace in a city like Bradford.

There was little traffic at six a.m. and the bus moved swiftly down Leeds Road, dubbed the 'Curry Mile' by the locals. Almost every shop was a food outlet, not just curry houses but fried chicken, doner kebabs, upmarket establishments – it had the lot.

Halfway down was the city's major Hindu temple, next to a Christian church. A little further down were two Sikh temples, while the city centre itself was ringed by mosques. *Multicultural Bradford* – a city where brown and white faces had at times struggled to find a common platform.

The bus stopped at temporary roadworks in front of the colossal Guru Nanak temple with its towering orange flags displaying the *khanda*, the Sikh symbol of faith. In the centre was a doubled-edged sword surrounded by a circle (*kara*), and then finally two protective swords (*kirpans*), one on each side, acting as guardians.

The temple, or gurdwara, had featured prominently in Jack's early life.

Before his father died, Jack had gone there with him every day. Every fortnight his father had washed the orange flagpoles in milk to purify them. It was a job he had taken great pride in. Jack could recall vividly the smell of incense wafting in from the great hall where the Guru Granth Sahib was being chanted. A lump formed in his throat as he watched the mammoth flags flapping in the breeze, a colourful break from the general gloom that seemed to engulf the city. His father had been one of the Khalsa, a man who had taken solemn vows never to cut his hair, drink alcohol or eat meat, and to follow the strict code of honour passed down from the tenth Guru, Guru Gobind Singh, in 1669.

One day, Jatinder, you too will become one of the Khalsa. And then you will surpass me and become one of the Gurmukh – one who has reached the ultimate salvation and is completely at one with God . . .

Jack turned his head away from the orange flags, ashamed. If his father could see him now, a criminal who had cut his hair long ago, and often defiled his body with alcohol and sometimes cocaine, he'd have had no hesitation in cutting Jack's head off himself. For the few moments the bus stood stationary in front of the temple, Jack cowered away from it, disgusted with himself at betraying his father's memory.

You left me and I couldn't take it. I lost my way so badly.

Jack nudged Aisha awake as the bus pulled into the Bradford interchange. There were a few more people here but Jack reminded himself that, for now, no one would realize they'd got away.

They crossed the road and headed towards City Park, where England's largest urban water feature could be found – the Mirror Pool. Powerful jets of water soared high into the air before splashing on to the concrete below; the sound was strangely reassuring.

Jack and Aisha jumped into a cab at the taxi stand and Aisha gave the driver her father's address.

Baildon was an upmarket area of north Bradford, six miles from the centre but rich with quarries and hiking routes, with the moors close by. It was a rural area, mostly inhabited by affluent white communities.

The taxi crawled through a ghostly mist that got thicker as

the roads grew steeper. At nearly three hundred metres above sea level, Baildon was shrouded in fog almost every morning.

'We're here,' said Aisha, pointing though the mist to a large set of intimidating iron gates surrounding a huge plot of land.

Jack paid the driver and told him to wait, then joined Aisha at the gates.

'Impressive,' said Jack.

'I suppose,' replied Aisha.

'You can make it on your own from here,' said Jack. 'I'll take the taxi and get to where I need to be.'

'No, you have to come inside with me and tell my father what happened. He won't believe me – it's too absurd.'

Jack shook his head.

'You'll be safe in there,' she said, 'I promise you. He runs Elite Security – you must have heard of them?'

Jack had. They were a multinational firm with contracts all over the country. He'd read an article on them in the paper some months back.

'Please. *You* might be able to disappear but I want my life back. I need you to tell my father what you know.'

Her face was covered in bruises. She looked like someone who'd been worked over by an abusive partner. Her dad would not take her appearance well.

'No chance,' said Jack. He didn't need the extra headache.

A silence lingered and Jack was about to turn and leave, when Aisha said, 'I'll tell the police everything – about your cellar and everything I saw down there, and your last location. I could put that call in right now and you wouldn't make it far. Or you can tell my father what happened, and I promise I'll have a very selective memory.'

Jack was surprised at her brazen attitude. 'Blackmail? Really?'

'How far do you think you'd get if I made that call? We need to figure out what happened together.'

She had Jack over a barrel.

'OK,' he said, 'but I need to tell the taxi he can go.'

Aisha pressed the intercom and told the hoarse voice on the other end to let her in. The large iron gates slid open and Jack and Aisha headed towards the residence. Jack felt uneasy. Half-way down the path he had an urge to turn round and run, just as he heard the thundering clang of the gates closing.

They passed a striking lawn area, glistening with overnight dew. In the centre lay a water feature with an Islamic inscription carved in stone.

'What does that say?' asked Jack, pointing towards it.

'Welcome,' replied Aisha.

They were nearly at the front door when it opened and an obese Asian man filled the doorway. He had a neatly trimmed beard and a shaven head, but the rest of his face was in shadow. Aisha ran towards him.

Jack hung back and shoved his hands in his pockets, giving them a moment. He could hear Aisha sobbing. Her dad sounded alarmed and pulled her into the house. Jack waited, unsure of whether to follow or wait to be called. He was about to turn and leave when Aisha's father came marching out of the house towards him in four military strides.

Jack stared at the man, stunned.

As his past came screaming back to haunt him, all Jack could do was stand there, speechless.

'Jack,' Aisha's father said bitterly, 'what the hell is going on?'

TWELVE

HABIB IQBAL'S SITTING ROOM, or 'Drawing Room' according to the gold sign on the door, oozed grandeur, as befitting a man whose wealth was speculated to run into the hundreds of millions. He'd come quite some way since his stint as Jack's business partner – a relationship that had ended in abandonment. Jack had been sent behind bars, and Habib – or Asif Khan, as he'd been called back then – had clearly used the fruits of those labours to transform himself into one of the richest men in England, creating the Elite Security empire. He had always kept himself away from the media, almost a recluse, which is why Jack had never made the connection to their shared past. Jack had tried to track down his old partner on release from jail, but it was back before the internet and social media ruled the world. Habib had done a fine job of disappearing, and it had been a smart move – he had many things to hide.

Jack was sitting on a golden couch near a fifteen-seater dining table with a gilt border, his grubby trainers resting on a gleaming sunshine-yellow carpet. Obscenely huge crystal chandeliers poured light on to a grand drawing of Mecca taking up the whole of the far wall. The excessive brightness of the interior lay in marked contrast to the murky day outside the window.

At the opposite end of the room hung a huge studio portrait showing Aisha seated alongside Habib's wife, Sara – a woman Jack knew well. She'd been Habib's sweetheart when they'd all been in business together. Back in the 1990s, their interracial relationship had caused quite the stir: the privileged white girl who'd got herself mixed up with a foreigner.

Jack scrutinized the photo. Habib had positioned himself behind Sara and Aisha, seeming to lord it over them, his shoulders pinned back and his moustache curling across his plump cheeks. What struck Jack most vividly was the total lack of emotion on either of the women's faces. There was no hint of a smile – they both looked cold and distant.

Patio doors at the far end accessed the rear garden, and although Jack managed only a fleeting glance, his eye was drawn immediately to a water fountain as tall as the house. Habib had clearly not changed his taste for the absurd. As a young man, he'd worn designer suits way above his pay grade while working his humble job in one of the textile mills in Bradford. He still wore an earring, gold of course, and Jack had noticed majestic rings that adorned his fingers.

Habib and Sara entered the room and shut the door. The difference between them was striking. She had aged fantastically well. Too well, thought Jack; a lot of money must be invested in that kind of upkeep.

Sara had clearly converted to Islam since he'd last seen her; she wore the traditional headscarf – that was gold too. Her conservative white Asian-style suit sparkled under the lights. She was as slender as Jack remembered but the warm glow was absent now from her face. She looked pale and the few locks of hair escaping from her headscarf were jet black and not blonde, as he remembered her. She probably dyed her hair to pass as a fair-skinned Asian woman rather than a white convert.

'I've called for Dr Abdullah. Aisha's too frightened to go to the hospital,' said Habib, taking a seat opposite Jack. 'She's briefed me on what happened and I can't quite get my head round it.'

'I just can't believe it's you,' said Sara, looking stunned.

'Jack, my old friend,' began Habib.

'Don't you dare call me that,' said Jack flatly. 'And what the hell is with the name, Asif? You're Habib Iqbal now?'

Looking awkward, Sara stared at the floor. Habib carried on.

'Before we get into what happened tonight, Jack, I need to explain—'

'How you fucked me over? How you cut me dead?' said Jack.

Habib puffed out his cheeks and looked across at the picture of Mecca. His enormous hands swept away the beads of sweat breaking out across his forehead.

'When you went to jail, Jack, Sara and I swore we would change. We took our pilgrimage to Mecca and I left my old name in the past. I wanted to start again, leave our old ways behind us.'

'Old ways? You mean, your criminal past?' said Jack, refusing to let Habib sugar-coat his words.

'We started afresh,' said Habib and Sara, almost in unison.

Jack knew what Habib really meant was that after their warehouse had been raided and over a million pounds' worth of contraband seized, Habib had been put on a 'watch list'. Changing his name had made it easier to reinvent himself.

'I need you to know that whoever did this tonight, *they will pay*. For trying to kill the man who kept me out of prison, and for trying to kill my daughter. But I need to know, Jack, without any fear of retribution – what the hell is this all about?'

'Without any fear of retribution': is that how Habib worded his threats these days? Tell me how you got my daughter mixed up in your shit, Jack, and we'll call it even.

Habib's accent had changed over the years. Jack remembered him speaking with a heavy northern twang, yet now he spoke with a polished accent, like he'd spent a few years at Oxford. Clearly he'd put some effort into his reinvention.

'I have no idea what this is all about,' said Jack. 'Aisha and I have no connection. Except you,' he added as an afterthought.

'Yes,' said Habib.

'Who is Benedict Cave?' asked Jack, looking Habib dead in the eye.

Habib shook his head and held Jack's gaze. 'The name means nothing to me.'

'Sara?' asked Jack.

She shook her head. She still hadn't looked him in the eye. 'Are you still involved in . . .?'

'I'm clean. I don't deal in that shit any more. I have a small corner shop in Elmswood. I learned my lesson.'

The look on Habib's face told Jack he wasn't buying it.

'Aisha told me what happened tonight. Are you telling me you have no idea how she ended up at your place or why these people tried to kill you?'

'None,' replied Jack without hesitation.

'Benedict Cave. I've never heard this name either,' whispered Habib, shaking his head.

'Well then, since you're no wiser than me, I'll be on my way. I've done my bit for Aisha. Another goddamn debt you owe me,' said Jack, unable to hide the bitterness in his voice. He stared around the living room. 'You've done well for yourselves but I know you two better than anybody. This . . . situation is clearly something to do with both of you. I know you can't have built this security empire cleanly.'

'Someone tried to kill *you*, Jack. Not us. Stay a while. We need to try and work this out together,' said Habib.

'They used your daughter to get to you. That's pretty obvious.

Look in your closet. There must be a fair few skeletons in there coming back to haunt you.'

'But why you? Why now?'

Jack shrugged. 'I don't know and frankly I don't care.'

'When they realize you've got away, they'll hunt you down. I can make it so you're untouchable – untraceable even,' said Habib, with more than a little arrogance to his tone.

'I don't want or need your help.'

'Stay, Jack, please. I'm asking you as—' Habib began.

'Don't you dare say "as a friend",' said Jack, jabbing an angry finger at him.

'Would money change your mind?' said Habib.

'There's nothing you can give me. This is simply a bizarre case of mistaken identity. I don't want the answers, Habib, I really don't.'

Jack stood up and lifted his bag off the floor, leaving a patch of dirt on the plush carpet.

'Jack, please,' started Sara.

'What do you want from me? We were a team! One unit. We built that empire from nothing. All you have is blood money – my blood.' He felt the old rage that had festered inside him over two long decades start to flare.

Sara got up and walked quickly out of the room.

'How the fuck did I end up here, straight back in a nightmare I've tried so hard to bury?' Jack muttered.

'Kismet,' said Habib.

Jack gave a dry laugh. 'Kismet, fate – whatever you want to call it? Well, yours turned out OK,' he said, gazing around the room again.

Habib stood up. 'Why didn't you contact me when you came out?'

'Why didn't *you* try to find *me*?' said Jack, pushing a finger into Habib's chest, hard enough that the big man took a step back.

Habib looked away, sheepish.

'Thought so.' Jack took a step closer to Habib. 'You're an untrustworthy bastard, and always have been.'

Jack turned round and walked out. There was so much more he wanted to throw at Habib. So much blame he wanted to apportion, anger he needed to vent. But the clock was ticking and Jack just wanted to be as far away as possible from this mess. Outside, the day was starting to brighten and he wanted to be clear of the city by lunchtime.

'You can't leave!' shouted Habib. Two bulky Asian men, arms folded, blocked Jack's path in the hallway. One of them jerked his head for him to turn round and go back in.

'You're kidding me, right?' said Jack.

'Until I understand what happened last night, I need you to stay as my guest,' replied Habib, appearing in the hallway.

'Your guest?' said Jack.

'That girl upstairs is the dearest thing in the world to me. I need twenty-four hours to make my enquiries and then you are free to go. I will put you on my own plane to a destination anywhere in the world.' He took Jack by the shoulders. 'You have my *kasam* on this.'

Kasam, the Urdu word for 'life', was used when making a promise you could only break on penalty of death. It was an ancient pledge, steeped in history. In Asian circles, it was the most serious pledge Habib could have offered.

'And if I won't stay?' said Jack.

Habib glanced towards his bodyguards. 'Then, brother, you will force my hand.'

THIRTEEN

JACK THREW HIS BAG across the guest bedroom, smearing dirt across the pristine white carpet. He moved to the window and saw several of Habib's security team outside.

He had little choice but to remain where he was. If he kicked up a fuss and the police were called, it would open up a whole new can of worms. He'd let Habib make his 'enquiries', whatever that meant. Jack imagined that with the wealth and connections his old business partner had, he'd be able to find information on Benedict Cave, something that would prove beyond doubt that Jack had nothing to do with what had transpired at his shop. Jack remained convinced this was no more than a case of mistaken identity.

Yet of all the places he could have ended up – here he was.

Back with the man he detested most in this world.

Jack's mind was running over old deals they had struck, enemies they might have made. The list wasn't exactly short.

Habib had plenty of money and the Elite brand had its hand in everything: in security, healthcare, construction. Even so, he'd been robust in keeping his identity hidden. Now it had been revealed, Jack began to connect the dots.

During the 1990s, Habib had set up the largest black market racket of cigarettes and alcohol in northern England with Jack. They'd had over a million pounds a year passing through their hands. They had generated so much cash they couldn't get rid of it fast enough and had bribed banking executives to take it, finding more and more complex ways of washing it clean.

But like all power-hungry regimes, they'd got careless, and their main warehouse, which had been a fortress for years, had been raided. Jack had taken the fall and kept his mouth shut. Yet Habib had never even said thank you. Having built up massive amounts of wealth, 'sorry' was still too hard a word.

Elite Security now had the contract for protecting all those goods as they came into the country. With the average price of a packet of cigarettes now at over ten pounds, there was a massive underground supply network. Jack could picture Habib at the top of that particular food chain.

Habib Iqbal: whiter than white on paper, but in reality dirtier than a crack addict's needle.

On his way to the guestroom, Jack had come up a winding marble staircase. He'd seen dozens of pictures of Aisha, everything from baby photos to her graduation day. Also on the walls were more enormous group shots of Habib, Sara and Aisha. In all of them, Habib loomed over his wife and daughter, while Aisha's face remained flat and impassive. Jack found the pictures unsettling. He wondered about Aisha's mother and guessed that Habib would have undergone an arranged marriage to a suitable girl from his community in order to please the elders. The death of his wife in childbirth would have then inevitably allowed him the freedom to rekindle things with Sara.

Despite the obvious lack of warmth in the pictures, Habib

nonetheless had a family of his own – something Jack had never managed.

It was the one thing Jack regretted the most.

There was a knock on the guestroom door. Jack opened it to find Sara standing there carrying towels and fresh clothing. Once again, Jack found her appearance to be nothing short of miraculous, almost as if she'd stepped from 1997 into 2019 overnight.

Sara walked lightly over to the bed and placed the towels on the duvet. An awkward silence filled the room.

'Jack . . . the doctor's still here. Habib wants to know if you'd like him to—'

'I'm fine.'

'You look like you might need—'

'I said, I'm fine.'

'I'm sorry about all of this,' she said meekly.

'Habib wants the truth about what happened. I get that. He's got until this evening, or this situation is going to get messy.' There was an edge to Jack's voice, and by Sara's reaction he could tell she'd noticed.

She couldn't look at him, although Jack didn't take his eyes off her. He waited. She remained quiet, fiddling with her rings.

'So where's Aisha?' asked Jack.

'Asleep, hopefully,' replied Sara, daring to cast him a glance.

Another strained silence.

'I'm going to take a shower,' Jack said finally. 'I assume your husband won't kill me while I'm in there?' He marched over to the bedroom door and opened it in an unsubtle invitation for her to get out.

'Habib wouldn't hurt you,' said Sara.

Jack felt there was no authority to her words. 'It didn't seem like that downstairs.'

'He needs to find out the truth behind all this. Aisha is all he has.'

Sara walked towards Jack with her head bowed. He took hold of her arm as she passed. She paused but didn't look at him. Jack felt the heat from her burning cheeks and smelled citrus perfume. A bead of sweat trickled down her temple from under her headscarf.

When she still couldn't look him in the eye, he walked off into the bathroom and closed the door.

'He's aged badly,' said Habib, sitting down at the kitchen table opposite Sara. She'd made tea and was needlessly stirring it. 'Would you stop that?' he said, when his wife didn't answer.

Her reply was curt. 'Not everyone is as privileged as we are.'

She paused and Habib saw that she wanted to say more.

'Go on then. Get it off your chest.'

'I don't want him here, Habib. You *know* why.'

'I can't just let him leave after what happened last night.'

'I don't think he's got anything to do with it.'

'Yeah, because Jack never mixed with anyone dodgy, did he?' said Habib.

'That was a long time ago. Look at him! Do you think he's involved in the same thing? He looks like a down-and-out.'

'That doesn't mean he's innocent in all of this.'

'And Aisha?'

Habib shook his head. 'I'm completely baffled,' he replied.

Sara stopped stirring her tea. She sent her husband a questioning look.

He knew what she was implying. 'No chance. Not *at all* possible,' he said, shaking his head.

Sara nodded and went back to the incessant tea-stirring. 'So what will you do?' she asked.

'Find this Benedict Cave and see what this is all about.'

'Do you think you can?'

He shot her a dismissive scowl. 'I'm already on it. Just let me handle this, Sara.'

'Don't you dare shut me out,' she hissed, and stood up suddenly. 'This can only be about one thing. Don't pretend you can ignore it.'

Habib didn't respond. He felt the same. It was too much of a coincidence that Jack and Aisha had been thrown together. Sara was unable to control herself any longer. She leaned forward and placed both hands on the table, splaying her fingers like accusing darts at Habib. When she spoke, her voice was quiet but laced with menace.

'This is kismet, Habib, and you know *exactly* what I am talking about.'

Habib stood up, jabbed a finger at her and now also dropped his voice.

'You're going to have to control that tongue of yours while Jack is in our house. These . . . these . . . things that bother you don't need to be aired.'

'That man upstairs murdered his wife,' she replied, glaring at Habib.

Habib put a finger to his lips and looked towards the closed kitchen door, afraid that Jack might appear.

'And what would you like me to do about that, Sara? How exactly would I explain to him that we know what he did? Ever thought about that?'

Sara's pale complexion was burning with a fiery intensity, turning her normally passive expression into something far more sinister.

'He went to jail for us: that is *our* debt. And we *repaid* that debt by keeping our mouths shut. For seventeen years I've had to live with that shame. While he's in our house, I want him to know that we're even – that we don't owe him a thing,' she spat.

'Control your ego,' replied Habib dismissively. 'In a few hours I'll have the information I need, and as long as Jack has nothing to do with last night, I will not break my *kasam* and we will never see him again. The fact that he will never know that we repaid our debt is a burden you will have to live with – just as I do.'

FOURTEEN

SINGH HAD ARRIVED AT Baxi's burned-out store an hour earlier, and among the waterlogged ruins quickly realized that Baxi and the girl were not there. He'd known exactly where to look next. While crime scene personnel were still all over the site, Singh had followed the line of shops to the end of the parade and eventually found a manhole cover not quite in place.

He had lowered himself down the ladder and walked the short distance past the sewage channel, arriving at a corridor of well-hidden cellars. He was now standing in the room from where, only a few hours earlier, Jack and Aisha had made their escape.

Shortly it would be swamped with crime scene investigators, and soon after that, the news would break that Baxi had not died in the fire.

Only a Baxi could have proved this resolute.

Singh gave the room a once-over. Baxi, it seemed, had been back to his old tricks, dealing in contraband. An open safe lay empty at the side of the room. Singh wondered how much money it had held. Enough to get Baxi far away and quickly, he assumed. It meant the race to find him was more critical than ever.

On the floor, Singh found a cloth soaked in what appeared to be blood. Was Baxi injured, or had it been the girl? Singh made a note to put in a call to the local hospitals as soon as he was back at street level. He doubted Baxi would have gone to one, unless of course his injuries were life threatening, but the girl might.

Back in his car now, Singh did two things. He put a call in to some men who did the odd job for him when necessary, and gave them a location he knew Baxi might eventually visit – a church in Shipley that was vital to unravelling this mess. Singh asked them to keep the area under surveillance and to put a temporary roadblock in place to trap Baxi if he ended up there. It was no more than a fifty-fifty but he had to cover all bases. They needed to keep this contained. Singh didn't want to contemplate the fallout if it broke internationally. Baxi's behaviour could, to some extent, be predicted. The girl, however – she was an altogether different proposition. Her father was the wildcard here. If he mobilized his influence, shit, this might all blow up in everyone's faces and put at risk an organization with eighty years of secrecy behind them.

Singh made a final call – one he had hoped to avoid.

'Take the old man to the top floor of the building site,' he said. He paused, then added, 'And dig the damn hole.'

FIFTEEN

'GET UP, IT'S NEARLY five o'clock.'

Jack stirred awake and found himself staring into the pale face of Aisha Iqbal. She was standing in her pyjamas next to the bed, a clean black scarf around her head. Jack was disorientated until it slowly returned to him: a truth he had hoped was a nightmare.

'Sara said you need to come down for some food.'

Jack closed his eyes again. 'I must have dozed off.'

'I bet you were hoping it was all a bad dream?' said Aisha innocently. Recalling what she herself had been through the night before, Jack found her attitude surprising.

'What about you?' he asked.

Her innocent face was tarnished by a blossoming black eye and red scratches.

'I'll live. Dr Abdullah's given me an antibiotic shot and patched up my leg pretty well. My father is' – she raised her hands, making mock speech marks – 'investigating.'

'Habib dotes on you. You should count yourself lucky.'

She shrugged. 'He thinks money can buy him everything – even the love of his own daughter.'

Jack had sensed some degree of animosity between Aisha and Habib, and now he knew for sure.

'He hasn't changed then,' replied Jack, sitting up. He turned his head to the side and inhaled deeply as a potent scent drifted through the air. 'Christ, does he still smoke those awful Senior Service cigarettes?'

She wrinkled her nose in disgust. 'Yes.'

'I thought they'd been banned. Those things give you cancer just looking at them.'

'He imports them from Japan. They'll catch up with him eventually,' she replied.

'You don't like your father much, do you?'

'I like him just fine.'

'Sure you do.'

She chewed her lip and turned her head to the side like a sulking child. 'I don't respect him. There's a difference.' Every time she neared the end of a sentence, she quickened her speech to try and beat a cough.

'Tell me why you don't respect him then.'

'Why are you so interested?'

'I'm just killing time.'

Sara's voice interrupted their conversation, shouting for them to come downstairs.

'We should go,' said Aisha. She hammered her fist against her chest, trying to force the cough back down into her lungs. 'Damn thing.'

'Dinner's not running off without us.'

Jack watched as Aisha thought carefully about her next answer.

'My father's a selfish man. He's obsessed with money, even though he has wealth way beyond what he could ever need.' She gave a pretty good imitation of Habib's voice: 'Without money in this world, Aisha, you are and always will be nothing.'

'Habib always was a narcissistic son of a bitch.'

'Why's that of any interest to you?'

'I knew your father years ago . . .'

'He told me. Why did you lose touch?'

'I went to prison,' said Jack, and watched carefully for her reaction. She was calm under scrutiny but he saw the surprise creep on to her face. He was waiting for her to ask him for more details when Habib appeared at the bedroom door. He didn't knock and walked right up to the bed, looking alarmed. Aisha took a little step away, and Jack noticed. His mind went to the photos of her and Habib scattered across the house.

Jack remained where he was and met Habib's gaze. 'What is it?'

'Benedict Cave,' said Habib. 'I know who he is.'

SIXTEEN

FATHER BENEDICT CAVE WAS no ordinary man. This much Detective Singh understood. He was alone with the sixty-seven-year-old, who was tied to a chair. They were on the top floor of a derelict building, one of many in Bradford.

An icy wind circled them, their location brutally exposed to the elements.

'I forgive you,' mumbled Cave, his head bowed and dried blood all over his bare torso.

Singh was standing opposite and found the words uncomfortable to hear. He'd been torturing Cave for hours but the old man had refused to talk.

It wasn't that killing Benedict Cave would be difficult, but Singh needed the information he could give him.

'I will not kill the person you're protecting,' replied Singh.

Benedict Cave raised his bloodied face towards Singh. 'Liar,' he said.

'It was never intended to be like this. Mistakes were made. All we are looking for is a peaceful resolution to this matter. No more lives need to be lost.'

'Christ was on the cross from nine until three before he died. He died for our sins. Yours. Mine. Everybody's. When you kill me, it is not death you grant me but salvation.'

Cave's head sank back on to his chest.

Singh could tell that Cave wouldn't break. His eyes and his words held a resolve Singh had seen before. Religious men like Cave relied on a higher power for judgement, and believed in their cause just as passionately as Singh did himself.

'What did you tell Aisha? I know you visited the hospital she works at. And Baxi? Did you tell him the same things? The . . . location?'

Cave's voice was nothing more than a weak whisper. 'I've already told you. The girl was busy and Baxi never answered the phone. I never spoke to either of them.' Cave paused, and then added, 'You are nothing but a coward, living in a past you cannot forget. The world has moved on since 1947.'

Singh came closer to Cave and hissed his next words. 'It has not changed. It will never change.' He backed off, irritated at his loss of composure, and tried again, speaking more calmly this time. 'You know what we need. Is it really worth spilling your blood for?'

'You won't find the location. You're not the only one with power,' replied Cave a little more forcefully.

'What power do you think you have?'

Cave smiled at him. 'I have the Lord Jesus Christ on my side. You cannot possibly win.'

'Do you think it's simply by chance that of all the police officers you could have met down at the station, it happened to be me?'

Cave didn't reply. His lips were moving. Singh thought he might have been praying.

'The girl and the man you came here to find, they're both dead,' Singh said flatly.

Cave let out a quiet groan.

'It should never have come to this,' Singh continued, his tone angrier now. 'You tried to unite two worlds that cannot coexist. Their blood is on your hands, Father Cave.'

Still Cave made no reply.

They remained silent for several minutes while the gales howled around them.

'It doesn't have to be this way. You can save yourself, Father Cave. Tell me the location and I'll release you.'

The priest looked at him with an unflinching stare. He shook his head.

'In that case, you leave me no choice,' Singh said with a sigh. He took a syringe from his top pocket and unsheathed it. 'This is a high-strength dose of potassium – it stops the heart. You won't feel a thing.' Singh crouched beside Father Cave and slipped the needle into a vein on his arm.

'One last chance, Father.'

'I forgive you,' said Cave again.

'Go peacefully then,' whispered Singh, and injected the lethal dose into the old man's body.

SEVENTEEN

JACK WAITED FOR HABIB to take a seat at the kitchen table. Sara had laid out an impressive spread of samosas, rice and some sort of curry, but nobody touched it.

Habib spoke with the confidence of a man who was certain about the information he had received. 'Father Benedict Cave is a Christian missionary who arrived in this country from India three days ago. Last night a missing person report was logged by West Yorkshire police.'

'It can't be the same man. It makes no sense. A priest? From India?' said Jack.

'The coincidence is too great,' replied Habib. 'He entered the UK at Manchester Airport with a valid visa and on an open ticket. From what my contacts have discovered, he checked into a Catholic church in Shipley. When he went out and didn't return, a Sister Catherine Lowry filed him as missing.'

Aisha shook her head. 'This just gets more and more crazy,' she said, fighting another cough.

'Anything else?' asked Jack.

Habib shook his head. 'I've got a car arriving shortly. I'm going to take my men down to the church to see what I can find out.'

Sara looked at him in alarm. 'Why do you need to go? Surely the others can take care of it?'

Habib shook his head. 'I need to hear for myself what Benedict Cave was doing here.'

'Do we know any more details about Father Cave? Where was he from in India?' asked Aisha.

Habib ignored her. 'My men'll be here soon. I'll find out what I can.'

Jack checked his watch. It was just before six p.m. Twelve hours had elapsed since they'd escaped from his shop. Surely by now Singh and his cronies would have realized Jack and Aisha's bodies were not amongst the rubble. Jack was keen to leave but this development with Benedict Cave was an itch he needed to scratch.

'I'm coming with you,' he said, getting to his feet.

Habib remained seated and waved his hand dismissively. 'I don't think that's wise. The safest place you can be is here. It didn't take much for me to get hold of this information, which means the men who are after you can also acquire it.'

'I'm not asking for your permission, Habib. If Cave is connected to me somehow and told this Sister Catherine, then she may only be willing to talk to me. Or Aisha,' he said, looking over at the girl.

'She's not going anywhere,' said Habib.

'Oh yes, I am,' replied Aisha boldly. 'Jack's right. Maybe she will only speak to the two of us. I really can't see what can possibly link Jack, Benedict Cave and me, but I'm coming.'

'It is not open for discussion,' said Habib.

'I'm coming with you!' snapped Aisha and burst into a violent coughing fit. She was struggling to breathe and looked ready to keel over. Habib rushed to her side and rubbed her back, telling her to calm down. Aisha ignored him and got to her feet, her small frame overshadowed by Habib's vast bulk. She took a few moments before speaking.

'You're going to have to accept that I'm not a little girl any more. I'm capable of making my own decisions.'

Habib started to object but Aisha continued, speaking over him.

'I was abducted, and I have the right to speak to this woman. And frankly,' she said, looking at both Jack and Habib, 'a few burly men storming into a Catholic church is far from subtle.'

Habib looked at Sara, who in turn looked back at Aisha.

'Sara, explain it to her,' said Habib.

Jack felt awkward, a stranger stuck in the middle of a family dispute.

'I've said my piece,' said Aisha, walking away from the table. 'I'm getting changed and if you don't take me with you, I'll go alone. You've already told me everything I need.'

She left them and there was an awkward hush.

'She has a point, to be fair. It's possible she is the only person this Sister Catherine will speak with,' Jack said eventually.

Habib looked distraught. He dropped his voice to confer with Sara. 'Why must she always work against me? I only want to keep her safe.'

Sara put her hand on his arm. 'I don't like this any more than you do, but you know how she is. And quite honestly, she's safer with you than anywhere else.'

Habib turned to Jack, eyeing him suspiciously. 'Are you sure you've never heard of this guy, Jack?'

It was more of an accusation than a question. Jack got up from the table.

'We're wasting time here,' he said, and left the room.

EIGHTEEN

SINGH WAS PARKED ABOUT a quarter of a mile down the road from the gates to Habib Iqbal's house. He'd driven past and noted the clear presence of a robust network of CCTV cameras.

Hardly surprising, given Habib's position as CEO of Elite Security.

Through his binoculars, Singh had a clear sight of the house. He thought it likely that Aisha and Jack would have gone there. Singh imagined the reunion between Jack and his old business partner would have been pretty tense – a spectacular clash of past and present.

Yet neither Habib nor Jack realized just what lay at stake here. How could they?

Singh knew Benedict Cave had been residing at a church in Shipley, and that had been his original destination, to see if anyone there had the information he so desperately needed and hadn't been able to get out of the old priest.

The location.

But more than anything now, Singh needed to tie up the loose ends, and that began and ended with Jack and Aisha.

If Father Cave *had* confided in them, there was simply no other option but to see this thing through and end their lives, irrespective of the fallout.

The alternative didn't bear thinking about.

Singh tapped his fingers impatiently on the steering wheel, thinking it over. He wished that he could discuss the best course of action with some other senior member of the organization, but he'd been firmly instructed to keep the circle small and deal with this himself.

The fewer people who knew, the better.

Habib was wealthy, connected and secretive – an altogether different proposition to Jack. Getting close to Habib wasn't an option, which meant simply waiting.

It didn't take long.

Less than an hour later, Singh's grip tensed around the binoculars as Jack and Aisha followed Habib out of the house and climbed into a large Mercedes van. Another car pulled in behind them, both vehicles turning smoothly out of the gates.

Parked at the side of the road, Singh was no more than a passer-by.

He started his car, left a reasonable distance and then began his pursuit.

He had one chance to get this right.

One chance to avoid an international crisis.

NINETEEN

HABIB'S VAN WAS EQUIPPED with the same blacked-out windows and bulletproof glass as any of the drug dealers' vehicles that regularly trawled the streets of Bradford.

In the front sat two heavy-set men, Habib's 'protective detail'. Jack doubted how effectively they could deal with trouble. Their size was their main disadvantage – too cumbersome to react fast in an emergency. Far from subtle, their main function served as a visual deterrent.

Behind the van was another vehicle. Jack had immediately clocked the sporty S-Class Mercedes, not to mention the constant glances from their driver in his rear-view mirror to ensure he didn't lose his back-up.

Quite who was in the car behind wasn't clear, but Jack got the feeling that if the situation got out of hand, they were primed to deal with it.

Jack was sitting next to Aisha. She'd been quiet since leaving the house; there'd been more bickering between her and Habib. The atmosphere inside the van was charged.

Jack felt claustrophobic, his head pounding from trying to connect all of the dots. He was certain this was a case of mistaken identity, or even identity fraud. But the mere fact of him being in a vehicle with this man he'd known so many years ago was disturbing.

Elite Security, Elite Healthcare, Elite Construction – the tentacles of Habib's empire stretched in all directions. The substantial wealth he had acquired had originated from planting those seeds of corruption with Jack years earlier – the trips across the border, bribing customs officials, buying intelligence and keeping all the layers of the cake fresh with cream.

'Are you OK, Jack? You're grinding your teeth,' said Aisha.

'Nervous,' he conceded. 'Don't know why. It's a church – hardly a place to be afraid of.'

Aisha put her hand on his arm. 'Allah will protect us.'

'We could have done with him turning up last night,' Jack replied.

'You're still alive, aren't you?'

'More to do with my cellar than Allah.'

'You don't believe in God?'

Jack remained quiet. Images of him reciting the Sikh holy book with his father flickered across his mind. He forced them away.

The Roman Catholic Church of St Mary and St Walburga was located in Shipley, only a few miles from where Habib lived. The driver circled it twice then parked directly outside.

The shadow of the S-Class behind them gave Jack some comfort. Memories of the past twenty-four hours were vivid and he could still taste the fumes from the fire.

Aisha was trembling, trying her best to look brave.

'Shall we?' she said, in an attempt to take control.

'No,' said Habib, turning to face her.

She opened her mouth to protest but Habib's booming voice stopped her dead.

'You will listen to me, Aisha,' he said, pointing a finger at her. The shift in his mood was unexpected and frightening. 'I'm going inside with one of my men. We'll make a few enquiries. In the meantime, you're to stay here with Jack, out of sight. Do I make myself clear?'

Aisha remained quiet, looking at the floor.

'Do I make myself clear?' This time he hammered his fist into his seat, clearly angered by her apparent contempt.

Aisha nodded quickly.

'Habib,' started Jack, but he was cut short.

'Don't cross me on this, Jack. You stay with her – have you got that?'

Jack bristled at being spoken to like a child.

As the two men glared at each other, Aisha flung her door open and made an urgent dash for the church, coughing as she went.

'No!' shouted Habib.

He followed after her but was slowed by his bulk. Jack flew past him, hissing Aisha's name.

By the time he reached her, she was already hammering at the front door. He pulled her to one side.

'Are you crazy?' he said, turning to see Habib and his men approaching.

The church door swung open to reveal a plump middle-aged woman in a grey tunic.

'Aisha,' said Habib, grabbing her arm, but she shrugged it away.

Aisha spoke quickly as if she was afraid the nun would slam the door. 'My name is Aisha Iqbal and this is Jack Baxi. Last night we were kidnapped, tortured and almost killed, and a man named Benedict Cave has something to do with it. We know he was here. I want to know why he tried to find us. Please let us in.' Jack could see she was trying not to burst into tears.

The nun looked carefully at Aisha, and then at Jack. She took her time, giving each of them a measured stare. A tall woman, she crouched to meet Aisha's eye level and stared intensely at her face.

'What . . . what are you doing?' said Aisha, taking a step back.

The woman kept her eyes fixed on Aisha. The lamp over the door poured a mournful yellow glow over them both, sending a chill down Jack's spine.

'You have a coloboma in your eye?' the woman said. 'A mark like a dark tear below your pupil?'

Aisha nodded, uncertain as to what was happening.

The woman sighed heavily. 'I had hoped it wouldn't come to this.'

'What are you talking about? Who are you?' asked Jack.

'My name is Sister Catherine Lowry. I'd like you both to come inside, but only the two of you.'

Habib opened his mouth to object.

'I'm afraid it's not negotiable,' continued the Sister. 'If you'd like me to tell you what I know, then it will be to the two of you alone or not at all. Those are not my terms, they're instructions from Father Benedict Cave.'

'You don't make the rules here,' began Habib.

Jack placed a firm hand on his shoulder and pushed him away. 'Back off, Habib. Just back off.'

He then turned back towards the nun. 'We have endured a rough twenty-four hours, Sister,' he said. 'We've been to hell and back.'

Sister Catherine's tone was sympathetic but she didn't mince her words.

'You may have suffered much already, Mr Baxi, but I fear that the hell you are referring to is yet to come.'

TWENTY

THE CHURCH CORRIDOR LAY in eerie darkness, the lights on the walls offering scant illumination. Shadows seemed to claw at Jack from all sides, and his steps faltered on the fraying red carpet beneath his feet. A cloying scent of rising damp rose beneath the faint incense in the air. The corridor was narrow, so they walked in single file. Sister Catherine led them to a tiny office at the far end.

She took a seat behind the desk and indicated for them to sit opposite. There were no windows, which Jack found unsettling, just dark rows of what appeared to be ancient religious texts. The room was bitterly cold and his teeth started to chatter. The nervous energy flaring through his body didn't help.

Sister Catherine asked them to clarify what had happened over the past twenty-four hours.

'Who is Benedict Cave?' asked Jack impatiently when he'd finished briefing her.

'Father Benedict Cave's parish and refuge centre is located in a suburb of Delhi called Sadar Bazaar. One week ago, Father

Cave contacted this church asking for a place to stay. He arrived three days ago.'

Aisha was also struggling with the cold. Jack could see her knees knocking together. Sister Catherine seemed unfazed by the inhospitable environment, although she struggled with her words. After several moments of uneasy silence, she continued.

'Father Cave also happens to be a doctor. The refuge centre he runs is supported by the church. It looks after sex workers who have been exiled from their brothels and left to die on the streets of Delhi. A year ago, a particularly complex case was referred to him.'

Jack listened, sensing that she was building towards something he'd rather not hear.

'It was by all accounts a traumatic case for Father Cave. He has spent over a year with this lady trying to' – she searched for the right word – 'cure her.'

She pointed to a television next to the desk. It had an in-built DVD player.

'I have some footage to show you, courtesy of Father Cave. I must warn you that the nature of it is . . . quite disturbing. As part of his role, he was authorized by the Catholic Church to conduct exorcisms in India.'

The hairs on Jack's neck stood on end.

'Jack,' whispered Aisha, 'I don't understand what's going on here.'

'Show us,' said Jack.

'Possession is a sensitive subject within the Church . . . Quite simply, it frightens me. I have no wish to see this again. When it's finished, I'll return and try to help you where I can, but I'm afraid the information I have is limited.'

Sister Catherine made her way to the door. 'Father Cave left me with strict instructions that if the need arose, I was to show this DVD to the two of you only and to no one else. I don't know what dark forces are at play here, but I do know that Father Cave was to some extent able to help this lady. The rest, well, he could not explain.'

She left the room and closed the door behind her.

Jack stared at the blank screen. The DVD was waiting to be played.

'This is freaking me out,' said Aisha.

Jack was breathing heavily. He couldn't bring himself to reach over and hit the start button. He turned to face Aisha. 'Before we watch this, do you have *any* clue what it's about?'

'No,' she replied. 'This is way beyond anything I can explain. They *must* have the wrong people.'

Jack wanted to agree, except that Sister Catherine had known their names. She had looked for the distinguishing anomaly in Aisha's eye. He was scared to watch the tape but knew it was vital if they wanted answers.

Aisha looked nervously at the screen then reached out and grasped Jack's hand, giving it an encouraging squeeze, before nodding for him to proceed. Jack forced a smile and hit Play.

TWENTY-ONE

HABIB STARED UNWAVERINGLY AT the front door of the church. He'd sent two of his men round the back of the building to make sure no one else could get inside.

Jack had taken charge, relegating Habib to the vehicle. It had reminded him of when they used to work together: Jack always taking the lead and Habib always in the shadows. It was this need to be at the forefront of everything that had led to Jack's downfall.

There was something deeper troubling Habib. A seed embedded long ago in his mind. A memory he had planned on taking to his grave.

When he'd first seen Jack that morning, the shocking state Aisha had been in had not been the thing that troubled Habib the most.

Even though he and Sara had sworn never to speak of it, the image of Jack murdering his wife was burned into Habib's memory. Jack's hands around Kirin's neck . . . the way he had dragged her towards the river, where she'd been found a fortnight later. The waiting was killing Habib. Only he knew how Jack and Aisha were linked, and it had nothing to do with a priest from India.

Habib closed his eyes, his head pounding from a puzzle he was unable to solve.

Singh had parked his Range Rover far enough away from the church to remain unnoticed. He had planted a few men from his organization at both ends of the road. They were dressed as workmen, making it look as if rudimentary roadworks were being carried out. If Singh failed here, there would still be no escape for Baxi and the girl.

He peered through his binoculars at Habib's Mercedes. He'd bet it had bulletproof glass – standard for someone as powerful as the CEO of the Elite empire. It gave Singh a headache. He'd need to take Jack and Aisha out on their exit from the church and he didn't have the right calibre of weapon to hit them at this range. His pistol meant he needed to be closer, and that meant compromising his position.

Singh got out of the car and headed towards the rear of the church.

He walked quickly, welcoming the bitter chill against his face. At the side of the church, he entered a snicket. Thorny trees on either side closed in around him; the entire church was surrounded by thick hedges. He peeked through a gap and spotted two shadows by the back door. He'd expected that.

He hurried to the other side of the church and saw another gap in the hedging, this one low on the ground and much larger. Singh crawled through and then made his way silently towards the building. He was only a few metres away now from the men at the back door.

They were facing away. One of them was smoking. They never saw him coming.

Singh crashed the grip of his gun into the back of the first man's head. He was unconscious before his body hit the ground.

Singh then whipped round to point his gun at the other man.

He raised a finger to his lips, the gun saying everything that needed to be said.

The man's cigarette fell from his lips in shock. Singh directed him away from the back door into the shadows next to the building.

A swift kick in the groin and the man dropped to his knees. Singh pushed the gun into the man's mouth so he couldn't speak.

'I don't want to kill you,' he said, 'but I will if you give me reason to. Answer my questions and all you'll wake up with is a headache.'

The man mumbled in agreement.

'Jack Baxi and Aisha Iqbal. Are they inside the church?'

The man nodded. Any resistance he might have posed seemed to have melted away with the taste of metal in his mouth.

'The van in front of the church. How many men inside?'

Singh removed the gun from the man's mouth.

'Two,' he mumbled.

'Is Habib Iqbal in the car?'

The man nodded.

'So, three of them in total then?'

Another nod.

'Are they armed?'

The man shook his head.

'How long have Jack and the girl been inside?'

'T-ten . . . fifteen minutes.'

Singh cracked the gun into the man's skull and gently lowered his head to the ground.

He darted to the back door and tried it, but it was locked.

His best chance would be to take out the van, then wait inside it for Baxi and the girl. Singh dragged both bodies to the side of the building and secured them with duct tape.

Then he headed towards the front of the church: to Habib Iqbal.

TWENTY-TWO

THE FOOTAGE SHOWED A darkened room, with a woman in a torn robe lying on a single mattress.

The narration was given by a man – Benedict Cave, Jack assumed.

'It is the twenty-fourth of September 2018 and present are Father Joseph Dunn and Father Benedict Cave. The subject has been non-responsive for the last twenty minutes and respiratory rate has returned to normal. The exorcism was carried out successfully and the footage logged as V4.24.11. All three personalities were present.'

Cave moved over to the woman. She was Asian but that was all Jack could make out. Her hair was strung chaotically across her face, she was painfully thin and had restraints across her torso.

'Can you hear me?' asked Cave, taking a seat next to her.

The woman's breathing became more animated. A twitch started in her neck, veins pulsing powerfully. She splayed her fingers and the noise of them cracking was revolting. The woman spoke in a deeply masculine tone with no stable pitch.

'They're all dead,' boomed the voice.

Aisha tensed and moved closer to Jack.

'If they're all dead, who are you then, child?' asked Cave.

'I am whoever you want me to be, baby,' said the voice, and burst into a girly fit of giggles. Then it started screaming expletives in Punjabi that Jack hadn't heard for decades. The language was so foul he cringed. It screamed of rape and sodomy.

'I don't want to watch this,' whispered Aisha into Jack's ear.

He didn't either. Nothing spooked Jack more than shit like this. But they had to see it through.

The voice on the screen changed. Now the woman spoke softly.

'I'm tired of all this,' she said in English, turning her head towards the camera, her hair still strewn across her face. 'Tired of it all, father.'

'What is your name, child?'

'I have so many, I don't know any more.' Her voice was old and withered. 'Let me die,' she said.

The DVD showed Cave's hand move towards her face with some water.

As he did so, the woman launched herself forwards, eyes bulging, and screamed like an animal. She bit Cave's hand and he yelled in agony, snatching it away and disappearing from screen.

The woman continued screaming and thrashing, trying desperately to free herself from the restraints. Her body convulsed, her hair finally slipping from her face. The noise coming out of her mouth was blood-curdling, and she had a triangular birthmark on her top lip.

Jack released a wounded cry as he paused the tape. He'd know that birthmark anywhere.

He knew this woman.

He didn't understand how, but he was looking at a ghost.

'Kirin . . .' he whispered.

A strangled noise came from Aisha. The girl was trembling. Before she even opened her mouth, Jack knew what was coming. It hit him all at once – the girl's familiarity now as clear as the fear etched all over her face.

'No,' she whispered, 'that is my mother.'

TWENTY-THREE

JACK AND AISHA WERE sitting in stunned silence. The freeze-frame of Kirin's face seemed to watch over them as they stared suspiciously at one another.

The room had been ice-cold, but now felt uncomfortably hot. Jack opened his mouth to say something but it was so dry he felt as if he was choking.

'How can this be?' said Aisha.

'It can't,' whispered Jack.

Aisha took out her phone, hands trembling, and scrolled to her pictures. Jack saw her access a file called 'Mum'. She turned the phone to face him and Jack's mouth fell open. He was looking at an old picture of Kirin, lying in a hospital bed with a newborn baby in her arms.

Jack took the phone from her and stared at the screen.

It was undeniable.

The room started to spin. Jack's mind was struggling with images of his wife's dead body, identifying it at the police mortuary, the police investigation and the funeral.

'I cremated my wife,' he said, trying to regain some composure.

'My mother died when I was born. I have the death certificate at home,' Aisha insisted.

Sister Catherine knocked on the door and entered. She walked past them, turned off the TV and retook her seat.

'You'll have many questions,' she said gently. 'I'll tell you everything I know. This lady was referred to Father Cave as a difficult case and all I can tell you is that it bothered him enough to bring him here. He gave up his post at the centre and started working exclusively with her. She had three personalities when she was exorcized. At different times throughout the year she claimed to be Kirin Baxi, Hasina-Ali and a third, more disruptive personality.'

Kirin Baxi. Just hearing her name made Jack wince.

'Father Cave contacted me six months ago, asking me to verify a few simple details about her life in the UK.'

'What sort of details?' asked Jack.

'She described her life with you, Mr Baxi: snippets of information at least. Your shop, for example. She knew its location and external appearance – details I checked for Father Cave when I visited your store a month ago. But Kirin also described living with Aisha's father, and she described you, Aisha, and the fact that you have a coloboma in your left eye. It's a rarity, no?'

Aisha nodded, everything Sister Catherine had said swirling around in her mind.

'But my wife is dead,' Jack said firmly. 'I cremated her.'

Sister Catherine ignored him and continued. 'Lastly, she described her life working as a prostitute in India. There were many contradictions. Father Cave came here to find out the truth.'

'And what *is* the truth?' asked Aisha.

'Father Cave arrived in Bradford three days ago, determined to find you both and explain what he knew.'

'But he didn't tell you?' asked Jack.

'No,' she replied. 'It was not my business and frankly the story so far is beyond anything in my experience. Like you, I am utterly perplexed as to how a woman you cremated may have ended up working for years in a brothel in India, only to then arrive at Father Cave's refuge. But this woman wants to be saved – that much I do know. Father Cave told me that his calling in life was to establish the truth and set her free. He became troubled, unable to sleep. He needed the two of you to complete the puzzle.'

'This is absurd – my wife is dead,' Jack said.

'How did she die?' asked Sister Catherine.

'She drowned. By the Leeds and Liverpool canal.'

'Did you see her body?'

Jack started to reply and then paused. He thought back to 2002, to a night he could picture as if it had happened yesterday. Kirin had told him she was leaving him. A bitter argument had got out of control. Jack had struck her and almost strangled her before he had stopped, horrified at his behaviour. Jack's mother had intervened and tried to restore order, but Kirin had called a taxi and left. A short while later, when Jack had pulled himself together, he had called the taxi firm, told them his wife was vulnerable and gone straight to where the taxi had left her.

The Leeds and Liverpool canal.

Jack had hunted high and low and eventually found her shoes and scarf by the waterside. He had assumed that she'd taken her own life and had not known what to do, his judgement clouded by regret. Jack had simply . . . gone home.

'Mr Baxi, did you actually see her body?'

'Yes,' said Jack. 'I identified her body when it was found. It . . . had badly decomposed.'

'Did you see her face?'

'I just told you, the body was decomposed,' Jack snapped, losing his cool.

Sister Catherine frowned at him. 'How can you be so sure it was her?'

'Her *mangalsutra* was round her neck. It is a wedding gift, a necklace Sikh men give to their wives as a token of marriage, and it was a one-of-a-kind piece my mother had commissioned in India. And her wedding ring was on her hand.'

Sister Catherine opened her mouth to speak.

'And finally,' Jack said, raising his hand to cut her off, 'a DNA match was done to confirm her identity by the coroner.' As these facts came back to him, his resolve hardened. This was all just some kind of sick joke.

Sister Catherine shook her head. 'Then I don't know what to tell you.'

'That woman is not my wife.'

'Her twin sister maybe?' asked Aisha.

'She was an only child and this is not a Bollywood movie,' he replied tightly.

'Yet a woman who knows intricate details of our lives and looks exactly like her is still alive and we have people trying to murder us,' Aisha shot back.

'Is there anything else?' asked Jack, heading for the door. 'I need to get the hell away from here.'

Sister Catherine nodded. 'I have a few photographs here and a medical file,' she said.

'May we take a look, please?' asked Aisha.

Sister Catherine opened a drawer in her desk and handed the file to Aisha.

'You say Father Cave had a refuge in a suburb of Delhi?' asked Aisha.

'Why? You planning to take a trip?' Jack said mockingly.

Aisha ignored him.

'The address is on the back of the medical reports in there,' replied Sister Catherine. 'The location of the refuge is not made public for its own security – some of these women have escaped brutal prostitution rackets.'

'This has gone on long enough. I'll see you outside,' Jack said, and left the room.

Aisha turned to Sister Catherine. 'Can we take this with us? It's all we have to go on.'

The nun hesitated. 'Father Cave didn't . . .'

'Please,' Aisha implored.

Sister Catherine eventually nodded.

'Thank you. I'll be in touch if we find anything.'

'May God be with you, Aisha, and be careful,' the nun said.

Jack and Aisha hurried down the path, waves of icy rain stinging their faces. They were almost back at Habib's fortified van when a Range Rover came tearing down the road and screeched to a stop.

Detective Singh flung open the door, jumped out and pointed a gun at them.

'Shit!' whispered Jack, paralysed with shock.

From behind the van, the Mercedes screamed forward, blocking Singh's line of fire as he pulled the trigger. The bullet cracked into the windscreen and became lodged in the glass.

Habib, meanwhile, threw open the side door of the van and shouted for them to get in.

Jack grabbed Aisha and they ran for their lives. Before the door was even closed, the van and the Mercedes had pulled away.

Singh fired two more shots, both of them snared by the bulletproof glass. He threw himself aside just before the van smashed into the side of the Range Rover, ripping the driver's door clean off its hinges before accelerating wildly away.

At the end of the road, the van slowed down, roadworks

blocking their exit. Two Asian men, both in turbans, raised their hands, one brandishing a red STOP sign at them.

'Go through them!' shouted Habib and the driver put his foot down. The men waved furiously for them to stop but jumped clear of the plastic barriers just as the van and the Mercedes behind crashed through and sped away.

Detective Singh stood up and brushed himself down. A few house lights had come on, curtains twitching. He didn't have long.

Singh leapt inside his car, leaving the door on the road. He called his men and told them to pack up and leave. The phony licence plates on his Range Rover would afford him some level of cover, but he knew that in the moment he'd pulled the trigger, his life in the UK had changed for ever.

The matter he was overseeing was more complex than anything he'd dealt with before. He would not be turning up for work tomorrow. The case files on his desk would remain untouched. This matter took priority, and if it meant he had to sacrifice his life for it, then he was honoured to do so.

Kismet had led Baxi and the girl to the church. And now, no doubt, they knew secrets that should have stayed buried.

They would try to find the woman.

Singh was now on a direct collision course with them. Baxi and the girl didn't know who they were up against. A global network of shadows was primed to be called upon. This would all come down to one simple matter.

Who would find Kirin Baxi first?

TWENTY-FOUR

HABIB HAD TIGHT HOLD of Aisha as they pulled up to the house. Jack was staring out of the back window, convinced that Singh would be in pursuit. He was gripping the file Aisha had been given by Sister Catherine. While Habib barked orders at his men to mobilize a team and secure the house, Jack flicked through the file. The ramifications were beyond anything he had thought possible. Everything was in there.

Same blood type.

Same thyroid disorder.

Irrefutable pictures.

His wife, Kirin Baxi – slave to a brothel in a notorious red-light district of Delhi.

Jack and Aisha's names were inside the file among tattered transcript papers.

Jack was disorientated. It felt like he'd been concussed for the past twenty-four hours. None of this felt real.

As the gates to Habib's mansion closed behind them and

security vehicles swarmed, Jack could only stare at the crumpled figure of Aisha Iqbal, huddled inside Habib's enormous arms.

How could she be Kirin's daughter?

Deep down, Jack thought he knew the answer but it was too horrifying to contemplate. For now, he persisted with denial.

Inside the house, Habib carried Aisha into the kitchen and sat her down at the table. He checked her over and shouted for Sara to call the doctor again, something Aisha vehemently refused.

Habib's men rushed around the house, barking orders about tracking the Range Rover. Suggestions about involving the police were quashed; this would be dealt with in-house.

Jack was standing bewildered by the door, still clutching the file. Habib pointed to a chair next to Aisha.

'Sit down, Jack,' he said firmly.

Jack closed the kitchen door and made his way over to the table. He slumped into a chair, denial still overruling a truth he could not face.

Habib sat down opposite. 'Start talking. What the hell happened in that church? Why is this fucking Detective Singh trying to kill my Aisha?'

'He's trying to kill both of us,' Jack replied absently. He opened the file and slid a photo of his wife across the table to Habib.

Habib stilled. Sara peered at it over his shoulder and let out a whimper of incredulity.

'How is it that my mother and Jack's wife are the same person?' asked Aisha coldly.

Habib shared a troubled look with Sara.

Jack kept his gaze on their faces.

'I . . . I . . . need to find this Detective Singh,' mumbled Habib. 'P-perhaps he knows what—'

Jack slammed his hand on the table, making them all jump. He leaned forward, dropped his voice and hissed at Habib.

'Start talking, Habib. *Now!*'
Sara rushed to the sink. She retched noisily.
Guilt: it was written all over her – crippling, shameful guilt.
She started to cry.
'Tell him, Habib,' she whispered. 'Tell him everything.'

TWENTY-FIVE

THE ATMOSPHERE IN THE kitchen could have been cut with a knife.

Habib was involved.

Jack, his mind clear all of a sudden, saw his only option.

He stood up slowly, but once on his feet, sprang past Habib and grabbed Sara, pinning his arm round her neck. In one swift move, he grabbed a kitchen knife from the stand and held it against her throat.

Sara screamed and Habib lunged towards them.

'No more fucking lies,' Jack hissed. 'You tell me right now what's going on or I'll cut her throat.'

Habib backed away, his hands raised. He glanced at the kitchen door, hoping members of his team were still in the house, but it was deathly quiet.

'By the time you call them in from outside, it will be too late. Now, for the last time, start talking.'

'Jack,' said Aisha, getting to her feet and holding her hands up as if to calm things down, 'what are you doing?'

He didn't take his eyes off Habib when he answered her. 'Playing the only hand I've got left.'

'Please, Jack, you're hurting me,' said Sara.

Jack tightened his grip around the knife. 'Shut up. In about five seconds I'm going to draw blood.'

Habib nodded and backed away. 'I'm sorry, Jack. I . . . I . . . never thought it would come to this.'

'Tell me what you people did,' said Jack. He felt Sara's tears drip hot on his hand but didn't relax his grip on the knife.

'When you went to jail, Jack, we . . . looked after Kirin. As you'd asked,' said Habib, clearly struggling with what came next.

Sara continued for him, her words coming out choked because of Jack's arm around her throat. 'Habib and Kirin had an affair, Jack.'

He'd known it must have happened. But hearing it said out loud made it real.

'How could you?' he shouted. 'You fucking animal! Brother – that's what you used to call me. I spent three years in jail, three fucking years of my life for you bastards. *I'll look after your wife* – isn't that what you said, Habib? *Don't worry, Jack, she's my sister – I'll look after her.*'

Habib's colour rose.

Jack spat on the floor. 'Only you could be so filthy as to take a woman as a sister and then take her to your bed. And after everything I did for you.'

Habib glared at him. 'Don't act like you didn't know.'

Jack was taken aback.

'You knew she was having an affair,' continued Habib. 'She told you on the night she vanished. The night you . . .'

He fell silent and looked at Jack.

A knowing look.

Jack was stunned. He loosened his grip on the knife. Dark memories he had suppressed for so many years flooded back.

Habib carried on, knowing things Jack had never told anyone. 'Kirin told you she was leaving you. That she'd been unfaithful.'

As the pieces of a jigsaw Jack had never completed finally fell into place, he lowered the knife and let go of Sara.

She didn't dash away from him as he'd expected, just stood there.

'Kirin told you she was leaving you,' repeated Habib. He put his hand out, took Sara's and pulled her to safety behind him. 'And you know what you did.'

'I hit her,' whispered Jack, more to himself than anyone in the room. It was the first time he had ever admitted what happened that night.

'You did more than that,' said Habib.

Jack closed his eyes. Visions of his hands around his wife's neck flashed across his mind. How could Habib have known? Jack had almost convinced himself it had never happened.

'Kirin called me,' said Habib, 'that night, after she'd fled your house. She told me what you'd done and asked me to collect her. I was supposed to meet her by the stream, at the bottom of the railway line.'

Aisha was listening to the revelations, as stunned as Jack was.

'Why there?' asked Jack, his eyes wide. The room felt like it was spinning, so many untruths surfacing at once.

Sara stepped away from Habib and stood in the middle between both men. She spoke quietly, pain in her voice, recalling a past she clearly did not want to relive. She told Jack that when she'd found out about the affair, she had left Habib. Kirin had told her it had been nothing more than one night of foolishness but the pregnancy made the situation so much more complex. For a time, Kirin and Habib had tried to make a relationship work for the baby's sake, but there'd been no love there. Just . . . consequence.

'Kirin loved you, Jack. It's why she tried to make it work with you when you came out of jail. Habib convinced her it would be better for Aisha to stay with him but Kirin hoped that when the time was right, she could tell you about the affair and about Aisha and we might all work something out. But she couldn't stand to be away from her little girl and it all started to unravel.'

Habib stepped closer to Jack now and took over the story. 'I drove to the bridge and followed the path down to where Kirin had asked me to meet her. She couldn't come to the house because Sara and I had just reconciled and things were . . . well . . . delicate.'

Jack could not believe what he was hearing. He had protected them and this was how they had repaid him.

'When I got there, I saw you strangling her.' Habib raised his voice, angry now. 'You choked her until she was unconscious and then carried her body away towards the river.'

Jack shook his head. 'That wasn't me.'

'I saw . . .' Habib faltered and stopped. 'Your car was parked by the road, Jack.'

'But did you actually see me? My face?' said Jack, almost shouting.

Habib shook his head, confused.

'Christ,' whispered Jack and leaned back against a countertop, his legs feeling weak. 'I . . . did go there. I phoned the taxi company she'd used, told them she was vulnerable and forced them to tell me where they'd dropped her. I felt bad about what I'd done . . . I lost control. I tried to find her and followed the path down to the canal . . .'

Jack fell silent. He'd thought about this moment ever since that terrible evening. 'I couldn't find her, only her scarf and shoes by the side of the canal.' Another pause. Then: 'I assumed she'd jumped in and I . . . I . . . panicked because of what had gone on before.' Jack took a moment and then said softly, 'I left.'

The room fell quiet, everyone glancing at each other.

Jack broke the silence. 'I was disgusted with myself that I'd hit her – my rage got the better of me. I've thought for years that I caused her death with our final argument. She was a mess and I . . . I lost it. But I did not kill my wife, Habib.'

'You're a liar. I might not have seen your face but everything else points to it.' Habib's next words were delivered with contempt. 'You went there to finish off what you started in your home. Coward.'

Jack lunged at Habib, everything he had learned igniting a fury he needed to unleash.

'Bastard!' he screamed. 'I sacrificed my life for you!'

He crashed his palm into Habib's throat and kicked his feet from under him. The big man went thundering to the floor, causing the whole room to shake. Jack put one knee on Habib's throat and the other on his chest, then punched him in the face, breaking his nose.

Sara came running towards him, screaming for him to stop. He threw her off. She went crashing to the floor and lay there winded, gasping for breath.

It gave Habib a chance – he brought his fist towards Jack's groin and struck him between the legs.

Jack stumbled backwards and tripped over a chair. Habib snatched the knife from the counter just as Jack got to his feet.

The two men were panting heavily.

'Don't be stupid, Jack,' said Habib, blood dripping from his nose. 'Don't make me do something I'll regret.'

Images of Habib in bed with Kirin were running through Jack's mind. His body was trembling. He could hear Aisha's voice, timid and afraid, but couldn't make out the words. All he wanted was to spill Habib's blood. To exact revenge for a story he still couldn't piece together.

They had fucked him.

In the worst possible way.

When Jack spoke, his voice was calm, even if his head was a

The Blood Divide

mess. 'I'm coming for that knife, Habib,' he whispered. 'Of that you can be damn sure. Because one of us is not leaving this room alive.'

Habib shook his head and raised the knife, pointing the tip at Jack.

As the red mist darkened, Jack lunged for Habib with everything he had.

105

TWENTY-SIX

'STOP!' SHOUTED AISHA, LEAPING between the men. Habib dropped the knife to avoid hurting her. No sooner had he done so than Jack was on him, both men grappling, Aisha's delicate body trapped between them. Sara was still lying winded on the floor, trying to catch her breath.

Blood continued to flow from Habib's nose and Jack punched him there again, compounding the injury.

'Stop it!' screamed Aisha again. 'Can't you see there's something else going on here?'

Grabbing Jack's arm before he could land another blow, she pulled him off Habib with all the strength she could muster.

'Jack, you have to help me!'

He backed off but only to look for the knife. Aisha scooped it from the floor. She stepped between the two men again, brandishing it.

'Stop it, or I'll hurt one of you!' she screamed.

Jack was out of breath and needed to regroup. Thoughts of going through Aisha to get to Habib crossed his mind but a stronger voice told him he needed to get out of here before he did something he'd later regret.

He backed away, pointing an angry finger at Habib. 'We're done here,' he hissed. He grabbed the file from the table and at the kitchen door turned back to Habib, who was nursing his broken nose.

'I tell you one thing. If I ever see you again, no matter where we are, I will fucking kill you.'

Upstairs in the bedroom, Jack got his things together. Habib's residence felt toxic and he couldn't think straight.

They had all lied.

He couldn't believe a thing they said; their every word was coated in deceit. Only one woman could tell him the truth and Jack meant to get it from her, even if she was five thousand miles away.

Sara knocked on the door, one of Habib's thugs at her side.

'Out of my way,' said Jack.

She stepped into the room. 'Jack – look, none of this—'

'Shut up! You people are incapable of telling the truth.' Jack slung his bag over his shoulder.

'You don't think this was hard for me?' said Sara angrily. 'The man I loved having a dirty little affair with your wife? She wasn't innocent in all this.'

Jack lunged towards her but the guard stepped between them and he drew back. He glared at Sara. 'Don't you speak about Kirin that way.'

'We were both betrayed,' said Sara, not letting it go.

'It all makes sense now – why you fucked off and didn't find me when I got out of prison.'

Sara stepped past the guard. He tried to hold her back, but she slapped his hand away. 'You think it was easy for me? I had to endure their affair and then raise that bastard child as my own.'

Jack was taken aback by the ferocity of her outburst.

'So don't walk away thinking you're any better than me. It wasn't me who couldn't keep my woman out of another man's bed.'

Aisha's voice from the doorway grabbed their attention. 'None of that explains why Detective Singh is trying to kill us both.' She glared at Sara, who had jumped at her voice. 'It's only me – the bastard child.'

Sara didn't respond, and for the first time Jack could clearly see the tension between them.

Aisha walked past the security guard towards Jack, and stuck out her hand. 'Before you go, I wanted to say thank you for saving my life,' she said. He shook her hand, surprised when she tightened her grip.

'I'll walk you to the gate. No one will stop you.'

She swung round and spoke to the guard, who was still hovering clumsily in the room. 'Get out of my way or I swear this will be the last day you ever work here.'

He stepped aside and Aisha turned to Sara, her words cutting like knives. 'This *bastard child* will walk Jack to the front gates so he can leave in peace. Only then can we all sit down and talk this through. I suggest you go and get my father.'

Outside, she led Jack past a group of six men, all clearly itching to get their hands on him. The girl was doing him a favour. There was no way the men would engage with Jack with her at his side. For a moment, he saw a ferocity in her that reminded him of Kirin.

Shoulder to shoulder, they headed down the gravel path towards the open gates.

'Why are you doing this?' whispered Jack.

'You broke Habib's nose. I heard him ordering his men to grab you and make sure you don't see sunrise. He's madder than I've ever seen him.'

'So, you leading me out is some sort of "secure passage"?'

'They wouldn't dare try anything with me at your side.' She glanced at her watch. 'It's nearly midnight. Where will you go?'

'That's none of your business,' replied Jack.

'How is that not my business? I was lied to as well,' she hissed.

'Habib has a habit of that.'

'But he'd never want to hurt me. There's no connection between him and this Detective Singh, as you thought earlier. There's something else going on, and we need to find out what it is.' Aisha looked over her shoulder. There was movement outside the house.

She checked her watch again.

'Does Cinderella turn into a servant at midnight?' asked Jack.

'Huh?'

'You keep looking at your watch.'

She nodded but was clearly on edge.

'There are two cars back at the house. One is my father's, the other his security.'

'I don't need a ride. Look, we're practically at the gate. I can take it from here. Go back inside. I can handle your father and his cronies.'

'You're foolish if you think you can escape without my help.'

Jack came to a standstill. 'What do you mean?'

Aisha took hold of his arm. 'Keep walking. They're watching.' She glanced at her watch again.

'Do you want to tell me what's going on?'

'The security lights are on a timer. I changed it so that in about two minutes they'll turn off. Both sets of car keys are in my pocket, along with my passport and three hundred pounds in cash. I can get more when we stop at an ATM. I've also taken Habib's passport. It'll slow him down.'

'What?' said Jack, completely perplexed.

'This affects me too,' hissed Aisha, 'and I will not cower away from this. We need to go to India and find her. We both deserve to know the truth.'

'Aisha . . .' Jack began.

'I'd rather work with you than against you, but when these lights go off I'm coming through those gates with you whether you like it or not.'

Jack was about to set her straight when a thought hit him.

If you have Aisha with you, then you have Habib's most prized possession.

A bargaining chip like no other.

He looked at the determination on her face. Jack had seconds to make this call and it needed to be the right one.

'Look at me,' said Jack, glancing at his watch.

23:58.

'This is no comic book adventure,' he said coldly.

'And I'm not a child so don't you dare treat me like one. This is my mother we're talking about – I need the answers as badly as you do.'

'Fine,' said Jack, securing the rucksack on his back and getting ready to make a run for it. 'Give me your phone,' he said to her.

'Why?'

'No time – just hand it over.'

Aisha gave it to him and Jack turned it off and put it in his pocket. He looked at the approaching gates.

'When the lights go out, which way do we go? You may have their car keys but they'll be on foot and on us within a few minutes.'

'There are two jogging tracks snaking through the woodland just outside the gates,' Aisha said.

'So which one do we take?'

'Neither – but they will.'

'Why?'

'Because I'm going to drop my headscarf on the ground next to one of them.'

'And what about us?'

'There's a bus stop at the foot of the hill. Next one arrives at five past midnight. We have five minutes to catch that bus.'

'A bloody bus?'

'Same way we escaped from Thornbury, remember? If we can manage to keep our cool, they'll lose the scent and we can get away. You've seen them: all brawn, no brains.'

'What happens if the bus doesn't turn up?'

'Then we're on foot.'

'Are you up to this? They'll be hunting us.'

'They already are,' Aisha replied. She pushed him towards the gates.

At that moment, the lights switched off and the compound plunged into darkness.

'Run!' she whispered.

PART TWO

PART TWO

TWENTY-SEVEN

THE LIGHTS WERE DIMMED in the Air France flight 226 from Paris to Delhi. It was the middle of the night and the plane was surging steadily through a prolonged stretch of turbulence. The business class cabin was full, everyone asleep apart from Jack Baxi and Aisha Iqbal.

They'd escaped from Habib a little over seventy-two hours ago, Aisha's plan catching her father completely by surprise. They had fled to the bottom of the hill, caught their bus and then taken a taxi from Bradford city centre to Leeds Bradford Airport. They'd booked on to the next flight out to Paris. Aisha stealing Habib's passport had been a stroke of genius, but while it might slow him down, Jack knew the delay would be twenty-four hours at most. Getting a visa for India would be a whole different story though, and it was that bit of red tape that made Jack hope they had enough of a head start.

Unlike Jack, Aisha was not in possession of a valid visa to enter India. As someone of Pakistani heritage, obtaining one was not straightforward. India routinely denied entry to anyone with Pakistani origins, the countries being sworn enemies. Fortunately, Jack had strong connections in Paris, as it was the main route for his illegal goods entering the UK – from Calais to Dover and then up to the north of England. One of his many contacts in Paris pulled a few strings to get Aisha fast-tracked at the Indian embassy. A bribe of six hundred euros and an hour in the queue had secured Aisha a six-month emergency visa.

Jack had applied for a permanent visa long before going to jail, some part of him thinking it might be a handy back-up plan should he ever need to flee the UK. It had been easy to obtain one in the 1990s; global terrorism had been a relatively minor concern and 'computers-saying-no' hadn't yet ruled the world.

Jack had intended to travel to India many times to reconcile with his mother, who had moved there permanently. She was widowed; Jack had disgraced her within Bradford's close-knit Sikh community, and after Kirin's death, she'd had no more reason to stay in England. She had disowned Jack, cursing his immoral ways, the denial of his faith and his descent into criminality.

Your father would be ashamed of you.

They hadn't spoken since.

Each time he'd thought about getting on a plane, he had remembered the bitter way they had parted and his anger stopped him from going. As far as he was aware, his mother was living the life of a hermit in the small rural village of her birth.

Nursing his whisky on ice, Jack closed his eyes, flashes of his mother's cutting last words intertwining with lewd images of Habib with Kirin.

Christ, he had been played for such a *fool*.

Jack had mourned his wife for years – regretting the violent end to their last night. Since learning the truth, he'd been replaying the events of that night on a constant loop.

Kirin had fled the house after Jack had struck her.

He had regretted it immediately, and tracked her via the taxi company.

Kirin had called Habib and asked him to collect her from down by the Leeds and Liverpool canal.

On arriving there, Habib had seen a man he believed to be Jack with his hands around Kirin's throat and dragging her off towards the canal.

Who was that man? And why had he tried to kill Jack's wife?

When Jack had arrived, he had searched for Kirin, finding only her shoes and scarf by the side of the water. Fearful that his rage earlier that night had pushed her to her limit, Jack had fled.

Habib had seen Jack's car as he was leaving the area; the two men must have missed each other by moments.

When Kirin's decomposed body was found almost two weeks later, it had seemed like an obvious suicide.

The coroner had come to that same conclusion, but clearly much darker forces had been at work.

Whose body had that actually been? And why?

The person Habib had seen must have returned to dump a second body in the canal and then somehow gone on to fool or maybe bribe the medical examiner into saying it had been Kirin Baxi.

That felt like too audacious a thing to happen to a simple woman like Kirin. Something was missing, and as Jack sipped his whisky, he searched for that missing link. The one thing that kept coming back to him was that only Habib had seen Kirin being throttled and dragged away by this mystery third party.

While many things remained unclear, one fact was crystal: Habib Iqbal was not to be trusted. And yet the idea that he was behind all this was a stretch.

Murdering Kirin?

Sure.

Somehow selling her to a brothel in India?

No chance.

Jack knew him too well. Not even Habib would sink that low and there was no reason for him to have actioned such a thing.

'Jack?' whispered Aisha, tapping his arm.

'Yes?' he replied, eyes still shut.

'Thank you for letting me come,' she said.

'You didn't exactly give me a choice,' he replied, opening his eyes and turning to face her.

'I know, but you could have left me to do this on my own.'

Jack's silence was more telling than he realized.

'It's because I'm her daughter, isn't it?'

'Isn't what?' he replied edgily.

'The reason I catch you looking at me like that.'

He sipped his whisky in response.

Aisha tore a small length of fabric from the hem of her Asian suit and slipped it over his wrist.

'What the hell are you doing?' he said, pulling his arm back.

Aisha leaned in closer. 'Changing the nature of our relationship. Please, let me tie this *rakhi* round your wrist . . .'

Rakhi was an annual tradition carried out by Hindu and Sikhs, when a sister would tie a piece of string round her brother's wrist and in return he would promise to look after her and ensure no harm came her way.

'A *rakhi* is a Hindu tradition, later adopted by Sikhs. It is not an Islamic one,' Jack said coldly.

Aisha smiled and shook her head. 'I think you'll find that in folklore, Rani Karnavati, the Hindu queen of Chittor, sent a *rakhi* to the Islamic Mughal emperor Humayun, asking for his help. This bond of protection crosses religious barriers.'

'I know that story but the barrier between us isn't religious.'

'Perhaps. But if you let me tie this, you might see me differently. I need to know I can trust you.'

The plane hit a spot of turbulence and the seat belt signs

flashed up. Jack waited until things had calmed before continuing.

'I got you this far, didn't I?' he said.

'Jack, I'm not stupid. Having me here with you means you have my father at your mercy.' She fixed him with a perceptive stare. 'I'm insurance, aren't I?'

His hand stilled before the glass had reached his lips.

'Aren't I?' she repeated.

'And knowing that, you still got on this plane with me?'

'I don't think you'd hurt me,' she replied.

She touched Jack's wrist again. 'A *rakhi* is tied between a brother and sister to demonstrate a bond of protection. All I want to know is that, while you might bluff my father into thinking you'd hurt me, that you won't. Once I tie this, you'll be bound by it – like people have been for centuries.'

'I don't buy into that crap,' Jack said.

Aisha didn't relent. 'Then I have nothing to lose by tying it.'

He looked away from her, irritated, but relaxed his arm. Aisha slipped the length of cloth around his wrist. She tied the ends in a secure double knot.

'Feel better?' asked Jack when she'd finished.

'I do.'

'So, tell me something – as my new-found "sister". Tell me about Habib and Sara's relationship. Tell me about *you* and them. Take me into those four walls and for the next, say, thirty minutes or so, allow me a peek into your world.'

Aisha spoke earnestly and not once did Jack think she was holding something back. She had a naivety to her that he almost envied. He'd pretty much expected what she told him – that Habib was the boss and, boy, did everyone know it. Sara was and always had been the dutiful housewife, obedient to his every demand. She had never shown Aisha anything more than the most perfunctory affection.

Aisha had been given very few photos of her mother. Habib had told her they'd been destroyed in a house fire and Aisha had never had any reason to question it. Habib had referred to Kirin as Hasina-Ali and had always spoken fondly of her. He'd told Aisha that her mother had been his first true love and that when she had died in childbirth he had been a broken man, but then eventually started a new relationship with Sara. Aisha had never suspected that those were anything other than the facts.

Aisha, though, had always felt that Sara disliked her more than made sense. Now she knew why. She continued.

'Sara couldn't have children of her own and I think that bothered her more than she let on.' Aisha turned away from Jack, who could sense she was trying to figure out the best way to say what was on her mind. 'I think the real reason, though, Jack, was that while their affair didn't last long, Kirin falling pregnant meant that she and Habib bonded in a way that Habib never could with Sara.'

A silence filled the space between them, Jack thinking about what she'd said. It hurt more than he could say. Jack had never shared those experiences with Kirin either.

Or with anyone.

'So, I've told you all about me, Jack. What about you?'

'What about me?'

'Did you ever meet anyone else? Remarry? What's your world like? I feel like I don't really know a thing about you.'

Jack looked away, uncomfortable. He turned back to Aisha when she gently tapped the *rakhi* on his wrist.

'Sister, remember?'

Jack drained the last drops of his whisky and beckoned to the steward for a top-up. He took a sip and then turned to answer Aisha's question.

'You want the truth?' said Jack.

'Always.'

'I never recovered from what your father and Sara did to me. That was *my* sacrifice. *My* commitment to our friendship. Kirin was really the only person I had left.'

He sipped again at his whisky, seeming to struggle with the next part.

'I became needy towards her. She was distant and I couldn't understand why. When she left me . . .' He paused, collected himself and continued. 'After what happened, I retreated into my shell. Everyone I had ever trusted had betrayed me. Your father, Aisha, ruined me. I was never the same man again.'

TWENTY-EIGHT

JACK AND AISHA MADE their way in silence towards the immigration checkpoint at Indira Gandhi International Airport. Aisha had covered herself in an Islamic burka she had picked up in Paris; she felt safe, hidden away.

Her heart was racing. She doubted her visa was properly valid. It had all seemed so rushed. What if Jack had purposely engineered a fake and she was detained in customs? She watched Jack disappear through the checkpoint at immigration. A few seconds later, he was past the gate, and Aisha was on her own.

The immigration officer opened her passport, asked her a few generic questions about her stay and then asked her to lift her face veil. Aisha obliged and felt a visible flush of guilt spread across her face.

He gave her a cursory glance and then hammered a stamp into her passport.

It was really happening: she was in India.

*

Jack left Aisha by the carousel in the baggage hall and took himself off to the men's room. He entered the disabled toilet and locked himself inside.

More than anything, Jack wanted to get Aisha off his back, book into a five-star hotel and get pissed until everything that had happened faded into oblivion – the shop, Detective Singh, Habib, Sara and Kirin, all of it.

He was afraid.

How had he managed to get wrapped up in this?

There was a small mirror over the sink. Jack splashed water over his face. His eyes were bloodshot and his breath stale. He wanted to rinse his mouth out, but Indian tap water was a sure-fire way to end up in hospital.

He stared intently at his reflection. He'd spent so many years loathing Kirin for her affair and hating himself for the violent way in which he'd reacted.

Was he somehow to blame for this whole chain of events?

Now he was here, he didn't know how he felt about her any more. There were too many other thoughts whirling inside his brain. He closed his eyes and whispered:

'You *are* going to find her. You *are* going to get the truth.'

Jack and Aisha exited the arrivals lounge through the green customs channel, each of them carrying a single bag.

They were greeted by a large group of men, mostly taxi drivers holding placards with the names of people or hotels. They all looked strangely similar: dark trousers, light jacket, moustache, jet-black hair. The air reeked of sweat, beads of perspiration on every brow.

Jack walked quickly along the metal railings protecting them from the boisterous crowd. He made his way over to the Bureau de Change, Aisha in her burka staying close to him.

Jack changed two thousand pounds into Indian currency, his

eyes flicking nervously around the room. Fifteen minutes later, the cashier handed him four thick bundles of cash. Jack placed three of them at the bottom of his rucksack and stuffed the remaining roll in his pocket.

'Oh, madam, I am truly sorry!' he heard a voice say behind him. Jack spun round to see a middle-aged man with a bald head and thick round glasses apologizing profusely to Aisha. He'd bumped into her and spilled mango juice down the front of her burka.

'What the hell? Can't you watch where you're going?' said Jack.

'It's OK,' said Aisha, holding the dripping burka away from the clothes beneath. 'Don't make a scene, Jack.'

The last thing Jack wanted to do was draw attention. He nodded for the man to move on and grabbed Aisha's arm.

'Sir, I am feeling truly terrible about this mess. You are landing in India only to be insulted by my careless mistake,' said the man, not taking the hint. 'The most hospitable country in the world is making a very bad impression,' he said, shaking his head.

'It's fine. Just watch where you're going next time,' said Jack.

'Sir, I am needing to make this up to you. Please,' he said, handing them a laminated taxi ID card, 'allow me, Mr Kapoor, to be escorting you to a destination of your choosing,' he said, and then emphasized the words, 'for free.'

'That's quite all right, we can make our own—'

'You are being picked up?'

'No,' replied Aisha.

'Yes,' said Jack.

The taxi driver laughed – a cheerful sound – and stuck out his hand. 'I am not hassling you, sir. It would be allowing me to head home after my shift, feeling no guilt about causing madam here such distress. But if you are choosing another taxi, I am understanding,' he said, nodding his head.

A free ride.

Jack had over two hundred thousand rupees in his pocket, but the shopkeeper in him couldn't resist a bargain.

'Fine. You can restore your karma by taking us to a hotel,' said Jack.

The man scooped Aisha's bag from the floor and apologized again. 'I am carrying this for madam, and we are leaving.'

He stuck his hand out to Jack.

'Mr Kapoor, at your service.'

As they left the terminal, the humidity wrapped itself round them like a thick blanket. The smell of sweat was overpowering, a fitting stench for the metropolis of Delhi, where over eighteen million people toiled daily. The new arrivals were assaulted by a sea of taxi drivers, all noisily vying for business.

Holding Aisha's arm, Jack walked with her after Kapoor. They crossed the road, deafened by the endless blaring of car horns from every direction. The car park was no more than a barren expanse of dirt, with no organized bays or order, just cars scattered haphazardly.

Kapoor made his way to a white Honda Civic. It looked new, with blacked-out windows and gleaming paintwork.

'Nice motor,' said Jack, noticing that most of the other cars around were wrecks.

'Lakshmi provides,' said the driver, referring to the Hindu god of wealth. He opened the boot and threw their bags inside.

Jack took his seat behind the driver. Aisha got in the other side.

'Does sir want to sit in front?' asked Mr Kapoor.

Jack shook his head.

Inside the car, the driver passed them two bottles of mineral water. 'Indian hospitality.'

'Thank you,' replied Aisha. 'I had no idea it would be this warm at five a.m.'

'Ah, you are being first time in India?'

'Yes.'

'And your name, madam, if I am being so bold?'

'Her name is Farida,' replied Jack. 'Let's get going, Mr Kapoor.'

'Certainly, Jatinder. I am just sending my wife one text message informing her that Kapoor is picking up his last fare. She is always worrying.'

He went to start the car when Jack sprang forwards and thrust his arm around the man's throat in a chokehold. He squeezed powerfully, trapping Mr Kapoor's head against the headrest.

Aisha screamed. 'Jack! What are you doing?'

'Shut up. Don't make this any worse.'

TWENTY-NINE

KAPOOR STRUGGLED BUT HAD little resistance against the vice-like hold on his neck. His windpipe was being crushed and his face turning a flushed red. He punched his fists into the steering wheel, blasting the horn, but it wasn't unusual around here and no one paid any attention. Quickly, Kapoor started to fade.

Aisha screamed for Jack to stop. She moved towards him and tried to grab his arm, convinced he had lost it.

'He works for Habib,' said Jack.

'What? Don't be ridiculous – we only just got here!'

It took just under a minute for Kapoor to be rendered unconscious. His head wobbled for a moment on his chest, before coming to rest. Aisha was too stunned to speak.

'When I introduced myself in the airport, I told him my name was Jack, but this son of a bitch just called me Jatinder.'

She looked sceptically at Jack.

'I bet this'll prove it,' said Jack. He reached forward and snatched up Kapoor's phone, a cheap and ancient Nokia. Jack flicked to the most recent text messages.

'Bingo,' he said, showing Aisha the last message received.
Bring them to the house. Unharmed.

'Is that your father's number?' asked Jack.

Aisha looked at the phone, bewildered. She nodded. 'But how did he manage to . . .?'

'Money,' said Jack. 'We may have checked Habib's progress by taking his passport but his kind of wealth reaches far. We need to get out of here. Now.'

Jack grabbed the driver's seat belt and wrapped it around Kapoor's head, pinning him to the headrest. He took the keys from the ignition and shoved Kapoor's phone in his pocket.

'But what if he has more men close by?'

'We have no choice,' he said. 'Let's move.'

They hurried back towards the melee where taxi drivers were touting for custom. Aisha almost had to jog to keep up with Jack. He was looking around constantly for any further sign of Habib's men.

They crossed the road and ended up back in front of the airport. Jack looked for someone with a car right there so they wouldn't need to double back and risk a confrontation with Kapoor.

Three middle-aged men set upon him, all tugging at his arms. There was an overpowering scent of body odour and Jack shrugged them off. He beckoned Aisha to follow him across the front of the terminal to the other side, each step taking them further away from Kapoor.

Aisha was being hounded by every man she went past – some even trying to carry her bag for her. She snapped at them to stop and kept close to Jack.

'Sir! Sir!' shouted a voice. Jack turned to see a young boy who couldn't have been more than eighteen sitting in a grey BMW, all the windows down, waving wildly at them. The first thing that struck Jack was the kid's amazingly white teeth, gleaming like pearls. The boy mounted the kerb, forcing some of the other drivers to jump away, cursing him. He ignored them and focused his attention on Jack.

'Sir! I am being best taxi service in India! Not Delhi – but whole of India! I am speaking English, Hindi, Punjabi, Gujarati, Tamil, Bengali, Marathi, Urdu, Mirpuri, Sindhi, Rajasthani, and my car is being fully air-conditioned with DVD players and I am giving you mineral water for journey, plus I am . . .'

The kid spoke faster than an auctioneer, all the while creeping along the kerb, dismissive of the angry crowd hurling abuse.

There was something innocent about the boy and Jack was impressed with his brazen attitude to getting his business.

The boy yelled for them to get in quickly as a security patrol rushed towards them.

'In!' said Jack, ushering Aisha into the back seat. Jack got in the front and hadn't even closed the door before the boy floored the accelerator and whisked them away from the airport. He was laughing to himself as he manoeuvred closely between cars, blasting his horn.

'Sir, you are making an excellent choice. My name is Cruise and I am being with you for as long as you are needing. I am having discounts at all the major hotels and tourist attractions and I am also being able to take you to the best places to eat in Delhi, from Khan Market to Connaught Place.'

Two miniature statues of the gods Rama and Krishna toppled from the dash and fell to the floor by Jack's feet.

'Oh yaar,' said Cruise, 'you are both cursing me every time. Sir – you are minding?' he said, putting his hand out.

Jack scooped them from the floor and handed them to the boy. Cruise stuck them back on two wads of sticky tape on top of the dashboard. 'Bad karma,' he muttered, 'but I am polishing them extra shiny tonight and we are winning the karma back.' He nodded, swerving hazardously between rickshaws. 'Just like Cole Trickle, no?' he said, glancing at Jack.

'Who?' replied Jack, clinging on to the edge of his seat. Aisha was checking behind them as the airport faded from view.

'Cole Trickle. He is being the character Tom Cruise played in *Days of Thunder.*'

'What?' said Jack, perplexed.

'Don't worry. I am seeing all of Tom Cruise's movies, from his first one, *Endless Love* – although it was not really his movie, he just had, what you call it, a cameo part. His first real movie was *Risky Business* in 1983 and—'

'Do you ever shut up? And you weren't even born in 1983,' replied Jack.

'Oh yaar, I am following his movies for long time.'

Jack attempted to steer him on to a more relevant subject. 'Tell me, how well do you know the area of Sadar Bazaar in this city?'

Cruise smiled. 'Sir, I am knowing it very well.'

THIRTY

THE ROAD LEADING AWAY from the airport was quiet. The horizon was still dark, the cat's eyes on the road flashing orange.

Cruise drove quickly, a little too quickly for Aisha's comfort, changing lanes at will even when there was no need.

'*Days of Thunder*, Sister? You are seeing this movie?' said Cruise, back on his favourite topic.

'No,' replied Aisha.

'*Great* movie,' he said, sounding awestruck. 'Tom Cruise is being Cole Trickle in this film. NASCAR driver. You are thinking of me as your Cole Trickle. Safe, fast and always number one.' He flashed Aisha an exaggerated grin.

She smiled at his enthusiasm, even if she didn't understand the reference.

Jack was inspecting the driving licence handed to him by the kid.

'Cruise Om Veda Prakash Narayan,' said Jack, shaking his head. 'No wonder you just go by Cruise.' He gave the boy his licence back.

'My mother is giving me this name, thinking I am going to be a high priest in our temple one day.'

'Is it a religious name?' asked Aisha.

The boy nodded. 'I am adding the Cruise part after realizing that India is needing a Tom Cruise and—'

'Is that why you have such white teeth?' asked Jack.

'You are noticing!'

'The planes landing at the airport could see them,' replied Jack.

'All leading stars in Hollywood are having these teeth. I am bleaching them every week to keep them like this. Sir, I am being only nineteen and already I am making connections in Mumbai – film industry capital of India, home to Bollywood.'

'Connections?'

'Ah,' said Cruise, waving his hand at Jack, 'no faith. I am escorting film producers in Mumbai only last month for two weeks. I am telling them my ideas for many, many movies.'

'How much do you charge?' interrupted Jack.

'Daily rate?' replied Cruise.

'Yes.'

'Flat rate two thousand rupees per day.'

Jack sniggered. 'Try again, hero.'

'Sir, two thousand is—'

'Impossible,' finished Jack.

'Discounted rate,' continued Cruise. 'This is equalling only twenty-three pounds per day, which divided by twenty-four is less than two pounds per hour. Sir, I am knowing that the minimum wage in the UK is around eight pounds per hour, so you are getting three hundred per cent reduction. When you are also factoring in—'

'Try again,' said Jack sternly.

'Sir, this price is including all sightseeing destinations around Delhi, express queue access, mineral water and I am also having—'

'Stop the car,' said Jack.

'What?' said Cruise.

'Stop the car. Now.'

'Sir, we are on the freeway. It is not permitted to—'

'Stop right now or I'm not paying you for this trip.'

Cruise pulled the car into the left lane and brought it to a halt.

'It is difficult bargaining with you, sir,' said Cruise.

'I'm not some bullshit tourist you can fleece. Now, imagine this is your movie, Cruise, and you have one shot to get it right. One number, no second chances. Get it right, I keep you for a week. Get it wrong and we'll part company.'

Cruise glanced at Aisha, but she remained quiet.

'Give me your number,' said Jack, clicking his fingers in front of Cruise to focus his attention.

Cruise paused, clearly trying to figure out just how clued up Jack really was.

'OK, sir, I am giving you one-time offer based on one week's rental. One thousand rupees per day—'

'Done,' said Jack without hesitation.

'So, where are we going, sir?'

'We need a hotel,' replied Jack.

'You are not having any bookings?'

'No, it was a last-minute trip,' said Jack.

'Sir, Delhi is having thousands of hotels – are you needing to stay near anywhere in particular?'

'We need to be close to Sadar Bazaar,' replied Jack.

'Sadar Bazaar is being in Old Delhi. Very crowded area. Not many nice hotels. Long way off tourist route.'

'We don't need nice. Just somewhere cheap and quiet where we can have a shower, maybe sleep for a few hours and then attend to our business.'

'In this case, sir, I am wanting to make a suggestion. You see, I am having this friend – Ankur. He is renting out the top floor of his building. Two-bedroom apartment, two bathrooms – very clean and first-class price.'

Typical wheeler-dealer taxi driver, thought Jack.

'You are getting freshly made home-cooked food, first-class service for anything you need and it is being located centrally in Sadar.'

'I think a hotel would be better,' said Aisha quickly. She needed a hot shower, a comfortable bed and her own room. Shacking up in some stranger's house sounded risky.

Jack, on the other hand, thought it was a great idea. No prying hotel staff, no need to show their passports at reception and little chance of Habib tracking them down.

'I'll trust you on this, Cruise – deal.'

For a moment Cruise looked as stunned as Aisha. It was probably the first time this pitch had ever worked.

'Really?' he said, before quickly correcting himself. 'I am meaning this is *fantastic* news. His rate is being a very reasonable two thousand rupees per night for both the rooms.'

'Do you know any other number?'

'Sir . . . but this is—'

'Another number, Cruise,' said Jack firmly.

'OK, OK – I am negotiating on your behalf first-class exceptional rate of eleven hundred rupees per night.'

'It had better not be some shit-hole with two beds.'

'No, sir, I am not taking you to any such a place. He is renting this place to many, many people who are not liking hotels. I am promising you that it is clean. How do you call it in UK – boutique hotel?'

Aisha leaned towards Jack. She looked outraged at the proposal. 'How do we know he's not going to take us to some place where they'll rob us?' she hissed.

'We don't,' said Jack.

'And you think that's acceptable?'

'Yes,' he replied.

'Why are you doing this?' she whispered urgently.

'Look,' he said, trying to soften his tone and diffuse her fears, 'your father's going to phone every hotel in Delhi, trying to find out where we are. Let's remember that our goal here is to find Kirin. It is not about comfort or star ratings. If we arrive and it looks suspect, we'll leave. But we need to keep under the radar and this is the best possible way. I don't know what contacts Habib has around here.'

She mulled over what Jack had said and finally nodded her head. 'I'm just afraid. I have no idea what to expect here, you know?'

'I know,' he replied.

'Is that the sun rising over there?' asked Aisha, pointing. They'd been driving on the freeway for about half an hour.

'No, Sister, this is the orange glow of a Delhi morning. It is dust rising into the air. Street lighting is making it look orange. The sun will rise in around half an hour at six.'

'I'm cold,' said Aisha. 'Can you turn the air conditioning off, please?'

'No problem, Sister,' said Cruise.

'My name is Aisha.'

'But in our culture you are like sister to me, so if it is OK with you, I am calling you Sister.' Cruise glanced at Jack. 'I am not calling you Sister – Uncle?'

'You call me Jack, or we are going to have a falling out.'

'OK, Mr Jack.'

Jack was too tired to argue. 'How do you want paying?' he asked. 'Daily? Weekly? Cash?'

'Sir,' said Cruise, 'I am wanting to let you into a secret.'

'Secret?'

'Well, it is more of a mission statement – hell, it is being a family motto,' Cruise said, putting on a terrible American accent. 'Show me the money,' he whispered softly, dipping his shoulders and bobbing his head in imitation of the character Rod Tidwell from *Jerry Maguire*. He started laughing and then repeated the line over and over, getting louder each time. 'Show . . . me . . . the . . . money!'

Aisha creased over. It felt liberating to laugh after the nightmare few days she'd experienced.

'Jesus Christ,' said Jack.

Aisha's giggles ceased abruptly as Kapoor's mobile started to ring. On the display it said 'Habib England Mobile'.

Cruise was about to start another rendition but Jack cut him short.

'Jack, answer it,' said Aisha, but the phone stopped ringing and a text message arrived.

'Shit,' whispered Jack, dismayed that Kapoor had not remained secure for longer. The phone rang again and this time Jack picked up. 'Habib?'

'What the hell are you doing, Jack?' shouted Aisha's father. His tone was seething with anger. 'Goddamn you!'

Jack hung up and put the ringer on silent. He asked Cruise to pull into an approaching Indian Oil petrol station, knowing Habib would call again.

Cruise brought the car to a stop next to a petrol pump.

'Do you need something?' asked Cruise.

'Just some fresh air,' replied Jack. Before Aisha could say a word, he got out of the car and headed past a couple of stray dogs snoozing by the entrance to the back of the store, following the sign to the toilets. This time when the phone rang, he answered on the first ring.

'Jack, listen to me, you son of a bitch—' started Habib.

'No,' hissed Jack, 'you listen to me. I've got Aisha. In the middle of India, with nowhere to hide.' He was shaking. 'I swear to

God,' he continued, 'if you come after us, you'll never see her again. She thinks I won't hurt her – hell, she even tied a *rakhi* on my wrist, thinking it means something – but you and I both know what I'm capable of. I see you – the girl dies.'

Jack cut the call, dropped the phone on the floor and smashed it with his foot.

He knew Habib was coming.

And in a city where everything had a monetary value, Jack knew the odds were stacked against him.

THIRTY-ONE

'WHAT DID YOU DO?' asked Aisha.

Cruise was back on the highway. The road was busier now, the six a.m. commuters starting to surface. Jack had joined Aisha in the back of the car this time.

'Dumped the phone,' replied Jack.

'Did you speak with him?'

'I told him to back off.'

'Was he angry?' asked Aisha agitatedly.

'Lots of whispering happening back there,' called out Cruise. 'Is everything being OK?'

'How long till we reach Sadar?' asked Jack.

'Sir, we will be there in approximately forty minutes, depending on traffic. You are remembering that Delhi is having almost a third of the population of UK. Traffic always terrible.'

He clicked the radio on, leaving the volume low. The weather report was on: another day of thirty-degree heat.

Delhi was starting to wake up. Cars were spilling on to the dusty road from every side street, it seemed.

On Jack's side of the road, cramped rows of white residential tower blocks were topped with enormous billboards, advertising everything from the latest Bollywood movie to ladies' fashion garments. Some of the flats had balconies on which bright garments hung from makeshift clothes lines.

The weekly wash displayed clues as to the social status of each family. One had nothing but old withered Asian suits. The flat above had a row of Manchester United football tops and three official Team India cricket jerseys. A family of three boys, deduced Jack. In India that was akin to a lottery win – three males to look after their parents in old age. Jack heard his mother's voice in his head: *Boys are to be cherished and nurtured, girls wept over and protected.*

'Do they have a Tube network in Delhi?' asked Aisha, spotting the red Metro sign.

Cruise sniggered. 'Sister, they are having *everything* in Delhi. Metro has been here for a long time. Every year we are having new stations. We are having *every* facility now – all models of cars, BMW, Range Rover, Mercedes, and now we are even having a Ferrari garage.'

Aisha was surprised at the explosion in traffic in the space of a few minutes. Cars were gridlocked along the dual carriageway, the air thick with ceaseless honking.

'Why are they bothering when there's nowhere to go?' asked Aisha.

Cruise blasted his own horn and laughed. 'It is necessary,' he replied. 'In the UK you are having this wonderful system, my old client is telling me – mirror, signal, manoeuvre. Am I right?'

'Yes,' replied Aisha.

'Here, Sister, it is manoeuvre, horn, signal, horn. You are only looking in the mirror if you are wanting to check your hair.' His face cracked into a broad grin.

'It's giving me a headache,' muttered Aisha.

'This is being mild, Sister.'

'Where are we?' asked Jack, frustrated at the lack of progress.

Cruise turned down the volume on the radio. 'Pitampura. North Delhi. It is taking another thirty minutes to get to Sadar.'

'God, look at this place,' said Aisha, amazed at the volume of cars and people, all jammed against each other. There was a scooter on either side of the car, both of them touching the side panels.

A woman wearing a tattered blue sari approached, carrying a Harry Potter balloon in one hand and a Hello Kitty one in the other. Her face was lined with coarse wrinkles, her complexion a burned charcoal in colour. Her eyes were jaundiced yellow and she looked dangerously malnourished. She smiled at Aisha, revealing several gaps in her teeth, and tapped on the window for money.

Aisha stared at her, feeling helpless.

'Argh! These beggars, always wanting something,' said Cruise dispassionately. He yelled for the woman to move but she lingered at the window, pleading with Aisha to buy a balloon.

'It's awful,' said Aisha, dropping her gaze to the floor.

A small girl in tattered clothing now appeared at the woman's side. She was holding a Mickey Mouse balloon and smiled innocently at Aisha.

'Jack, give me some money,' Aisha said, looking pitifully at the child, who couldn't have been older than six.

He shook his head. 'If we start like this now, we'll be broke by the end of the day.'

'Please, she's just a baby.'

'Sister, the money is not going to her. She will be having a boss who is taking whatever you are giving to her,' Cruise said.

Aisha put her hand in her pocket and pulled out a five-pound note.

'Don't be stupid,' said Jack, reaching out to take it off her.

'Hey!' she snapped, jerking her hand away from him. 'You might be in charge of our journey but not what I do with my own money.'

Before Cruise could intervene, Aisha wound down the window and handed the note to the child.

'No, this is causing us chaos, Sister,' said Cruise.

Aisha closed the window. 'Don't be so dramatic.'

'Look,' said Cruise, nodding towards the crowd of children flocking towards the car, arms outstretched. They surrounded the vehicle, grappling with each other for prime position next to Aisha. One of them pulled out a tooth and tapped it on the window. It left a streak of blood right in front of Aisha's face.

'Oh God,' she said, flinching.

'Sister, I was telling you this is bad idea,' said Cruise. He revved the engine and moved the car forward a few inches. The kids didn't budge.

Aisha sat frozen in her seat. The tooth-child stuck a finger in his mouth and used it to smear more blood on the windscreen, grimacing all the time and imploring Aisha to give him money too.

'Sister, please, don't look at them. Only then are they leaving.'

The cars in front started to move. Cruise started to drive and as quickly as they had arrived, the children melted away. Aisha stole a last horrified glance at the little boy, who continued to wave his bloodstained tooth at her.

Half an hour later, having driven past Keshav Puram, Inderlok and then hit Kanhaiya Nagar, Jack saw a sign that said 'Sadar Bazaar'.

'Sir, Sadar is mostly a Muslim area,' said Cruise, pointing towards a mosque on the left. 'Old Delhi is entirely different to New Delhi. This area is not designed for tourists. I am suggesting that if you are needing to go out anywhere, for *anything*, you are taking me with you.'

'Is it dangerous?' asked Aisha.

'Sister, I am telling you what I am telling all tourists, especially the women. In busy tourist areas in New Delhi like Connaught Place – no problem. But in non-tourist areas, Delhi is *not* safe city. Rape is being a huge problem in this city and the police are no use. Never,' he said, turning to face her, 'venture out alone. *Never.* Especially in Old Delhi. Sadar Bazaar is having the largest markets in Asia – very easy to get lost. Even I am not finding my way out sometimes.'

'Markets?' asked Jack.

'Trade markets. Like here on left, this is totally metal market.'

Jack and Aisha gazed beyond Cruise's outstretched finger. There was nothing obvious, just rows of shabby huts and some impoverished children playing cricket by the side of the road.

Cruise took an abrupt right turn down a narrow alley and a startling darkness replaced the sunlight. The transition was unsettling.

'There are narrow roads and then there's this,' said Aisha, alarmed that the wing mirrors were scraping along the walls to either side.

They arrived at the end of the street and Cruise sounded his horn three times. He took out his mobile phone and sent a text. Aisha was surprised to see it was a new iPhone.

The gate was opened. Cruise parked the car and switched off the engine. 'We are here.'

Jack and Aisha glanced around. Cruise saw their reluctance.

'It is appearing dark and perhaps a little scary, I am knowing. The sun is not shining at the back of these buildings. I am giving you my word that upstairs is the apartment you are wanting and I am being with you until you are feeling comfortable.'

He flashed them a smile and stepped out of the car.

THIRTY-TWO

THE BUILDING WAS ON three storeys. Ankur, the 'manager', looked about the same age as Cruise. He lived in the ground-floor flat and had converted the top two floors into rental units.

He proudly showed them to a spacious apartment with two bedrooms at opposite ends, a lounge, dining room and small kitchen. Ageing white tiles on the floor were heavily marked and the magnolia walls needed a fresh coat of paint.

The electricity was off, which Ankur told them was routine in Delhi, demand constantly outstripping supply. Ankur told them it would be restored within the hour as soon as the electrical generator in the basement started up.

Aisha had borrowed some money from Jack and asked Cruise to go into the Sadar Bazaar market and get them some neutral Asian clothing. She'd bought a few things in duty free but they were Western-style clothing and she'd stick out like a sore thumb if she wore them here.

'I am being deeply honoured that you are trusting Cruise with this money. I am informing you now—'

Jack put his hand over the boy's mouth. 'Cruise, less of the commentary and more of the doing?' He sent him packing, telling the boy there was no rush – that he and Aisha would rest before heading into central Sadar in a few hours after lunch.

Before leaving, Cruise had handed Jack a cheap mobile with his number in the memory, in case he needed to contact him. It was a nice touch and endeared him to Jack even more.

'Apartment looks OK?' Jack said, when the boy had gone.

Aisha shrugged and handed Jack a bottle of mineral water. 'These were in the kitchen,' she said. 'Keep away from the tap water. I can't afford you getting Delhi belly on me.'

Aisha closed the creaking door to her bedroom and slid the bolt across. The room was generously sized with a double bed, a wardrobe and a chest of drawers. She was relieved there was an en suite and, more importantly, it looked clean. An antiquated ceiling fan started to rotate; Ankur must have started the generator.

Aisha opened a set of double doors and stepped out on to a small balcony over the street. The sunshine hit her hard, momentarily lifting her spirits. Shielding her eyes from the glare, she searched for Cruise but the street was crammed with people. Cars blared their horns, children darted across the road and wild dogs roamed everywhere. Overwhelmed, Aisha stepped back inside, closing and then locking the doors.

She sat on the edge of the bed, sunshine streaking through the window, warming her body. This was a world away from Bradford, and yet here she was, alone with a strange man, attempting to track down a woman she had thought to have died in childbirth. There were so many unanswered questions, not least why Detective Singh, if he even was a detective, had twice now attempted to kill them.

Aisha rested her weary head in her hands, trying to pull her thoughts straight. The flight had been comfortable enough and she had even slept for a few hours, but the comfort of the bed was inviting. The day ahead was uncertain at best.

Aisha laid down and closed her eyes. She fell asleep thinking only one thing.

Her mother was close.

The shower worked poorly but Jack was pleased to have the sensation of hot water on his skin. He stayed under until the water was cold.

With a few hours to spare, he didn't intend to waste it on sleep. He had work to do. He and Aisha had purchased new iPhones in the duty-free shop in Paris and Jack now started the set-up routine. He didn't know much about mobile data but enough to recognize that he couldn't log on to anything he'd previously been connected with. Jack wasn't sure how far Habib's reach extended, nor that of Detective Singh.

Next, he created a new email address, Facebook and Twitter accounts. He went online and started to research Detective Singh. Jack was aware that police officers were not supposed to have social media accounts, and with only 'Detective Singh' to go on, he found no information.

He then combined a search for Bradford's local newspaper, the *Telegraph and Argus*, with 'Detective Singh'.

Bingo.

Singh had been telling the truth and was indeed a homicide detective. Jack found an article about a triple homicide in Bradford. It showed a picture of Singh and listed his full name as Kuldeep Singh. Jack inputted those details into social media sites and although it returned many hits, none of them was the same man.

Jack tapped his fingers on the iPhone, thinking. There had to be some other digital trace of this guy. He thought of his own cyber existence. His prison sentence had made him an outcast in his community, and Jack had pretty much lived in isolation since Kirin's death. He found it impossible to trust people. His social media accounts were and always had been dormant. He'd been cautious about what he put out online, especially since he'd been obsessive about staying under the radar with his illegal contraband business.

He looked again at the newspaper image of Singh.

The turban, the long untrimmed beard.

He was a religious man.

Jack typed in Singh's name and the words 'Sikhism', 'Bradford' and 'Gurdwara'.

The search revealed dozens of articles. Jack scrolled through them.

He smiled and clicked on a large feature entitled 'Shastar vidya, the forgotten Sikh martial art form'.

Singh, it turned out, taught classes at the Sikh temple in Bradford. Jack was well versed in *shastar vidya* but read the feature anyway. It had been developed by Sikhs in the seventeenth century, in the early days of the religion when it was coming under attack from Hindus and Muslims. Jack's father had been a master in the art form and taught classes at the very same temple in Bradford – ones Jack had been forced to attend.

Singh, it appeared, had been a student of Jack's father – a protégé, no less. When Jack's father died in 1984, Singh had continued his learning and was now one of the world's leading authorities.

Something stirred in Jack's mind. He scanned the article again and learned that Singh was fifty years old.

The same age as Jack.

Shit.

Jack closed his eyes and cast his mind back to those classes.

He stayed like this for several minutes, reliving them. Slowly it came to him.

Kully Singh.

Jack opened his eyes.

For the first time, he'd found a solid link with the man who had tried to kill him.

THIRTY-THREE

IT WAS JUST PAST two p.m. when Aisha emerged from her bedroom to find Jack sitting at the dining table. She was wearing a cheap green Asian suit, which Cruise had purchased for her from the markets.

'Could I pass for a local?' she asked.

Jack shook his head.

'Why not?'

He took a sip of Indian tea, which Cruise had also purchased. The boy was definitely growing on him.

'Your makeup,' replied Jack bluntly.

'What about it?'

'We're in a poor part of Delhi and it's over thirty degrees out there. That shit on your face will have melted before you've gone fifty yards and, more to the point, I don't see any of the locals wearing it in this part of town.'

Aisha opened her mouth to say something, then seemed to reconsider. 'You're right,' she said and retreated to her bedroom.

Jack had sent Cruise back into Sadar Bazaar to pinpoint the

location of the refuge where Kirin was supposedly being held. The last thing he wanted was to have to ask people for directions. People tended to remember things like that and Jack was mindful to be as discreet as possible.

The tea was good – sweet and milky, just like it should be. It reminded him of his mother's tea and, for the second time that day, he thought back to his youth.

Aisha returned, having wiped the makeup from her face as best she could. She'd also put on a black headscarf and now looked considerably more like your average girl on the street.

'Better,' said Jack.

'How's the tea?' she asked, pouring some into a plastic beaker and taking a seat opposite.

'Tastes like home. You ever have authentic Indian tea?'

She rolled her eyes. 'God, all the time. My father will not drink anything else.'

'And Sara makes it for him?'

She smiled. 'Hardly. He makes it himself.'

Jack whistled. 'Just when I thought he was the same prick I used to know.'

He slid a piece of paper over towards her with Cruise's mobile number on it. 'Put that in your phone in case we get separated, as well as the address of this place.'

Aisha did as he asked.

'It's a new SIM and phone, but remember: no calls unless it's life-threatening. God knows what reach your father has over here.'

They sipped their tea in silence, waiting for Cruise to return. Aisha asked Jack what their plan was when they found Kirin.

'I have no idea,' he said truthfully.

They went back to drinking their tea, but Jack could tell there was something on Aisha's mind.

'What is it?' he asked her.

She shrugged. 'I've never met her – my mother. I mean, up until a few days ago, I thought she was dead.'

'That makes two of us.'

'My point is that I don't know how to deal with seeing her.'

Jack understood her nerves. He finished his tea and pushed it aside. 'Aisha, I don't think either of us is going to know how to react until we come face to face with her.'

'Did you love her?' asked Aisha timidly.

Jack stood up, walked over to the window and stuck his hands in his pockets. He leaned against the wall, watching the life in the courtyard below – stray dogs asleep in the shade and children playing cricket in the street.

When he spoke, his voice was soft and rueful. 'When I was younger, my friends used to tell me that at the end of a long day, they dreaded going home to see their wives. They struggled with even putting the key in the lock and turning it. Some of them would spend ages just sitting in their car, building up the nerve to enter their own house and face a life they no longer had any interest in.'

'OK,' said Aisha, getting up from the table and closing the distance between them.

'That never happened to me. I never hesitated in putting my key in the door. I loved my wife. And she loved me. While I was in prison, I used to dream about opening that same door to start over again with Kirin. And when I arrived home after my three-year stretch, sure, things were different. But I never saw this. I never saw the dishonesty.'

Jack turned to face her and heard the door of their flat open. He saw Cruise step into the hallway.

'I did love my wife, Aisha. The reason it ended badly between us was because she said she was leaving me for someone else – it broke me in half.' He paused and then added, 'There are many questions I need answering but the one at the forefront of my mind is this – just how much of my life with her was a lie?'

THIRTY-FOUR

HABIB WAS STANDING ON the eleventh floor of the luxurious Leela Palace hotel in New Delhi, located in the diplomatic enclave and only a thirty-minute drive from the airport. He, Sara and his most trusted bodyguard, Rehaan, had checked in a few hours ago.

The rooftop infinity pool was quiet, with only a few residents enjoying an afternoon swim. From here, Habib had far-reaching panoramic views across the city. While Delhi was known for its congestion and smog, here, in the midst of the diplomatic quarter, Habib could mostly see lush greenery, with trees in full blossom and colourful flowerbeds.

He leant on the glass barrier surrounding the rooftop and closed his eyes. It was surprisingly peaceful up here, the only sound that of a train rattling past on the tracks adjacent to the hotel.

Their search for Aisha and Jack was already under way.

Delhi had a population of over eighteen million people, so finding just two was going to be a Herculean task. Fortunately, though, India was a country where one thing ruled supreme.

Cash.

The one real advantage Habib had over Jack.

Over anyone who crossed him.

The forty-eight hours after Aisha's decision to flee with Jack had been intense. His rebellious daughter might have hoped to block him by taking his passport but it had only resulted in a slight delay. Habib's influence in the international trade sector meant that not only had he got an emergency passport the following day, but had also arranged urgent business visas for himself, Sara and Rehaan.

Money made everything easy.

Habib's Elite empire had a large subsidiary in healthcare and held the contract for exporting medications from India into the United Kingdom. It meant that while he hadn't visited the country in almost five years, he could still summon influential connections with a phone call.

Aisha leaving with Jack had wounded Habib. He knew she had always thought of him as a tough, controlling father. And he had been. Raising a child born from the result of an affair had been a challenge, to say the least. Habib truly loved Sara and he had tried desperately to get her to see Aisha as no more than an innocent child and not a poisonous reminder of his infidelity.

He had not succeeded.

Habib's grip on the railing grew tighter, his knuckles turning white. This whole debacle had stirred bad memories for Sara. The affair with Kirin had been foolish, a short-lived act of sheer idiocy. It had been a tough road back.

The immediate aftermath of Kirin's death all those years ago remained vividly etched in Habib's memory. His pleas with Sara to raise Aisha as her own daughter and hide the fact that she was not her mother had fallen on deaf ears. Love was blind to many things – infidelity could be forgiven – but to raise another woman's child as her own? That had been a step too far.

He had tried to love Aisha enough to make up for the loss of her mother, yet for Aisha it appeared to have manifested as an overly protective and at times bitter relationship.

Habib didn't know any different. Sara had always provided for Aisha but had never been able to love her like her own daughter, and things had only deteriorated when it became clear that she couldn't carry her own child.

And now here they were. Starting all over again: the lies, the manipulation, the loss.

While the past was playing heavily on his mind, one memory held firm above all others. It was of Aisha, aged four, falling off her bike and hurting herself. Habib had held her close like a newborn baby and tried to comfort her. If he could, he would have taken on all her pain, something he had always tried to do – to be there for her.

Somewhere, he had gone badly wrong.

Was Habib about to lose Aisha to an event that should never have resurfaced?

And all because of Jack – *this was his doing*, Habib was certain of it. He didn't yet know how or why, but it was inconceivable that Jack was innocent in this mess.

Habib opened his eyes and glanced towards the tracks as another train hurtled by. He had established the Elite brand as a global force, yet always staying in the shadows, an intensely private man. He needed cash in the bank, not fame and popularity. Habib regarded himself as a visionary, able to predict what came next in business deals.

He now applied the same thought process to their current predicament.

There was only one solution: the death of Jack Baxi.

Delhi was the perfect place to make it happen – a city so overpopulated that no one would register another person disappearing off the radar.

Habib was joined by Rehaan, the two men standing side by side and observing the city. The silence lasted a few moments before Rehaan said the only words Habib needed to hear.

'Everything is set. They will meet with us shortly.'

'Good,' replied Habib.

THIRTY-FIVE

THEY WERE ALL SET to go and Cruise was giving them firm, final instructions.

'Daulat Ram Marg is being the main market road. And I am meaning thousands of peoples. Underneath the main square is the largest underground market in India and today is being their busiest day of the year.'

He stopped talking and stared at them both to ensure they were paying attention.

'This is because today is being the Islamic festival of Eid—'

Aisha gasped. 'Of course it is,' she said, more to herself than to anyone else.

'—so, it is being extra busy outside,' continued Cruise.

'How far is it?' asked Jack.

'Maybe one half kilometre from here. We are walking, because no cars being allowed in this area.'

'Walking?' said Jack in dismay.

'Mr Jack, it is totally, how are you saying, jim-jam packed. We are ready to leave now?'

Jack and Aisha shared a look.

'Let's go,' said Jack.

At the front door, Aisha paused. 'Is there a safe in here?' she asked Cruise.

'Safe?' he replied.

'A locker? Somewhere I can put my passport.'

'Oh, Sister, it is being *totally* safe in here. We are locking this door and Ankur is making sure of the safety.'

Aisha looked at Jack.

He stuck a hand in his pocket and took out his own. 'I'd carry it with you,' he said.

They emerged on to the street in front of the building. The heat was unyielding; the sun's rays burning the sides of their faces. Aisha pulled her headscarf down her forehead to block the sun from burning the skin on her temples, while Jack drew out a pair of sunglasses from his bag and put them on.

Cruise continued to give instructions. 'Stay close to me, please. If you are getting lost in here I am being unable to locate you.' He handed them a tattered business card each for the apartment they were staying in. 'If you are losing me or each other, then you are asking for directions back here or catching a rickshaw.'

He looked at them both with a serious frown. 'Understanding?'

They nodded.

'Keeping close then, please,' he said.

Sadar Bazaar was the location of one of India's largest trade markets. In this section, the shops were selling metal goods: nails, door handles, copper pipes and padlocks. There were hundreds of stores, each one limited to only a few square feet. The locals didn't walk so much as march down the path, heads down, urgency in their every stride. The air hung heavy with exhaust fumes and smoke from a nearby fire, and Jack could definitely smell marijuana in the air.

At the end of the row of shops, they turned into the heart of the market. Aisha and Jack hovered behind Cruise, who had come to a standstill. The chatter of thousands of people crammed into the main square was deafening.

They were stopped beside a yellow metal barrier on which was clumsily scrawled: *No cars, motorcycles.*

'Welcome to India,' said Cruise, laughing.

Aisha was gobsmacked. There didn't seem to be any space to walk. People barged past one another, some balancing enormous parcels on their shoulders. An entrance on each side led down to the underground markets. Traders poured out from these, continuously adding weight to the crowd.

Packed rows of tiny shops jostled for space, offering a mesmerizing variety of goods from bright orange garlands and glittery tassels to curtain rails or clothes. There were no signs on any of the stores, just stock hanging from the ceiling and on every wall, and no doors – just open shutters that led directly inside. Hungry dogs darted between shoppers' legs, scrounging for morsels of food. To complete the chaos, plodding across the heart of the square, seemingly without a care in the world, was a donkey pulling a cart.

'We're going into that?' shouted Aisha, her voice faltering.

Cruise nodded. 'Are you wanting to hold my hand, Sister?'

She was grateful for the offer. Aisha held her other hand out to Jack. He ignored it, as she knew he would.

The three of them struggled through the crowd. Aisha was afraid of losing Cruise and clutched his hand tightly, while constantly glancing over her shoulder to make sure Jack was following.

The babble of the crowd buzzed in her ears: chattering voices, shouts of vendors and the bleating horns of traffic close by.

A deafening crash in front of them brought Cruise to a standstill, causing Aisha to career straight into him. A huge wooden cart had toppled over, shedding its load of yellow flower garlands. The labourer who had been pulling it was trying desperately to gather them while the owner hurled abuse at him.

The crowd didn't stop, some trampling the garlands while others shouted insults at the owner. Cruise led Aisha and Jack safely around the spectacle and towards a row of shops selling food. The sharp smell of onions and chilli powder stung Aisha's eyes.

Cruise stopped and pointed to a tiny dhaba – a food stall. He gave them a thumbs-up but was waved on by Jack.

About a hundred yards later, Cruise took a sharp left turn into a darkened alleyway. Towering buildings to each side blocked the sunlight and the atmosphere felt hostile compared to the vibrancy and colour of the main market square.

They were now forced to walk slowly in single file and Aisha let go of Cruise's hand. The boy was using his finger to count off each building on his left.

'We are here,' he said eventually, pointing to a sign on the peeling blue door.

'Room 5205c,' muttered Jack, and checked the piece of paper in his hand.

Aisha took a step closer to read the inscription.

'Look, Jack,' she said. She reached out and brushed the dirt from beneath the numerals, revealing a faded cross.

Jack looked around cautiously. Floor upon floor of flats rose steeply on either side of the alley.

'Are these all residential?' he asked.

Cruise shrugged. 'I am not knowing, Mr Jack,' he replied. 'Should I be waiting here?'

'Yes,' Aisha said quickly. She looked at Jack, who seemed hesitant to knock on the door. 'Jack?'

'Maybe you should both wait—'

Aisha pushed past him and rapped loudly on the door.

THIRTY-SIX

INSIDE THE BUILDING WAS a small courtyard with a statue of Christ on his cross protruding from the centre of an ancient-looking water feature. The nun who had opened the door had been welcoming and asked them to wait while she fetched Sister Florence.

Aisha was fidgeting furiously, her eyes darting nervous glances around the yard.

Jack wasn't faring much better, breathing heavily and grinding his teeth while staring at the large wooden doors through which the nun had disappeared. It felt surreal to be sitting here with Aisha next to him. The magnitude of the old deception kept slapping him in the face.

'It'll be OK,' said Aisha.

Jack wasn't sure if she was seeking to reassure him or herself.

The doors opened and a tall, painfully thin nun in a white tunic approached. Jack and Aisha rose on unsteady legs to greet her.

'My name is Sister Florence,' she said. 'Could I see some identification, please?'

They handed over their passports. Sister Florence checked their details and handed them back, satisfied with what she'd seen.

'I know why you're both here. Where is Father Cave?'

Jack and Aisha shared a troubled look.

'Er . . . he's in England,' replied Jack, stumbling.

Sister Florence gazed intently at them both and then sighed. 'Mr Baxi, you're in a house of God and wanting my assistance. Please do not lie to me again.'

She waited for Jack to respond but he couldn't find the right words. Sister Florence turned to Aisha.

'We're not sure,' whispered Aisha. 'He . . . he disappeared.'

'Why don't you tell me how you both arrived here?' said Sister Florence.

She organized for some tea to be brought out to them but it remained untouched as Aisha recounted their journey, from the attack as she left the hospital, to their meeting with Sister Catherine Lowry in Bradford. Jack stayed quiet, his focus on the doors through which he would soon come face to face with the woman who claimed to be his wife.

Aisha finished their story and then asked the only question to which Jack wanted to hear the answer.

'Is she here?'

'Yes. She's inside, resting,' replied Sister Florence.

'Well, can you wake her up?' asked Jack abruptly. 'I have believed for seventeen years that this woman was dead. We haven't come all this way to hang about while she takes a little nap.'

He hadn't meant to snap but his mind was a mess. Sister Florence reached out and took his hand.

'Mr Baxi, I know you're suffering, I really do.' The nun's eyes were sympathetic but her face held a steely resolve. 'But I assure you that whatever pain you are feeling, it is nothing compared to what she has been through.'

*

Sister Florence spoke to them for almost half an hour, explaining that Kirin had been kicked out of a brothel on GB Road, a notorious red-light district near Sadar Bazaar. She'd been suffering from serious mental health issues and the trauma of working as a prostitute had finally taken its toll. Jack found it hard to listen to.

'It's a common trait,' said Sister Florence. 'The women are abused and treated like animals until they can no longer function. Then they're fed on to the streets of Delhi, and I can tell you from experience that this is not a city that treats its vulnerable well.'

Kirin had been taken into the refuge and immediately started causing problems. She had a severe psychological disorder, referring to herself as different personalities. She'd lived a reasonably comfortable life within the brothel, being the favourite girl of the owner, Thakur, but like all sex workers, that had changed when her age and the severity of her delusions had outstripped her use. Kirin had spoken fondly of a best friend called Yasmina, a fellow prostitute, whom she missed and thought of as a sister. She spoke too of being abducted from England. Her stories had become intertwined and often confused, but the tale of her capture remained consistent. She became disruptive when her multiple personalities struggled for supremacy.

'We referred her case to Father Cave,' said Sister Florence. 'The rest, well, you know as much as I do. He worked with her and extracted some information, which led him to England to find the two of you.'

'How did she end up at the brothel?' asked Jack. 'Surely you must know that?'

Sister Florence's demeanour changed and she looked uncomfortable. 'Kirin told us that was your doing, Jack.'

Jack's blood ran cold. He felt as if he were under suspicion. Aisha and Sister Florence both stared at him. Jack focused his attention on Sister Florence.

'Aisha knows that's not true. There's something else going on here.'

He looked to Aisha for confirmation and she nodded weakly at Sister Florence.

'Surely she must have been able to tell you more than that?' said Jack, becoming irritated.

'When you see her, you'll understand, Mr Baxi,' replied Sister Florence, but her tone had changed. Jack felt as though she still viewed him as responsible for Kirin's downfall. Aisha saw it too and spoke up.

'Sister Florence, Jack did not do this to his wife. I'd not be here with him if I didn't believe that. As he said, there's more to this than any of us realize.'

Reassured, Sister Florence smiled and nodded.

Jack stood up. 'Well, let's get on with it,' he said.

'Please, sit down, there are a few more things I need to brief you both on. Kirin hasn't spoken a word for several weeks now. It happens with her. She becomes silent and withdrawn. I'm not sure how she'll respond to seeing you both. How do you want to proceed?'

'We're going in together,' said Aisha.

'No,' said Jack sharply, 'we are not.'

Aisha started to object but he glared at her.

'Aisha, show me some damn respect. I need to do this part alone.'

She accepted that he was right. 'I'm sorry. You go ahead,' she said.

At first, Jack thought he was in a hospital. The large hall he'd been led to had ten beds on each side and windows that filtered in the warm sunlight. The atmosphere was calming, and it was quiet, with just three ceiling fans humming as they circulated humid air.

There was an office at either end of the ward, their doors open. The nuns gave Jack a courteous nod and went back to their work.

Sister Florence pointed to the left-hand side of the room. 'Bed four,' she said. 'I'll be in the office, if you need me.'

Jack hadn't expected an open room. Having the nuns keep a watchful eye put him on edge. He wanted to go into the office and ask Sister Florence for a private room but his legs were weighted to the floor. There was a sharp taste of bile in his throat and he was sweating profusely.

Overwhelmed, he dropped to one knee, the room closing in around him.

Sister Florence came out of the office and knelt down beside him.

'Are you all right?' she said, putting her arms around him.

'I just need a moment,' he whispered.

'Don't move. Let me get you some water.' She left, and quickly returned with a plastic cup. 'It's bottled,' she said.

Jack remained on his knees and took a sip.

'Do you think perhaps I could have a little privacy? I just don't want an audience the first time I see her.'

'Of course. I'm so sorry. I should have offered that before.'

She helped Jack to his feet and took him into the office, asking the two other nuns to leave. 'Do you want a little longer?' she asked.

'No,' he replied. 'I'm ready.'

Jack stared at the back wall, focusing on articles documenting the birth of the charity some ten years earlier. The woman claiming to be his wife was sitting in a chair right behind him. Until he actually laid eyes on her, he'd not really believe this was happening. His heart was racing. He tried to breathe steadily and build the courage to turn round. It seemed like the most difficult thing he'd ever ask of himself, simply to move his feet a hundred and eighty degrees and look her in the face. He couldn't do it.

And then he felt her presence.

Behind him.

Close. To the side.

In his peripheral vision, he glimpsed a white robe.

Jack was trembling. The pressure was immense, buckling his mind. Everything hit him at once – the smell of smoke from his store, Habib's face, and the decomposed image of a corpse he'd identified as his wife seventeen years ago.

Finally Jack turned, and in those first few seconds it all became clear.

Standing there, with the deadest of eyes, was indeed his wife, Kirin Baxi.

THIRTY-SEVEN

THE MAIN POLICE STATION in Sadar Bazaar was a small claustrophobic space. Habib was in the main office, a place full of chaos and disorder, with papers and files scattered everywhere. A ceiling fan clanked around laboriously, interrupted every few seconds by a loud click as if it might at any moment detach itself from its fixing.

Habib had left Sara and Rehaan back at the hotel. This was a meeting he needed to conduct alone. He'd been waiting almost half an hour now and a headache was brewing. The damn fan was making more of a racket than affording any real respite from the searing heat outside. Habib wiped the sweat from his brow and was just getting to his feet to leave when stopped by a voice from behind.

'My apologies, Mr Habib, Saab,' said the voice.

Inspector Khaleel Akbar stepped past Habib, eating a mango. He took a seat at the desk, grabbed a tissue and wiped his mouth.

'Are you wanting one of these? Ripe from the market. We have some outside,' said Akbar.

Habib thanked him and shook his head. 'Could we turn this fan off? It's too loud for us to speak discreetly,' he said.

Akbar shrugged, swivelled his chair and flicked a switch. The fan shuddered to a halt. Habib got up and closed the office door before retaking his seat. 'I thank you, Inspector Akbar, for seeing me at such short notice.'

Akbar nodded and continued to savour his mango, rolling his hands along each side and squeezing the juice and flesh through a small hole at one end. It was the conventional Indian way to eat a mango but the technique took some practice and was one Habib had never mastered.

'You paid a lot of money for this meeting,' said Akbar. 'What is it I can help you with?'

Habib picked up his bag from the floor and put it on his lap. He opened it and removed several photographs of Jack and Aisha – high-definition digital stills taken from the CCTV network around his house in England. He slid the photos on to the desk past a huge stack of papers. Akbar continued to slurp at his mango and glanced briefly at the pictures.

'Daughter?' he asked.

Habib nodded.

'And the man?'

'Someone who has taken her.'

'Against her will?'

Habib started to reply, reconsidered, and said, 'Children are easily led.'

Akbar nodded and tossed the mango skin into a bin. He wiped his hands and face with another tissue and threw this one on the floor.

'This is a matter of great importance,' said Habib sternly.

There was a brief silence, Akbar waiting for more details.

Habib knew which card he needed to play. He'd done his research and knew that Sadar Bazaar was a conservative Muslim

166

area. 'My family honour is at stake here. I am sure you understand what this means? The man in that photo is not Muslim. He is dangerous and a criminal back in England. I was told you'd be helpful in resolving this matter.'

He opened his bag again and this time removed four large bundles of cash, stacking them one on top of the other on the table. He pushed the money towards Akbar.

'One hundred thousand rupees,' said Habib.

The amount was a small fortune in India but in the UK only about one thousand pounds.

'This is to show you how serious I am and for your understanding in this matter. If you find my daughter and this man, there will be another hundred thousand for you.'

Akbar's eyes narrowed on seeing the money and Habib saw the hint of a smile. Akbar glanced through the glass window of his office, then opened a drawer in his desk and swept the cash inside.

'I think, Mr Habib, that we understand one another perfectly.' He smiled and nodded towards his officers outside. 'I have twenty-six officers working each day. For the next few days, I will make this a priority. Sadar Bazaar is not a small area. If you are able to give me some clue or direction as to where your daughter might be, that would be most helpful.'

Habib forced a rueful smile. He told Akbar that Aisha was probably headed towards a Christian refuge centre located somewhere near or in Sadar Bazaar but that he did not have the address. Habib had glanced at the file Jack had taken from Sister Catherine but couldn't recall the precise details of where Kirin was currently being held.

Akbar told Habib that there were several such places located in and around Sadar and that his officers would keep a lookout near all of them and stop and search all taxis and rickshaws. Anyone who appeared to be a foreign national would be questioned.

He was clear with Habib that there were no guarantees, especially with the sizeable population of the area.

'And what about this man?' said Akbar, tapping the photo of Jack.

Habib remained quiet and continued to stare at the inspector until he got the message.

There was a silence and then Akbar said, 'For this matter, the money you have given me will not suffice.' He looked around his office and raised his finger to the roof. 'This is still a police station, and doing this . . . other thing . . . is not what we do.'

Habib waited, sensing there was more.

'There are people around here who may take over, once we have them.'

Akbar was choosing his words with care, clearly cautious now. 'I can give the man to some people I know and they can be in charge of, let us say, sending him where you would like him to go.'

He opened the drawer where he had put Habib's money and pointed to it. 'Their cost though, Mr Habib, is going to be ten times what you have given me here,' he said rather sheepishly.

Habib's response was anything but.

'We have a deal, Inspector.'

THIRTY-EIGHT

KIRIN BAXI'S SUNKEN EYES were vacant. She was looking through Jack, not at him. She gave no sign of knowing who he was or the past they had shared. With her jutting jaw and gaunt cheekbones, she looked anorexic. Gone was the long silky black hair he had loved – it was now exclusively grey. She looked so much worse than the grainy video footage he had seen.

Jack stared at her, unable to find an opening.

He had wondered how he might feel when this moment arrived. For years he had thought of her infidelity, her leaving their home and finally of her suicide – the death to which he had believed he'd driven her. Anger mixed with so much guilt.

Jack now felt empty and that was far worse than anger or sorrow.

He took in more details of her appearance: the grey hair scraped back into a tight ponytail and the scars on her neck that crept down her chest like arrows.

'Kirin?' His throat was dry.

She remained motionless, unresponsive to his voice.

'Kirin, it's Jatinder,' he said.

He looked for any sign of recognition. If he looked hard enough, he might convince himself there was a spark, but she remained silent.

Jack had spent every minute since he'd found out she was alive working out how he would handle this meeting. He had so many questions, but now she was in front of him, his mind was a blank.

He moved to the desk, picked up his cup of water and took a long sip. Sweat trickled down his face, catching at the corner of his mouth, the taste salty.

Kirin stayed still.

'Can you hear me?' he asked, returning to her. 'I'm your husband. Jatinder Baxi. From Bradford.'

She turned to face him but still didn't speak. Her eyes blinked repeatedly, like a camera shutter clicking. Then the blank stare took over again.

'Kirin?'

Jack reached out and held her hands. He had hoped he might feel something when he touched her, but there was nothing. Her skin felt coarse as sandpaper and the third finger on her right hand was missing. His gaze fell to the floor and he felt his anger betray him. Anger at everything that had happened over the past few days.

'Kirin, can you hear me?' he whispered, dejected.

'Yes,' she said loudly. Jack jumped and let out a small yelp of shock. He let go of her hands and backed away.

'Sixteen Parsonage Road. The back door leaks when it rains. Ruins the newspapers,' she said.

Jack was gobsmacked.

'She wants to know if it still leaks,' said Kirin.

'Who does?' asked Jack.

'Kirin does.'

'I . . . I fixed it. Kirin, it's me – Jack.'

'Jack tried to kill me,' she said softly, and took three sudden paces towards him. Taken by surprise, Jack jumped back, but was cornered against the desk behind.

He put his hands out, ready to push her away. She was staring at him, glaring into his eyes. The vacancy had vanished.

'Jack tried to kill me,' she whispered again. She grabbed his hands and put them around her throat. He tried to break free but she was freakishly strong. 'Like this,' she said.

'Let go!' Jack cried.

'Jesus loves me. He saved me. Saved everyone. Died like me and then came back.'

She still held his hands gripped around her throat. Jack struggled and managed to free himself just as Sister Florence came hurrying into the room.

'What's going on?' she asked in alarm.

'I . . . I don't know. She just grabbed my hands and put them around her throat,' said Jack.

'Kirin?' said Sister Florence.

Kirin's poisonous stare remained on Jack. There was history in her eyes.

She saw him.

Sister Florence was now sitting in the office with Jack and Kirin. A few minutes had passed since she had entered the room and Kirin was once more a mute statue.

'How did you get her to speak about her past?' asked Jack.

'Father Cave hypnotized her. He quickly established three personalities living inside her. Often they would fight for superiority and at those times she became violent. When that happened, she was impossible to control. We were forced to tie her to the bed.'

Jack wondered how he could possibly make sense of what he was hearing.

'Father Cave managed a period of a few weeks where he got a lot of information from her about you and Aisha, but the puzzle of how she ended up in India has never been solved. It's buried so deep inside her that I'm not sure even she can access it any more.'

'There *must* be a way,' said Jack.

'Father Cave tried everything. It was why he travelled to England. He was hoping to find answers. I assume he stumbled across something people did not want unearthing.'

'Do you have transcripts of what Kirin told him?'

'Father Cave kept an audio file of their meetings.'

'Could you give me a copy?'

There was a commotion outside. Jack heard raised voices and then a scream from Aisha.

'What the hell's going on?' he said, jumping to his feet.

The wooden doors leading into the hall were flung open as two burly Asian men dressed in black appeared. They pushed their way into the office.

Sister Florence went towards them and began to ask what they were doing. One of them, unshaven and bulky, struck her in the face. She was unconscious before she hit the ground.

Jack started to run at the man but stopped when the second one pointed a revolver at him.

Kirin remained motionless on the chair, observing the drama.

'What is this?' asked Jack. He saw the blood trickling from Sister Florence's nose. 'You bastards. What do you want?'

The man ignored him.

'Just the woman. Leave him alone,' Jack heard him say in Punjabi to his accomplice.

Where was Aisha? What had they done to her?

The man turned his gun on Kirin.

'Get on with it,' said his accomplice, his eyes displaying little emotion.

There was a dramatic crack, and the man who'd been pointing his gun at Kirin dropped to the floor.

Cruise whirled round and smashed his wooden plank into the neck of the second man, who crumpled, landing on top of his partner.

'We are going, Mr Jack?' said Cruise, panting heavily.

Jack nodded. 'Hell yes.'

He grabbed Kirin roughly by the arm and dragged her to her feet.

'Quick, there is being a car waiting for them, for sure,' said Cruise.

They rushed into the courtyard and found Aisha lying face down on the ground.

'She is alive,' said Cruise, kneeling beside her. 'I am checking her when I came in. But she is out.'

'Here,' said Jack, passing Kirin to Cruise, 'take her.' Jack scooped Aisha's body into his arms. 'Cruise, get us out of here safely and I'll make you a rich man.'

'Come quickly,' said Cruise and led them out of the courtyard, through the front doors. He stopped briefly and checked the alleyway. There was a Jeep waiting at the far end.

'We are having to go in Sadar market. The car will not be allowed there, so they will be coming on foot. We need to move fast.'

'How far is it?'

'It is a few minutes away. We can be losing them in the underground markets; it is, how are you saying, a maze. Thousands of peoples. We will be having a good chance.'

'Let's go,' said Jack.

'Wait – they are having guns too? We will be easy target in the alley.' Cruise surveyed the immediate area. There was little to help them out. 'Are you knowing how to dodge bullets, Mr Jack?'

'What?'

'Be moving in a zigzag. Understanding? I am seeing it in *Mission Impossible*.'

Jack shot him a disbelieving stare.

'OK, sir, follow me,' Cruise said, and with that he grabbed Kirin's hand and dashed into the street, dragging her behind him.

Jack followed, carrying Aisha against his chest. There was a few seconds' delay before shouting and urgent footsteps started behind them.

Jack turned his head, expecting to see Habib.

The reality was far worse.

Detective Singh had found them.

THIRTY-NINE

THE GROUND WAS UNEVEN and twice Jack nearly stumbled. The voices behind were getting closer. He was struggling to keep up with Cruise, who was still dragging Kirin like a rag doll.

Jack tripped over three cats fighting in the middle of the path. Fatigue was creeping into his legs and he knew he wouldn't be able to carry Aisha much further. The humidity was crippling, sweat dripping down his face and making his eyes sting.

They emerged into the carnival atmosphere of the Bazaar, streaming sunlight welcoming them out into the open. Cruise disappeared into the hubbub, with Jack close behind. Glancing behind him at the alleyway, Jack let out a cry as Singh, escorted by two other men, came into view.

Jack started shouting at the crowd to get out of the way. He barged forwards, sending people sprawling. He ignored the angry curses as he kept moving.

At the other side of the square Jack followed Cruise down a narrow path leading down into Sadar Bazaar's underground labyrinth. He risked another look behind and saw that they'd gained a little distance from their pursuers.

The air was stifling, like there was no oxygen. The heat from thousands of bodies had simply nowhere to go.

Jack spoke urgently to Cruise. 'We need to split up. Whatever happens, do not lose Kirin. I'll double your daily rate. Meet me back at the apartment, but *do not* lead those men there. Can you do that for me?'

'Sir, I am not letting you down but we cannot be going back to the apartment. It is not being safe there any more. There is a mosque at the bottom of this market. I am heading there. You are cutting right here, then loop all the way around. OK?'

'Yes,' said Jack. He wasted no time in taking the turn. More abuse was hurled at him, everyone seeming oblivious to the fact that he was carrying the limp body of a girl. She probably looked like a child to them, asleep in his arms.

Jack shouted again for people to get out of the way. He took a left turn, then a right, hoping desperately he wouldn't hit a dead end. He hurtled past stalls selling pens, tin openers, padlocks and clocks. It was too risky to check behind him now. Every second he had was about putting distance between him and the men with guns.

Aisha was a dead weight in his arms and kept sliding down his body. Jack could go no further. He took a final right-hand turn and entered a small shop, stumbling past the counter and into the room at the back. He sank to his knees and hid behind the counter, clumsily rolling Aisha's body to the side. He could hardly breathe.

A chubby Indian boy, no older than ten, was sitting cross-legged in the corner, on top of a mountain of handkerchiefs, eating a chocolate bar. He gazed down in amazement at Jack. There wasn't an adult in sight.

Jack touched his finger to his lips, pleading with the boy to be quiet. The youngster tilted his head to one side, and although clearly perplexed, remained silent.

Jack waited for the men to lean over the counter and put an end to the chase. He looked up, expecting to see Detective Singh glowering down at him. Dark spots danced in front of his eyes.

Aisha was stirring. She moaned incoherently and opened her eyes, bewildered. Jack clamped a hand over her mouth. She didn't move. Confusion written all over her face, she peered at her surroundings. Jack didn't take his eyes off her, terrified she was about to scream.

He placed his lips to her ear. 'We were ambushed at the shelter. You were knocked unconscious. We're in the underground markets. I couldn't carry you any more. Are you OK?'

She nodded. Jack took his hand from her mouth.

'Mum?' she whispered.

It hit Jack like a sledgehammer.

Mum.

'We've got her. Can you walk?'

She drew her knees up to her chest and then stretched them out. 'I think so.'

'OK, good. We're going to head towards a mosque at the other end of the market,' he said. 'Kirin and Cruise will meet us there. Are you ready?'

Aisha manoeuvred herself into a crouching position. 'Let's go,' she said.

Jack helped her to her feet and they took stock of their surroundings. The little boy beamed at them but stayed silent.

'Do you know who's chasing us?' asked Aisha.

'Detective Singh,' said Jack. 'That bastard is better connected than we realized. And he's somewhere around, so when we move, we do it calmly and try to mingle into the crowd. Got it?'

'He really followed us here? How?' said Aisha, her bottom lip trembling.

'I have no idea. Come on, we're not beaten yet.'

They stepped nervously on to the main track. The ground was littered in food wrappers and unfinished beverages. Hundreds of shoppers continued to move like a conveyor belt heading deeper underground.

They blended in, taking small steps away from where they'd been hiding, tucking themselves close in to the shoppers. All at once, the smell of sweat, chilli powder and urine hit Jack. The melody of the market was the incessant chatter of people, buying, selling, everyone contributing to a symphony of chaos.

Jack held tight on to Aisha's hand, every few seconds glancing over his shoulder, trying to spot Detective Singh amongst the crowd. He prayed that Cruise had managed to get away. The tenacity of the kid gave Jack hope. Cruise by name and by nature, it seemed.

They'd been flowing along with the crowd for several minutes now without any drama. Jack needed to find the mosque. He asked a couple of store owners but they ignored him, only interested if Jack was buying.

It was sixth time lucky when a tea vendor finally pointed him down the path and told him to follow the route to the bottom until he could go no further. They would reach a food square and from there they needed to go up some steel steps, round to the left and then they'd reach the mosque.

Jack checked to see if Aisha was OK. She looked pale and told him she needed water. He reassured her that the mosque was close by.

It took fifteen minutes to reach the other end of the market. It felt like they'd descended miles into the underworld of Sadar Bazaar. The air had grown even hotter and more stifling. Jack wondered if this was as close to the realm of the devil as you could get. His feet were sweating and he imagined the flames of hell warming the ground.

They were standing in a large square, their senses assaulted by the pungent fumes of a vast spice market. Jack's eyes watered as he spotted the mountains of chilli powder at the front of almost every stall. The yells of the vendors were deafening, each one trying to outdo the others.

'*Garam masala!*'

'*Mirchi!*'

'Over there,' said Jack, spying steps in the distance. They hurried towards them and climbed to a path at the top, which led into a winding dark passageway. Aisha's steps became smaller and more hesitant.

'We can't see what's down here, Jack.'

'It'll be fine,' he said. 'It has to be close now.'

Hugging the wall, they made slow progress. The spiralling dirt track seemed to go on for ever.

'This doesn't feel right, Jack. We've not come across anyone for a few minutes now. There are thousands of people out there, so why are we on our own?'

The air had grown stale and the ground damp and powdery beneath their feet.

With hesitant steps, they trudged on towards a light at the bottom of the tunnel. On their left was a pink door with an Arab inscription on the glass pane over the top.

'Mosque?' asked Jack, pointing to it.

Aisha took a step forward, read the inscription and nodded.

'Thank God,' he said.

Aisha pulled her scarf straight, pushed open the door and they stepped inside. Jack closed the doors behind them.

'Is this a mosque?' asked Jack, peering around the dimly lit room. There were no lights on, just sunlight filtering in through a far-off window.

'I'm not sure,' replied Aisha.

Jack knocked loudly on the plastered wall to his right.

Footsteps in the distance, getting closer, brought them to a standstill.

'Someone's coming,' she hissed.

Cruise rounded the corner, towing Kirin behind him. He looked as exhausted as Jack.

Jack hugged the boy, unable to contain his relief.

Cruise was out of breath and slumped to the ground when Jack released him. His words came out short and urgent.

'Mr Jack, sir, you are needing to tell Cruise just what exactly is going on here.'

FORTY

THE HOLIEST PLACE IN Sikhism, the Golden Temple, was as ever a calming site for the man everyone knew only as Sahib. He was sitting in his electronic wheelchair, listening to the soothing sound of the Granthis, the ceremonial readers who read continuously from the Sikh holy book, the Guru Granth Sahib. Their prayers were being transmitted through speakers located in the lofty domes of the temple, a few kilometres from where he was sitting.

On first appearance, Sahib looked like a child, dressed from head to toe in a thin orange cloak on which were etched the religious symbols of the *Khalsa*: a circle and three swords. The cloak protected him from ultraviolet light, which was toxic to his skin, such as he had left. Seventy-two years ago, when he had been only twenty-one years old, Sahib had been doused in petrol and set alight – but not to die. That would have been too easy.

Sahib had suffered ninety per cent burns to his body and then been taken to the hospital by his aggressors and kept alive.

Not out of compassion.

No, as a reminder – a living message that would be spoken

about for decades until he eventually died and his story became legend.

But in saving his life, his aggressors had created a force far more powerful than they could ever have imagined.

The guards outside his residence were waiting for instruction. So far, Sahib remained silent.

He moved his wheelchair slowly across the marble floor to the other end of his four-storey residence. Heading out on to the balcony, he made sure his body was shielded from the sun. From here, he could see the farm and the young boys practising sword-fighting in the fields, training to become the Khalsa one day.

Khalsa, the Sikh warriors. Sahib was perhaps the oldest one alive today.

The farm was twenty acres of sacred land. The boundary was close to the border of Pakistan and was constantly patrolled, although bloodshed was seldom these days, unlike in the 1950s and 1960s when daily skirmishes had resulted in loss of life.

The fields were bare now. The rice had been harvested, leaving the soil naked and exposed. Sahib had a workforce of almost a hundred men. They looked after the land like it was their own. The soil was sacred. It was where so many battles had been fought, all of them successfully. Those were the times when men faced each other with a sword.

Painful memories.

Especially of the night that changed everything. A terrible night of consequences, engineered albeit accidentally by white men who had vacated the region.

The British had divided India without any consideration for what would happen when they were no longer in charge. They didn't much care. Through almost one hundred years of torment, they had ravaged the land and looted riches that would keep their empire wealthy for centuries to come.

No one perhaps could have foreseen the level of devastation that would be caused by the drawing of a single line on a map. The British lawyer tasked with doing it had never even set foot in India.

Sir Cyril Radcliffe.

How had that man slept at night, knowing what followed? How much blood was on his hands?

Sahib's mind had wandered, something that happened often these days. He came back to his present dilemma.

Jatinder Baxi.

Baxi had proved elusive so far. Chasing him was tiring.

Baxi wanted the truth and that would ultimately lead him to Sahib.

So why chase him?

Let Baxi come to them.

And what then?

Sahib didn't know.

More bloodshed?

He didn't want that. Of all the lives he had taken, he *did not* want to be the man who spilled Jatinder Baxi's blood.

That would be bad karma.

The others couldn't understand why he didn't just give the order to end it.

They wouldn't.

They were too young to remember.

It was the name that gave him the most trouble.

Baxi.

To kill him would be to cross a line.

Sahib had much pain to live with. The older he became, the more he thought about how much blood he had shed. How many lives he had been responsible for taking.

He didn't regret any of them but he didn't want to take this one.

Yet, deep down, Sahib felt he was destined to face Jatinder. Everything that had happened so far suggested it.

Back in 2002, Detective Kuldeep Singh had put everything on

the line to fake Kirin Baxi's death and bring her to India. He was a senior member of their organization and had been ordered by Sahib to abduct Kirin. Singh had planted a Jane Doe at the canal, where Kirin had seemingly disappeared, and then used their organization's vast connections to ensure it had been identified as Kirin Baxi.

It had been one of the most sensitive operations they'd ever attempted.

Everything had gone according to plan.

But then, several days ago, Father Benedict Cave had landed in Bradford and gone to the police station and asked to speak to someone about the historic death of Kirin Baxi. Detective Singh had been called to take the query, seeing as he'd been the investigating officer seventeen years earlier. On seeing Cave's evidence about Kirin's continued existence, Singh had alerted Sahib and everything after that had been about damage limitation.

'What a mess,' whispered Sahib in Punjabi.

He was rueful at not having taken Kirin Baxi's life. Her existence as a whore in Delhi was more troubling to him than the others realized. He had ordered her execution. It should have been clean and without consequence. She was a Sikh woman, whose death should have been honourable, even if her existence had been anything but.

Something had gone wrong.

Someone had betrayed him.

He knew who it was. *That was in hand.*

But the fact it had happened suggested something more than chance.

Kismet. Karma. Fate. Destiny. It had many names.

The silence was broken by a guard, who knocked lightly on the balcony doors. He brought a small table to Sahib and placed a cup of Indian tea on it, cardamom seeds floating on the top.

As the guard started to leave, Sahib stopped him.

'Jatinder Baxi,' he said.

'Yes, Sahib?'

'I have made my decision.'

'As you please, Sahib.'

'Leave him.'

'Sahib?' replied the guard, unable to hide his surprise.

'He will come to us. Have no doubt. It is written this way. Do you disagree?'

'Sahib, it is not my place to question your wisdom.'

'I ask you anyway. Give me your counsel.'

'Since you allow me, then I will state that I believe we should eliminate this risk immediately. If he were to take the woman to the British consulate and she were able to recall what happened, it would place us at great risk.'

Sahib digested the guard's opinion.

'We have our men in the consulate,' he replied.

'The media could hear of it. We have no control over them. If people look into her story – there is risk.'

'There is always risk,' said Sahib. 'But we have tried twice to silence this man. And twice we have failed. That is unheard of. Would you not agree?'

'It is unfortunate,' replied the guard.

'It is kismet. No?'

The guard didn't reply.

'You know who he is?' said Sahib.

'I know.'

'He makes you uncomfortable?'

'The situation makes me uncomfortable.'

'I have made up my mind. Alert Singh and call an end to the chase. Allow Baxi free passage. It will prove almost impossible for him to locate us. His journey to the truth is filled with danger. But if Jatinder succeeds, then he deserves the truth. After that, well, we will see what his kismet holds.'

FORTY-ONE

MY MOTHER, THOUGHT AISHA.

She placed her hands gently around Kirin's face and looked into her eyes, almond-shaped and green, the same as hers – a rarity in the Asian community. Aisha blinked back tears and tried to speak to her but Kirin remained silent, lost in her own world. After several failed attempts, Aisha made her way back over to Jack.

The imam of the mosque had sent a young boy over with a large bottle of cold water and four plastic cups. They sat there in silence, quenching their thirst, nobody really sure what came next. Cruise had told the imam that they were tourists who had got lost and just needed a few moments to gather their strength. The imam had been welcoming, telling them that any house of Allah was theirs also. Curious, the old man made his way over towards Kirin and sat down cross-legged in front of her.

'Cruise, what the hell happened back there?' asked Jack.

'I am not knowing, sir. I am seeing those men forcing their way inside the church. When I follow, I am seeing Sister lying on the floor and realizing that we are having some trouble.'

'Shit,' whispered Jack.

'Please don't use that language in here,' Aisha said quietly.

This irked Jack no end. 'Today is the third time in a week that someone's tried to kill us, and this time, five thousand miles from where it last happened. My wife over there has spent years working the streets of Delhi when she was supposed to be dead, and her illegitimate child is sitting next to me telling me not to swear because we're in a holy place? Any time God wants to start helping us out, I'll watch my mouth.'

Aisha didn't reply.

'Sir, this is being your wife?' Cruise asked, his eyes wide.

Jack nodded.

'This is being an incredulous development.'

'What are we going to do?' said Jack, more to himself than anyone else.

'Go to the police?' suggested Aisha.

'Oh no, Sister. If these peoples who are chasing you are connected, then the police are *definitely* the wrong place to go. You are being able to buy a police officer for *very* little money in Sadar Bazaar.'

'Then what do we do?' said Jack.

The humidity inside the mosque was punishing. Jack poured himself another glass of water and drank it down in one gulp.

'Cruise, can you get us safely back to our apartment?' asked Aisha.

'Sister, of course. I am—'

'No, we can't go back there,' said Jack.

'But all my things are there,' said Aisha.

'You have your passport on you. That's all you need. I don't know how Singh and those guys found us, but they must have been tracking us from the airport, hoping we'd lead them to Kirin.'

'But we didn't speak to anyone at the airport,' said Aisha.

'How could they have known which flight we would land on, on which date and what we look like?'

Jack massaged his head and sighed.

Cruise raised his hand.

'Speak freely, Cruise, we're not at school now,' said Jack.

'Immigration,' said Cruise.

Jack sat upright as a thought was triggered in his mind.

'When you are going through Immigration, Mr Jack, they are taking your picture, your flight – all of the details Sister was just saying. I am seeing it in a movie.'

Immigration.

Jack got to his feet and staggered away from them to the other side of the room. He rested his head on his arms, leaning against the wall.

'Jack?' said Aisha, but he remained as he was, his thoughts racing. Having worked through what Cruise had suggested, Jack stared across at Kirin. 'Who are you?' he whispered.

Aisha appeared at his side. 'She is nothing like the woman you or my father thought she was,' she replied softly. She placed a hand on Jack's shoulder. 'There are forces at work here that only she can tell us about.'

He turned to face her and folded his arms across his chest. 'Whatever *this* is, it's out of our control. Whoever's tracking her has *very* powerful connections. Think about it, Aisha – the police in England, immigration services here. That's a *global* network.'

'But who could possibly want her that badly and why?' said Aisha, looking across at her mother.

'Someone with a lot of money and a lot of power,' he replied quietly.

She took the bait instantly. 'My father?'

Jack nodded.

'But he helped us in England. My father would never, ever hurt me. *Ever*,' she said forcefully.

'Argh,' said Jack, massaging his head again. It felt ready to explode. 'You're right, it makes no sense. It can't be Habib, but then who else has that kind of power?'

'There's only one person who can tell us,' said Aisha, focusing her gaze back on Kirin. 'We have to get her to talk.'

The imam was still sitting with Kirin. The sunlight seemed to catch her face, lighting it up for an instant. For the first time, Jack saw glimmers of the woman he had married.

Curious, he approached the two of them.

The imam turned to face him, his voice soft. 'She is lost, no? How long has she been like this?'

'Years,' replied Aisha.

'Tell me about her, if you have the time. Perhaps I can help.'

Jack briefed the imam on their journey so far. He saw little point in hiding the truth. He explained that battling the different personalities within her had forced Kirin to become trapped in her own mind.

The imam listened patiently, nodding every now and again, constantly playing through the rosary beads in his hands. 'What your wife is running from – this is the same thing that brings you to my mosque today?'

They looked nervously at each other. Jack nodded.

The imam smiled. 'So, it is important you unlock her mind?'

'Critical,' replied Jack. 'Can you help us?'

The imam nodded. 'I have seen this type of case a few times over the years.'

'What can we do?' asked Jack eagerly.

The imam sighed and shook his head. 'Nothing. You are needing the help of the *khoon-saab*.'

'*Khoon-saab*?' said Jack hesitantly. 'Doesn't that mean blood-doctor?'

The imam nodded. 'It is the oldest type of therapy.'

'I don't understand,' replied Jack. 'What exactly do they do?'

'I do,' whispered Aisha, her face draining of colour. 'I've studied the ways of alternative medicine in Asia at university and I will *not* take her there.'

'I am in agreement with Sister,' said Cruise, more forcefully than Jack had so far heard the boy say anything. 'The *khoon-saabs* are *very* dangerous people.'

The imam was equally strong in his rebuttal. 'This lady's mind is locked. You will only help her when you take the mind past conscious thought.'

'We've tried that. She's been hypnotized,' said Jack.

'That is a very mild probe. *Khoon-saabs* work differently.'

'Imam,' said Aisha, crouching down opposite him, 'how can you suggest this? It's highly dangerous.'

'Aisha,' said Jack, trying to keep a lid on his annoyance, 'would you, please, for the love of God, tell me what on earth a *khoon-saab* does?'

Aisha dropped her voice and looked ill at ease. '*Khoon-saabs* believe that shedding impure blood brings people back to who they once were. It's used in some parts of Asia as a treatment for personality disorders – you insert an open-ended needle into the arm and bleed someone until they speak.'

'And if she doesn't?' asked Jack.

'In that case,' said Aisha, her voice a little shaky, 'she may well bleed to death.'

FORTY-TWO

THE *KHOON-SAAB*'S HOUSE WAS a half-hour journey from the mosque, at the far side of Sadar Bazaar. Jack was mindful that Singh and his cronies might be nearby but their escape through the underground markets had led them to the other end, almost a kilometre from where they had first escaped with Kirin. Even so, Jack was cautious and had sent Cruise out into the markets to find burkas for Aisha and Kirin. For Jack and himself, he had purchased traditional *shalwar kameez*, two skull caps and two cheap scarves to wrap around their faces.

'We don't look like we're trying too hard to cover up?'

'Relax, Mr Jack, we are being in a predominantly Muslim area, remember?' said Cruise.

Jack was grateful to be away from the underground furnace of the markets and back in civilization. He felt uncomfortable in the attire but Cruise was right, they blended in.

Cruise flagged down a bicycle rickshaw and they all climbed in, Cruise next to Aisha and opposite them, Jack and Kirin.

The rickshaw inched its way down the road, Eid celebrations

in full swing, people carrying huge shopping bags bulging with food and new clothes. Wandering amongst the indistinguishable burkas were women dressed in vibrant red, yellow and green outfits, while the front of almost every building was festooned with tinsel. Jack tried to speak to Kirin but her eyes were closed and she appeared to be dozing.

The rickshaw turned into a narrow side street, their skinny cyclist standing up and pedalling hard. They now entered a slum area, where small, feebly constructed shacks cowered beneath hazardous-looking power cables.

To their left stretched a vast area of wasteland, heaped with rotting litter and the occasional smouldering fire. The stench was sickening. Jack and Aisha followed Cruise's lead by pulling their scarves tightly around their mouths and noses. Kirin appeared to remain unfazed.

The rickshaw stopped for a Muslim man, struggling with a large camel just in front of them. A garland of pink flowers hung from the animal's neck and streams of green tinsel from its head. It was a wealthy man's sacrifice for Eid.

Jack's attention was drawn to a large group of slum children, playing cricket on the wasteland, seeming oblivious to its toxic stink.

Aisha suddenly yelled for the driver to change direction. He shrugged and told her it wasn't possible – the traffic was too busy for him to turn round.

Jack put a hand on Aisha's shoulder. 'What's got into you?' he asked, puzzled.

Aisha pointed into the distance and Jack saw what had got her so worked up.

A police checkpoint was stopping every vehicle, the officers comparing the faces of the passengers against the photos in their hands. Deep down, Jack just knew the whole charade was about them.

The rickshaw stopping in its tracks was now causing more than the usual traffic chaos.

Aisha hissed for them all to get out and now, but it was too late.

The officers ahead had evidently spotted their reluctance.

Within thirty seconds, their rickshaw was surrounded.

FORTY-THREE

THE POLICE OFFICERS HAD escorted the four of them into a disused retail shack, nothing more than four rusting metal sheets for walls and a roof that looked like it might fall in at any moment. So far, Jack and Aisha had refused to hand over any ID, playing the 'harassed tourist' card.

Cruise had done his best to tell the officers to get lost, but his outrage had been met with a swift slap to the face and he was now sitting beside Kirin, seething.

'You are showing us your UK identification and then you are leaving,' said the officer who appeared to be in charge. The ink on his name badge was smudged but Jack made out the name Nasir. The other two men were standing outside the hut, smoking cigarettes.

They were all armed, so any thoughts Jack had of overpowering them and making a dash for it were held firmly in check.

'Can't you at least tell us what this is about?' said Jack, wondering if this was Detective Singh's doing. So far, no one had made any calls and the officers' radios had remained silent.

Nasir was starting to get irritated. Sweat dripped down his brow and he wiped it with a meaty forearm. 'I no having time for this. You are showing us your identification or you coming to the *thana* with us.'

Thana – jail.

His English, while broken in parts, was surprisingly good.

Jack bowed his head and tried to think of some way out.

Aisha broke the deadlock by handing over her passport. Jack froze as Nasir opened it, checked her details and gave her a swift once-over.

Something changed in his expression.

His eyes narrowed, and as he returned the passport to Aisha, he grabbed for his pistol and pointed it at Jack.

Checkmate.

Jack took a deep breath of warm, stale air and put his head in his hands.

Christ, they really couldn't catch a break in this forsaken city.

Nasir's reaction on seeing Aisha's passport had told her everything she needed to know. The fact he had pointed his gun at Jack and not at her had been the giveaway.

This was her father's doing.

It had been the way the officers had manhandled Jack, Cruise and even Kirin, yet they had treated Aisha with respect. That and the gun pointed at Jack's head had made it clear what her only move was here. When she spoke, it was in Urdu.

'Habib. My father. He's the one who has done this, no?'

Nasir made no reply. There was no change in his face.

There was only one way to make sure.

Using every ounce of courage she had, Aisha stood up and made her move. Roughly, she shoved Nasir back towards the exposed doorway.

'Answer me when I speak to you!' she snapped.

Nasir looked at her angrily but did not counter.

Jack watched, perplexed, as Aisha acted with a level of bravado he hadn't known she possessed. While Urdu was not a language he spoke, he could loosely follow the meaning.

'I assume there's a lot of money riding on our capture?' said Aisha.

'Our orders are to take you to him. He is a powerful man,' said Nasir.

'Rich, you mean,' replied Aisha. 'But you won't be getting paid. You're just a lowly patrol officer. My father wouldn't have spoken to you. More likely, your boss, which means, if you take us in, you might get – what? A few hundred rupees? A few thousand?'

Aisha could see that her words carried truth. She played the only card she had left.

'It's Eid today, brother. And no matter what my father has told you or your boss, I'm in no danger of harm. You can see my age on my passport. I'm an adult and capable of making my own decisions.' She pointed to Jack and continued, 'If I'd wanted to escape from this man, I would come with you. Instead, let me make you a counter-offer. Allow me to go to that ICICI bank behind you and withdraw fifty thousand rupees with my card. It's the maximum I can do, and instead of your boss taking all the money my father's offered, you and your colleagues here can walk away and have a memorable Eid.'

Aisha glared at Jack, who took the hint and drew his own bank card from his pocket.

'Fifty thousand from me also,' he said.

Aisha stepped closer to Nasir. 'I'm in no danger. Let me repeat that. And this is your once-in-a-lifetime opportunity to walk away from here with a payday you will *never* see again. Your boss earns enough, no?'

Nasir nodded – the offer of such a sizeable amount of money had changed everything. Greed was written all over his face.

'What an Eid you and your family could have,' said Aisha.

Jack watched on, holding his breath as Nasir lowered his weapon. 'Let me see this money and then we will talk.'

The withdrawal from the bank took less than fifteen minutes, both Jack and Aisha watched over by Nasir, while the other two officers guarded Cruise and Kirin.

Jack had been fearful that their cards would be declined, but both he and Aisha had used an internet café in Paris to notify their banks of their trip to India. This had mostly been at Aisha's insistence. The last thing she had wanted was to be reliant on Jack for money.

With the cash in their hands, they followed Nasir back to the shack. Jack handed his money to Aisha and let her complete the deal.

'*Eid mubarak*,' said Aisha, and handed the money over to the policeman. He didn't count it but stuffed it inside a satchel round his waist. He stepped outside to his colleagues, exchanged brief words with them and then returned.

'Down this road, about a quarter mile, is another police block,' said Nasir. He pointed back the way they had come. 'You are taking that cut in the road and going around the outside of the bazaar. There is nobody to stop you there.'

Aisha smiled and thanked him warmly.

'Come on, Jack. We're done here,' she said.

FORTY-FOUR

BACK ON THE MOVE now, their rickshaw followed the route Nasir had cleared for them. Cruise was seated beside Kirin, his face still red from where Nasir had slapped him. Jack turned to Aisha and dropped his voice.

'That was . . . quite something,' he said.

With the veil from her burka tucked securely around her face, Aisha continued to stare ahead at the relentless energy of the Sadar Bazaar. Her reply was curt. 'People have so little here. I knew if we offered him a life-changing amount of money, he'd think of his family first.' She looked at him now, eyes narrowed. 'It's what we do, isn't it? Put our families first.'

Jack saw that she'd hardened since they had first met. He told her as much.

Aisha glanced towards Kirin, who was sitting abjectly, lost in her own little world.

'For what comes next, Jack, we need to be focused. *Khoon-saabs* are not to be underestimated. They are in reality no more than opportunistic witch doctors.'

Jack turned to face her. 'Is there any other choice in the short time we have?'

Aisha met his gaze and then looked away.

Her silence said it all.

Their journey took forty minutes. Blaring car horns, people flocking to the markets and stray animals cluttering the road had checked their progress.

The cyclist finally stopped by a row of fragile-looking metal huts. An old woman in a filthy red sari sat cross-legged outside one of them, next to a fire burning in a bin. She had piercing eyes, in stark contrast to her ashen face.

Cruise left his rickshaw and spoke with her. She waved lazily at the hut behind her. Cruise slipped her some money and then disappeared inside, telling Jack he'd return shortly. Not for the first time, Jack was thankful to have stumbled upon the boy. He was young enough to believe this was an adventure, but had clocked up enough Delhi miles to be street savvy.

Aisha made her way over to Jack. 'Are you really sure about this? I've a bad feeling about it.'

Jack wiped sweat from his forehead, pulled her gently to one side and said, 'Benedict Cave hypnotized her. He spent a whole year trying to find out what happened to her. What other choice do we have? Not to mention Detective Singh and his cronies are intent on killing us, and your father's now firmly in the mix as well. We *have* to try this. I've never heard of this practice before but I'm willing to give it a shot.'

'Even if it kills her?'

'Look at her,' he replied, his tone sharp. He grabbed Aisha and shoved her in front of Kirin, who was standing like a statue, staring blankly across the street.

'Is she alive now?' he asked.

'Get off me,' Aisha said, and slapped his hand away. 'There are good doctors in England, Jack. Trained psychiatrists. We should consider taking her to the embassy and bringing this whole thing back to Bradford.'

'Somewhere close by, people are trying to kill us, Aisha. We are shit out of time here.'

Cruise reappeared from the entrance to the hut, damp with perspiration. He told Jack the *khoon-saab* was expecting them but that Jack needed to pay him first.

'How much?'

'Four thousand rupees,' replied Cruise, shaking his head. 'He is telling me, it is Eid and rate is double usual amount.'

'Whatever, we're not in a position to bargain,' said Jack. He took the kid to one side. With what had happened to them at the refuge, their stay at Cruise's friend's makeshift hotel was not an option, nor even returning there to collect their car.

'I need you to arrange another vehicle, Cruise. Can you do that?' asked Jack.

'I have been thinking similar thing,' the boy replied, wiping the sweat from his temple. 'I am calling my colleague to collect our car but first he is dropping off another one for us, somewhere close to here.'

'They'll be watching our car, Cruise – you know that, don't you? Your friend might not be safe.'

Cruise dismissed Jack's concern with a theatrical wave of his hand. 'If anyone is asking my colleague any question, they are saying I am missing in action and they are taking the car back.'

'What are you going to tell your colleague?'

'That we are requiring a four-by-four vehicle and that you are paying me top price to sort this out.'

'Good,' replied Jack.

'Sir, are you wanting my help with the *khoon-saab*?'

Jack shook his head. 'Aisha and I will handle this.'

Cruise started to say something and then stopped himself.

'What is it? Spit it out.'

Cruise chose his words with care, glancing nervously at the old woman in the red sari. He lowered his voice. 'Sir, the *khoon-saabs* are witch doctors. I am warning you to be careful.' Cruise hesitated and then fixed both Aisha and Jack with a serious stare. 'Do not look into the *khoon-saab*'s eyes for long. There is being black magic in the eyes.'

FORTY-FIVE

INSIDE, THE *KHOON-SAAB*'S HUT was blisteringly hot. Jack felt like he was in an out-of-control sauna. The smell was putrid – almost like a pan of sweat boiling on a stove. Jack and Aisha immediately went back outside, taking Kirin with them.

'Goddammit,' said Jack, letting out a long breath.

Aisha looked ready to throw up.

'I can't take that,' said Jack.

'Me neither,' replied Aisha. 'It's like an oven.'

As ever, Kirin seemed unfazed by the feverish heat and the stench.

Jack took several enormous gulps of air. 'And I thought it was hot out here.'

He removed his shawl and undid two more buttons on his shirt. 'Aisha, maybe you should stay here?'

She was forceful in her defiance. 'Not a chance. We need someone medical in there, someone who can tell you when enough is enough.'

'How will you take the heat?'

Aisha scanned the area quickly. There were some children playing marbles across the street and a row of shabby-looking shops opposite.

'Wait here,' she said, and disappeared round the back of the hut.

There was nobody in the vicinity, just a few dogs asleep in the field. Aisha worked quickly, removing her clothes from beneath her burka. The warm air hitting her clammy skin was intensely satisfying. She made her way back towards Jack, who was standing outside the hut, holding two large bottles of water.

'Where did you get those?' she asked.

He pointed to the rundown store across the street. 'Makes my corner shop look like a palace. They're warm, but better than nothing.'

Aisha took one from him. Jack noticed the scrunched-up clothes under her arm.

'Good job that thing covers you from head to toe,' he said.

'I managed to avoid wearing one of these in Bradford, only to be defeated here,' she replied, attempting to lighten the mood.

Aisha tucked the clothes she'd removed just inside the entrance to the hut, pushing them into a dark corner. Then she took her mother's face in her hands, looked at her with sympathy and kissed her forehead.

'Come on, it's time,' said Jack.

The humidity was suffocating and Jack tried to take shallow breaths through parted lips so he didn't have to inhale the stink. The woman in the tattered red sari was now sitting in front of a veiled partition, behind which was a dim light.

The low roof over their heads meant that Jack had to stoop and shuffle forwards over a badly frayed carpet that showed the earth underneath.

'*Pasay?*' said the old woman rudely, sticking out her hand.

Jack handed over the money. She counted it quickly and waved them inside.

'You ready?' Jack whispered to Aisha.

She nodded and held Kirin's hand tightly, leading her inside.

The room they entered was larger, but the punishing humidity the same. Jack spied a bucket in the corner of the room, filled with what looked like blood and a lump of meat. He stopped dead, thinking the worst. Aisha saw what he was looking at.

'It's Eid, Jack. It's probably just goat meat, as an offering to him. He's going to be highly revered in this area.'

The *khoon-saab* waved for them to sit down. He was as Jack had imagined. A painfully thin old man with a sweeping grey beard and butter-yellow teeth, most of which were missing. Only one eye appeared to be functional; the other gleamed with cataracts.

The *khoon-saab* spoke hoarsely in Urdu.

'He's asking why we've come,' whispered Aisha.

'Tell him,' replied Jack.

Aisha spoke confidently, conversing fluently. Jack picked up the odd word.

'He says there are no guarantees,' said Aisha.

'Ask him what the odds of success are,' said Jack.

'He says it doesn't work like that. If she has any clean blood left inside her, she'll talk. But it's not absolute.'

'What did you tell him?'

'That she suffered a lot of trauma and speaks infrequently. That there are three personalities inside of her and we need to speak to the oldest one.'

'Good,' said Jack. 'That's good.'

'He wants to know how far to go,' whispered Aisha nervously.

'Meaning?'

'Should he stop if she starts talking?'

'I don't understand.'

'He says that usually when the body loses just the right amount of blood, it enters a state of shock. It's in this transitional phase that she might come back to us. If we stop the bleeding at that point, there is a chance she'd be lost for ever, perpetually confused in her mind.'

'Don't stop then,' replied Jack.

'He says the window is very narrow. If he doesn't stop the bleeding within a couple of minutes, she might . . . well . . . you know.'

'Die?'

Aisha nodded.

Jack stared intensely at the *khoon-saab*. Ordinarily he would never have entertained such barbaric treatment. But he was desperate. And out of options.

Jack stared at Kirin. He had been certain that the heat, stench and eeriness of the place would have drawn some kind of response from her, but it was like she wasn't there. He thought of all he'd so far learned about her – the secrets they simply had to unearth.

'Tell him to get started,' said Jack. 'When – if – she starts talking, we'll guide him.'

Aisha passed the message to the old man.

The *khoon-saab* nodded at Jack and displayed a troubling grin that spread right across his face. He leaned over towards Jack and handed him a wiry rope and a long dirty piece of cloth.

'What's he saying?' asked Jack, taking it from him.

She hesitated.

'Aisha?'

'He told you to tie her arms around her back, Jack. And that if she screams, to put the cloth round her mouth.'

FORTY-SIX

JACK TOOK A SIP of tepid water from his bottle. The only time Kirin showed any emotion was when the *khoon-saab* inserted a three-inch open-ended needle into her arm and placed a grimy blue bucket beneath it. The drip of Kirin's blood was immediate and alarming. Jack kept count: three seconds between each drop.

He looked across to Aisha, saw the sweat dripping off her face, and they shared a guilty look. This was barbaric, undoubtedly painful and, more than anything, potentially lethal.

The *khoon-saab* seemed unfazed. They had moved Kirin closer towards him and he sat cross-legged on the floor, inhaling deeply on a pipe filled with what smelled like cannabis. He was blowing out thick plumes of smoke, adding to the inferno-like nature of the room. Jack wanted to get the hell out of there, but they were committed. Watching a woman he had been married to, had loved, silently bleeding was torture to him. He kept telling himself it served a purpose.

*

Aisha was struggling with the same guilt as Jack. She was a trainee doctor – how could she sanction this? She wanted to stop it but was too afraid to intervene. The needle in Kirin's arm was in a major artery. Any damage to it would almost certainly result in her mother's death. Her focus flitted from Kirin to the *khoon-saab*. He seemed unearthly, humming gently and taking huge drags on what was obviously a cannabis pipe.

Aisha kept telling herself one thing: *this was the only way*.

Jack felt light-headed and desperately wanted to get out and fill his lungs with air that wasn't rancid.

This must be what it felt like to drown, he thought, suffocated by your surroundings. Each breath was a struggle and his throat felt tight. The room seemed to elongate and then rush at him, spinning as it came. His head dropped on to his chest. Images and memories from his past came into his mind, clear and precise as if they were being played out live, right in front of him.

He felt as if he could recall any memory he wanted – his upbringing, shrouded in a deep-seated understanding and commitment to religion. Reading the scriptures at the Sikh temple. The way his father had always spoken so reverently of Sikhism.

Now came images of his marriage to Kirin, the lavish ceremony in Bradford. He could see the five-hundred-strong crowd in the temple's main hall, the bright turbans and saris. Next, his father's ill-fated trip to India and his death. His mother crying, banging her wrists on the ground and smashing her plastic bangles all across the floor – a sign she was now a widow and would no longer wear jewellery.

Back to Kirin and their first night as a married couple with the heat of unexplored passion. Then their business dealings with Habib and the incredible level of wealth they had acquired.

Was he even conscious any more? Jack tried to open his eyes.

He could hear the *khoon-saab* rhythmically chanting 'Kirin' every few seconds.

Aisha's eyes were also closed. She was reliving the past few days: being abducted by Singh, the fire at Jack's shop, Sister Catherine in Shipley, and then running away from Habib. Everyone's faces seemed to flash in front of her eyes, their voices in her head.

Who is Benedict Cave?

What did he tell you?

Habib's angry face came to her. Memories of growing up under his strict tutelage and his obsession with money and power, seemingly more important to him than Aisha or Sara. Of his obvious extramarital affairs and his patriarchal view of their home life. Whatever was happening in the room, it was influencing Aisha's subconscious and bringing forgotten memories to the surface.

Was it the heat or the fumes from the pipe? Aisha knew one thing, she was being passively drugged. Yet, she *was* conscious. She could hear the *khoon-saab*'s mellow chanting.

Her thoughts were interrupted by Jack gently shaking her arm. Aisha forced her eyes open and the room came hazily into focus. She looked at Jack drowsily.

'I can't take this any more,' he whispered. 'I need to step out. There's something wrong in this room.'

His face was saturated with sweat, drops falling from his chin like rain.

He glanced at the *khoon-saab*, who remained motionless, inhaling on his pipe, staring at the blood dripping from Kirin's arm into the bucket.

Had anyone died in here?

He glanced around the room, his attention once more falling on the lump of meat in the corner.

'Step outside if you need to, Jack,' said Aisha. 'But don't be too long. I might need to follow you.'

'OK,' he said, trying to get to his feet, his head heavy. 'Keep an eye on her.'

He scrambled past Aisha, through the exit, but no sooner was he clear of the room, taking in great gulps of cleaner air, than he heard Aisha's urgent voice, calling him back in.

He rushed back into the room. 'What is it?'

Aisha was crouching beside Kirin. 'Hi, Mum,' she said, smiling warmly.

The *khoon-saab* retreated a little, giving them space.

'Kirin?' said Jack, reaching out to touch her face, but the *khoon-saab* stopped him angrily. Jack turned to Aisha for an explanation of what he had said.

'Don't touch her,' whispered Aisha. 'It may break the spell. But you can now ask her questions.'

Jack searched for an opening question, his mind suddenly blank.

Aisha broke the silence. 'What is your name?' she asked.

Kirin replied in Punjabi, a language Aisha was fluent in. 'Though I've had so many,' she said.

'Do you know who I am?' said Aisha.

'A child. A pretty one.'

Aisha smiled. Kirin looked weak and drowsy.

'How many times have you been married?' Aisha said.

Kirin's eyes were locked on the *khoon-saab* as she spoke, her eyes wide and strange. 'Three times. I married Jatinder first. Then Asif. And then Thakur.'

Asif – Habib's old name before he changed it.

Jack reminded Aisha of the fact, unable to recall whether he had previously told her.

'Why did you marry Asif?' asked Jack, trying to hide the hurt in his voice and keeping to the shadows. He was terrified she'd stop talking if she saw him.

'I was pregnant with Aisha. He said I had to convert to Islam and marry him before she was born – that we needed to do it the right way. We did a *nikkah* secretly. My baby was so beautiful. Green, almond-shaped eyes just like mine.'

Jack felt the devastation of both statements. A *nikkah* was a simple Islamic marriage ceremony carried out in front of an imam, and Kirin had now confirmed that Aisha was her child.

'Is that why you wanted to leave me?' he asked, stepping towards her.

There was a pause and Kirin turned to look at him, and this time he knew she saw him. There was a definite change in her eyes, a softening – a realization. Staring at Jack seemed to have burned the vacancy from her eyes. In the silence that followed there was only the slow drip of her blood from her wrist into the bucket.

'Jatinder?' she whispered.

He nodded, holding his breath.

'What kind of nightmare am I trapped in that I see your face?' she said. 'Am I dead? I must be.'

'No,' replied Jack. 'I really am here. I've come to take you home. Tell me – who brought you here? Who did this to you?'

She spat at him and her face burned with a terrible rage – a fury Jack had never seen in her before. She snarled at him and tried to bite his face. Jack recoiled, hearing the smash of her teeth in his ears. Kirin swore profanities at him in Punjabi, ones he never thought she knew. The dripping of her blood now started to quicken.

'We need to stop the bleeding,' said Aisha, gesturing to the *khoon-saab*. Jack didn't catch the reply but he understood Aisha's frustrated response.

'Take the needle out. Stop this now! I don't care if it stops her speaking.'

Jack readied himself, unable to take his eyes off Kirin's flushed face as the *khoon-saab* cut the rope binding her wrists. No sooner was she free than Kirin lunged at Jack before anyone had time to react. She flashed her wrist across his face, the open end of the needle cutting him with surgical efficiency. Jack fell backwards and Kirin was on top of him. She ripped the needle from her wrist with her teeth.

Jack heard Aisha scream in alarm.

Kirin brought the needle down towards Jack's face. He grabbed her wrist, blood spurting all over him now. The struggle was intense – she was possessed with a strength he would never have thought possible. The needle teetered inches above his eye, Kirin using all her bodyweight as leverage. The point of the needle grazed Jack's eyelid and the sensation gave him new energy. He threw Kirin to the side and got on top of her, pinning her to the ground. She dropped the needle, as her body went limp.

Panting heavily, Jack stared down at her. 'Why?' he asked.

Aisha came hurriedly to Kirin's side and checked her wrist. A pool of blood was gathering on the floor. 'Oh God,' said Aisha, 'she must have severed her artery.' She turned to the *khoon-saab*, asking for a cloth or something to wrap the wound with but he didn't move. She rushed past him to find something herself.

'Why?' said Jack to Kirin again. 'Who did this to us?'

'You did this, Jatinder. You took them from me,' she said hazily, her eyelids starting to flicker. Jack eased his grip on her and tapped her face lightly.

'What do you mean?' he said. He could hear Aisha ordering the *khoon-saab* to call an ambulance and his reply that no ambulance would come here and the nearest hospital was thirty minutes away.

'She won't make that,' said Aisha, returning to Jack and starting to tie a tourniquet on Kirin's wrist. 'She's dying, Jack – she's lost way too much blood.'

He didn't know what to do. Jack slid his hand under his wife's neck and gently raised her head.

'Kirin? Kirin? Don't let whoever did this to you win. I promise I'll get to the bottom of it, but I need your help.'

Jack lowered his face to Kirin's ear.

Her voice was faint.

'You did this to me, Jatinder,' she repeated. 'You took them from me . . .'

'No, I don't know what you're talking about, Kirin – tell me what you mean.'

'You organized for me to be taken from the river and then brought here, to India, just so you could have them. It was never about me, only about them. I loved you, Jatinder. Only ever you, nobody else. How could you do this to me? I didn't understand why.'

She was fading fast, her words no more than a whisper.

'I promise you, I did not do this. I need your help to understand it all.'

'They looked after me for months,' she said weakly, 'but it was never about me, only about them.'

'Who are they?' asked Jack.

Then she uttered her final words.

Eight words that changed everything.

He looked incredulously at his wife as her eyes closed for the final time.

'Our boys, Jatinder,' she murmured. 'You took our twin boys.'

FORTY-SEVEN

SINGH WAS SITTING ALONE in a cheap hotel room in Sadar Bazaar. The call with Sahib had been strained. He simply could not understand why the leader of their organization would allow Baxi free passage towards them.

He will not make it this far.

Sahib's words were clear in his mind, yet Jack had already made it all this way and Singh didn't like it one bit.

He had landed in Delhi twelve hours before Jack, taking emergency compassionate leave from work. He'd used their organization's key contacts in immigration at Indira Gandhi Airport to learn of Jack and Aisha's arrival, and then Singh had simply followed their taxi to their residence, and from there on to Kirin Baxi.

Singh was irritated that yet again Baxi had escaped him. The bastard was proving more elusive than he could ever have given him credit for. And now, having been reunited with his wife, he was bound to learn a truth so terrible it was impossible to predict what impact it might have on him.

They had taken his bloodline from him.

The decision all those years ago had not been taken lightly and had come at considerable risk. But the order had come, not from Sahib, but from the only other person who could have commanded such a move. Singh closed his eyes.

His head was throbbing.

A past that needed to stay buried was trying its hardest to surface.

He took a seat in front of a grimy mirror and unwound his turban. Sweat dripped down his temple and he allowed his hair, uncut since birth, to tumble down his naked chest. He massaged his scalp with his hands, allowing it to breathe.

Singh had been instructed to go back to the airport and board a flight to Amritsar. From there, he would travel to Sahib and stay with him until either Baxi arrived or they received news of his death. The latter was more likely.

Singh had played out the moves Baxi would need to make in order to arrive at the truth.

His likely starting point would be the GB Road, Delhi's red-light district. That in itself would prove almost impossible for Jack to navigate. He wasn't street smart and Delhi was no place for a novice. Even if Jack managed to get what he needed from there, he would then have to head out to one of the most militarized destinations in India.

The outcome there would be absolute.

Singh picked up his phone and punched in the number Sahib had given him. It rang six times before someone picked up.

The conversation was brief, the order simple.

If Baxi did somehow make it through to the most secure location in India, it would be his final resting place.

FORTY-EIGHT

JACK AND AISHA WERE standing alone on opposite sides of the pyre consuming the body of Kirin Baxi. The *khoon-saab* had arranged the cremation with Jack. In India, the dead had to be put to rest within twenty-four hours.

The sun had started its retreat and clouds covered the sky like purple bruises, a warning of imminent monsoon rains. The feverish heat of the day was giving way to the cool of evening. The flames raging before him gave Jack's eyes a fraudulent sparkle – but behind them lay only emptiness, a chasm so deep he felt like he might never hit the bottom.

The cremation was taking place in a field behind the ghetto where the *khoon-saab* lived. The fire had been burning for an hour or so, flames reaching into the darkening sky.

In the slums, there was no one to ask awkward questions. No one to pry as to why a body was being cremated. This was India, where among all the statues of religious deities, one reigned supreme.

Money.

It had exchanged hands, wood had been organized, and four teenage boys, looking as diseased as the wood on the pyre itself, had carried Kirin's body to the bottom of the field. She had been draped in a clean yellow sheet, symbolizing the death of a married woman. Around her lay blocks of ghee butter to facilitate the fire and ensure a swift transition from this world to the next. They had made sure her head faced north, the supposed direction of the dead.

Jack had lit the pyre without saying a prayer or any last words. Nothing seemed appropriate.

What he really needed right now was a drink and to lose himself until the past few days were nothing more than a mirage.

Everything he had known about his life was a lie.

And yet, with Kirin's death, more questions had surfaced.

Riddles he didn't have answers to.

Aisha felt numb, uncertain of how to act.

Is it our fault she's dead?

It was a question she feared would stay with her for ever.

With the flames crackling in front of her, Aisha wondered how they would move on from this. She had come to India to find her mother – and now she had lost her for ever. Uncovering the mystery of how and why Kirin had come to be here seemed too great a mountain to climb. There seemed only one thing left for Aisha – a tense reunion with her father, then a flight back to Bradford.

In her mind, she fixed the firm thought that Kirin Baxi had died, and not 'her mother'. She wanted to grieve, to feel something. But she felt anaesthetized. Aisha realized that in her mind, her mother *had* died when she was born.

The fire was intensifying and Aisha retreated a few steps. The revelation that Kirin had been carrying Jack's twin boys: *could that really be true?* She doubted her mother's sanity in her final moments of life.

Not Jack, though. She'd seen it in his face – he believed it.

The fire crackled and sent cinders scurrying across the ground. Aisha took another step back. Sweat trickled from her headscarf down the side of her face. She had put her clothes back on underneath the burka and they were suffocating.

There was a rumble overhead and large droplets of rain started hitting the ground. The build-up was almost seductive: one drop landing a few feet from Aisha, thudding heavily into the dirt. A couple closer still, to either side of her feet. Then a few more, daring to creep on to her clothes.

A few moments later, a brutish wall of rain swept across them as impressively as the flames dancing high into the night. Within minutes Aisha was soaked through, water dripping down her face and collecting in large muddy pools by her feet. The rain lashed heavily against the flames, causing them to cower, but they didn't die away.

Jack closed his eyes, welcoming the cool on his face. A single phrase repeated itself in his mind.

'Our boys, Jatinder; you took our twin boys.'

Those softly whispered final eight words had changed everything. It was the only thing Jack had ever wanted – craved even: a family of his own. All he had ever known was abandonment, whether by Habib, Kirin or his own parents. Everyone had left Jack.

Kirin had truly believed that Jack had done this to her – that this was *his* will.

A seed had been planted in his mind but it was buried so deep that there was only one way to reach it. In Bradford, he might have taken a line of coke, but here, in the middle of Delhi, he'd have to make do with whisky. Jack needed to descend to the place where conscious thought gave way to the whispers of his mind.

The rain lasted only a few minutes and then stopped as

dramatically as it had started. Jack looked to the heavens and saw more clouds heading their way, ready to continue the assault.

The ground had become boggy, squelching under Jack's feet as he made his way slowly towards Aisha. There was a menace in his approach, a slow prowl as he stopped in front of her. His hands were shaking and a terrible rage was starting to build.

This had all started with her: *the illegitimate child.*

It was becoming clearer to Jack with every passing second. This was Aisha's fault. If she had never been conceived, Kirin's affair with Habib would have gone to the grave with his wife. None of this would have happened.

Jack stared at Aisha, saw her fear and for a moment revelled in it – the narrowing of her eyes, the frown breaking across her face.

Their journey ended here. Whatever came next would be without her.

Jack slid his fingers underneath the *rakhi* Aisha had tied to his wrist. In one angry motion he ripped it away, the slip of cloth tearing at his skin. He threw it at her and said, 'Go home, little girl. You're not safe here any more.'

FORTY-NINE

CRUISE WAS STANDING WITH his arms folded, leaning against a newly acquired four-by-four.

'We are really leaving without Mr Jack?' he said. He was holding a bottle of whisky, something Jack had ordered him to bring before he settled his final bill. Cruise looked at it warily.

Aisha didn't share his concern. She'd left Jack standing by the pyre and made her way across the field back to Cruise.

'He wants to stay.' Aisha handed back the phone Cruise had given Jack.

'For how long is he staying out there?' asked Cruise.

'Until he's ready to leave.' Aisha glanced at the purple skies and thought of her *rakhi* trampled into the mud. 'He needs to be left alone.'

Aisha needed to find a hotel, take a long shower and maybe shed a few tears. She felt dirty and hollow inside. She'd even contemplated calling her father but couldn't face his wrath. She needed space too.

Cruise sighed and shook his head. 'He is taking chances out

here overnight. Slum area is never being safe. I cannot be allowing him to do this.'

'Leave him alone, Cruise. He's not himself.'

'But, Sister, this is—'

'I don't want to hear it,' she said, rather more harshly than she had intended. It made her sound like Jack. 'I'm sorry,' she added quickly. 'It's been a horrific nightmare and it's not over yet.'

He nodded sympathetically. 'I am understanding. It is being like one crazy movie.'

'Can you help me, Cruise?'

'Of course, Sister,' he replied.

'Can I trust you?'

He looked heartbroken at her suspicion but she didn't drop her gaze.

'I am calling you Sister. And I am always looking after my sister.'

After the harrowing events of the past few hours, being on her own with Cruise didn't seem like such a risk. Under normal circumstances, she would never have trusted a stranger but right now she had little choice.

'I need a hotel. A *decent* one. I have money and I want you to stay as my driver until I can organize a flight home. A day at the most.'

He nodded. 'I am doing this for you.'

Cruise opened the door of the car and Aisha got inside.

The two tiny statues of Rama and Krishna were already in position on the new dashboard.

Cruise jumped into the driver's seat and slammed the door, causing the statues, as per usual, to fall over.

'Shit, yaar,' he mumbled. 'You guys are needing to give me a break. Be cursing someone else!' He picked them up and placed them back into their holders, whispering profuse apologies.

'Sister?'

'Yes?' replied Aisha.

'I am really giving him this whisky?'

'If you want paying.'

He sighed again. 'It is being the devil's drink.'

'You're speaking to a Muslim woman. We've known that for years.'

He grinned, a wide innocent grin that perhaps only a nineteen-year-old could produce. 'Sister, I am seeing all kinds of people drinking this stuff. Even in Sadar,' he said, hinting at the predominantly Muslim population. 'But I am learning from my father that alcohol is being bad for health.'

'He taught you well,' replied Aisha.

Cruise began driving towards Jack. He threw the bottle of whisky on to the passenger seat. 'My father is teaching me nothing, Sister,' he said bitterly. 'He is dying from a lifetime of drinking this poison.'

The temperature had dropped to single figures but the wind made it feel colder. It whipped from the north side of the field along the mounds of litter until it hit Jack.

He didn't notice. He was still standing in front of the pyre. Each glug of Bagpiper whisky warmed his insides. Cruise had left him a blanket but it was on the floor by his feet, soaking up pools of water. The boy had also tried to give Jack some advice – but it fell on deaf ears.

Accepting the bottle from Cruise had felt like a lifeline. Cruise hadn't even left before Jack tore off the cap and knocked back an enormous mouthful. The alcohol helped numb the desolation in his soul.

'Thank God for whisky at least.'

God.

He laughed at the thought and stuck his middle finger high in the air. He screamed loudly into the night, his face as thunderous as the sky above. Expelling the rage felt good, so he did it again, this time screaming profanities towards the heavens.

Here, in the most god-worshipping country on Earth, Jack wanted a demonstration. He taunted the gods to strike him down. Show him he needed to fear them.

Jack bowed his head to the ground.

'My mistake, Kirin,' he whispered. 'You're probably down there rather than up with the gods. Who took the boys, Kirin? What didn't you tell me?'

A family he never knew he had.

A life he could have lived; a future he could have valued.

I could have spent the last twenty years feeling alive, instead of decaying a little more each day.

Locals were now starting to light small fires around the outskirts of the field. Jack was at the back, far away from them. He sat down clumsily, forgetting the ground was waterlogged, and cursed at his stupidity as muddy water saturated the lower half of his body.

The pyre was burning calmly now, his wife's body reduced to a mere handful of ashes.

He had cremated her once before. Seventeen years ago, at a crematorium in Bradford. The image of the closed casket slipping behind the curtains on its way to the incinerator was etched vividly in his memory. His devastation as he'd said goodbye for the last time. But it hadn't been Kirin in the casket.

Couldn't have been.

He cast his mind back.

An officer had arrived at Jack's store. Jack couldn't recall his name but remembered the face of the young white guy: strangely angelic with his blond hair and blue eyes. He told Jack that a body had been found and he was needed to identify it.

The body had decomposed badly, having spent almost a week under water. The face had been eaten by water rats and the rest of the skin spoiled. But Jack *had* seen a body. They had checked Kirin's dental records and confirmed her identification. How else could that have happened?

Kirin's *mangalsutra* had been round her neck.

The religious necklace he had given her on their wedding day.

It was planted.

The first sign of an elaborate deception.

Someone knew she was pregnant.

Someone who wanted those children.

Someone desperate to get their hands on them.

The realization was cloudy for a few seconds before it came hurtling at him.

Habib had been having an affair with Kirin.

Maybe they were his boys: not Jack's.

It would make sense. Kirin might have told him she was having an abortion. Aborting two boys – that was inconceivable.

But Kirin had said, '*Our* twin boys.'

Jack smacked his head, trying to piece it together.

Habib was involved, of that much he was certain. Jack wanted to hurt him, watch as he bled. There was way more to this than Habib had let on – some secret yet to be revealed that might bring this all together. Yet Habib was fucking untouchable. He had—

Jack's hand jerked to a stop before the Bagpiper reached his lips. Another thought was germinating, sneaking its sinister way into the forefront of his mind.

There was one way to get Habib to tell him the truth.

Jack needed his most prized possession.

He needed Aisha Iqbal.

FIFTY

THE CAR RADIO WAS playing classic *ghazals* by the late Nusrat Fateh Ali Khan, the world's leading singer of Sufi music. Aisha found the music soothing. It reminded her of Sunrise Radio in Bradford; they were always playing his songs.

They had reached the outskirts of Sadar Bazaar but were once again stuck in traffic. Aisha was irritated by the sound of car horns and the sight of a seemingly endless line of glowing red brake lights. The rain had left a trail of puddles across the pavements and kids were kicking water at each other.

Aisha was dozing, her head knocking against the window. It was the words of the *ghazal* on the radio that woke her, singing about money and loss. She knew even before she searched her jeans that her passport and credit cards were missing. She couldn't feel the bulge in her back pocket.

'Cruise,' she snapped, making him jump in his seat.

She was furiously scrabbling in her other pockets, the hem of her burka bunched around her waist.

'Sister,' he said, turning round to face her, 'what is happening? Are you all right?'

'My passport and my credit cards – they're gone!' she said.

'What?'

'They're gone! I . . . I . . . never thought to check, with everything that happened.'

'When are you last having these items?'

Aisha stopped the futile search and traced her mind back. 'I took my clothes off under the burka when we went into the *khoon-saab*'s house.'

'And you were not removing these items before doing so?' he said incredulously.

Aisha was doing her best not to cry. A pit had opened in her stomach. 'Cruise, we have to go back. They might still be there.'

'OK, OK, Sister, I am taking you back. No problem. But I am not being confident that these items are still there. They have value on the black market,' he said despondently.

Aisha swore.

Cruise hadn't heard her do so before and raised an eyebrow.

The traffic wasn't moving so he took the car over the middle intersection. Aisha gripped the seat as they drove on to the other side of the road.

'Cruise, you're driving the wrong way!' she said, alarmed.

'Relaxing, Sister, I am just taking this next cut in the road.'

Cruise took a sharp turn and swung the car around.

The tiny statues of the gods fell off the dashboard again. 'Seriously?' he hissed and picked them up.

'What am I going to do if my things aren't there?' said Aisha, sinking her head in her hands. 'I have no money – no passport. I'm stuck in the middle of India all on my own.'

'Sister, Sister, you are calming down, please. Cruise is not leaving you alone. I am helping you through this.'

She was grateful he was with her, but knew the timer on his patience would be ticking. Money was his language. Adventure was a bonus.

Cruise was tapping the steering wheel, clearly wrestling with something.

'What's wrong?' asked Aisha.

He picked up the statues of the gods and held them in his hand, spinning them round. He paused before replying.

'Sister, I am thinking that if we are not able to get your things, then I should be dropping you at UK embassy. I am not being able to help you without money. I am not leaving you alone, Sister, but taking you to embassy is best option. Mr Jack is paying me already for today's rate.'

He spoke sympathetically yet had clearly calculated his own risk in the matter.

Aisha put her head in her hands again. Of all the errors to have made. She could just imagine what Jack would say if he knew.

At that, a thought flickered across Aisha's mind. She did have one other option. Except that Jack's parting words to her hadn't exactly been welcoming.

'Sister?' said Cruise.

Aisha stared out of the window at the sky. Maybe this was how it was meant to be – going back to Jack. There was unfinished business. The mystery surrounding her mother's arrival in India was no closer to being solved. Did she still have a part to play in it?

Asking Jack for help would not be easy. He didn't want her around and she didn't want to be there. She thought of his dead eyes, heralding the rage and despair he would now be sinking into.

'Cruise, take me back to Jack,' she said.

FIFTY-ONE

IT WAS EIGHT O'CLOCK when Cruise and Aisha arrived back at the *khoon-saab*'s shack, and eight fifteen when they left empty-handed. Aisha had waited in the car, Cruise insisting that he would speak with them. She told him to offer them money. If it appeared they had her items, they'd go to Jack and get the funds. But Cruise returned empty-handed, promises of thousands of rupees falling on deaf ears.

Aisha tried to think positively. Jack would no doubt be angry but surely he'd lend her money for a hotel and a flight back to Bradford. She so desperately wanted to be home and away from the dust and humidity of Delhi.

Cruise drove through the deserted narrow streets of the slum. There was no sign on the only store that was open. It was a tin roof supported by two wooden sticks. The rows of bronze bottles and the drunken men loitering outside gave it away as an off-licence. Aisha looked quickly to see if Jack was there, but saw only old men huddled in thick grey blankets.

Cruise stopped the car at the bottom of the field where they'd left Jack.

'Sister, you are staying here.'

She shook her head, wanting to face Jack and not cower from him any more. She was through playing the victim.

'But, Sister, it is—'

Aisha cut him dead and opened the car door.

They left the car with its headlights on, beaming into the distance. The field was covered in swampy pools of water, thick with rotting refuse, making any kind of firm footing impossible. The rain had dampened down the stench but it was still vile enough to make Aisha's lip curl. Cruise stayed a few paces ahead, his steps small and careful, weaving his way between the puddles.

Aisha kept her eyes on the ground, picking her route, keeping Cruise in her peripheral vision. She didn't hear the steps behind, the squelch of mud hiding the sound of two men lurking in the shadows.

They were out of range of the car headlights now, the treacherous darkness twining around them like a serpent.

Cruise heard them first and turned just in time to see two men grab Aisha and pull her to the ground. She screamed but the sound petered out in the vastness of the empty field.

Cruise ran towards her, realizing immediately his foolishness in bringing her here. A rape happened every six minutes in Delhi and in the slum area there would be no one to help them. *He had been so stupid.*

Cruise had lectured tourists – even warned Jack and Aisha about wandering alone in the city. Yet in his eagerness to find Jack, he had forgotten his own cardinal rule.

He couldn't see the men properly, only the shadow of one of them pinning Aisha into the mud. The second man was hidden in the darkness somewhere. In Cruise's rush to protect Aisha, he was caught off-guard by the vicious kick that caught him square between the legs. Cruise dropped to the ground just as Aisha let out another scream.

The pain between Cruise's legs was unlike anything he had ever experienced. He was unable to catch his breath, blinded by the tears streaming down his face. Aisha was in trouble – he heard another scream. Cruise felt sick – he couldn't allow this to happen.

Aisha didn't know what was going on at first. But the presence of rough hands under her burka, groping at her breasts, brought the reality home.

'No!' she screamed, trying to fend the man off. She smelled alcohol on his breath and then the hideous sensation of bristly lips on her mouth. She shook her head like a rattlesnake and when it failed to deter the bastard, she tried to bite him. She missed but the clash of her teeth made him recoil for an instant.

The second man screamed suddenly and there was a loud crack of bone splintering.

Her assailant rolled off her and jumped up, ready to defend himself. The darkness camouflaged the details, but there was the shattering of glass and Aisha felt liquid splash all over her face. It was whisky. A body slumped to the ground and a shadow reached down towards her. She cringed away.

'Aisha, it's Jack,' came the voice. 'You're all right,' he said, kneeling beside her.

He scooped her rigid body from the ground and she wrapped her arms tight around his neck, her breath shallow and ragged.

Cruise appeared at Jack's side, looking both sheepish and in pain.

Jack held Aisha close. 'Don't worry,' he said. 'I've got you now.'

FIFTY-TWO

CRUISE LIVED IN RAJOURI Garden, a middle-class part of west Delhi with a predominantly Punjabi population. Jack learned that Cruise's father had passed away some years ago from liver cancer; it was now just Cruise and his mother. She suffered from multiple sclerosis and was mostly bed-bound. They had a full-time servant who lived with them: a petite girl of about thirteen who attended to everything. Jack couldn't remember when the decision had been made to hide out at Cruise's place, but then there wasn't an awful lot he did remember about the journey.

Cruise was more than just a taxi driver. He was due to start university the following year and was driving the taxi to build up his savings. The kid had wild ambitions to become a movie director and make Bollywood bigger than Hollywood, maybe to be lauded as the Tom Cruise of the Indian film industry.

The house felt secure, not some cheap hotel full of strangers. Jack was to sleep in the living room, giving Aisha the one spare bedroom. Jack had asked Cruise to make sure she was fully settled in. She hadn't said a word on the journey but Jack had noticed the way she'd been clawing at her hands.

Aisha was happy with the bedroom. It was basic but cosy, and most importantly, there was a lock on the door. Cruise spent a little time with her, making sure she knew to make herself at home. She could tell he felt responsible for what had happened at the slum, and was clearly consumed by guilt. Aisha didn't say a lot. She thanked him for bringing them here, because while it wasn't her own home, she did feel safe.

Aisha even had her own bathroom. She turned on the geyser for hot water and arranged a towel and some clothes of Cruise's mother's, which he had found for her. It wasn't much: a grey Punjabi suit and a pair of slippers, but they were clean. His mother, whom Aisha hadn't met yet, must be petite too – the clothes were a perfect fit.

It was eleven p.m. when Aisha started washing, and she was still at it forty minutes later when the water ran cold. Her face stung from her assailant's bristles and she could still smell the stench of alcohol all over her. She scrubbed her skin raw, then made her way to the bedroom. She sat down at a small dressing table and stared into a mirror for several minutes. Fresh bruising showed across her face along with several deep scratches. It hardly seemed possible that so much could have happened to her in such a short space of time.

Her mother had died. Again.

It didn't feel real. Aisha had never known the woman and didn't know how she should grieve. There were no tears, just an empty chasm where her emotions should have been.

She climbed into bed, curling her body into a ball, and fell instantly asleep, forcing all the images of the past twenty-four hours from her mind and dreaming of nothing except home.

*

Jack was lying on the living-room floor, where Cruise had made up a comfortable bed for him. An old silver fan rotated slowly on the ceiling, pushing a cooling breeze on to his face.

Cruise's home was so much better than a hotel. Jack felt in control at last – there was no way they'd be found here. In the simmering cauldron of Delhi, where crime and corruption were rife, he felt safe for the first time since they'd arrived.

There was a quiet knock at the door and Cruise stuck his head round. Seeing that Jack was awake, he let himself in and gently closed the door.

'Are you minding if we are talking, Mr Jack?' he said, taking a seat on the couch.

Jack sat upright and rested his back against the other end. 'Sure,' he said. 'And thanks for bringing us into your home, Cruise. After everything that's happened today, it can't have been an easy decision.'

Cruise dismissed it with a wave of his hand. 'In India, you are knowing this saying: "Guest is God, and no one is kicking God from their home".'

'I know it well. My mother used to say it to me all the time.'

'A wise woman.' Cruise smiled and then paused. 'What is happening today, Mr Jack? You are telling me about these people tracking you, but what is it all about?'

Jack could almost see the moviemaker in the kid at work. Plotting, weaving the angles, trying to come up with a scenario.

'I have no idea, truthfully,' said Jack.

'You must be having some clue?'

Jack thought about Habib.

Finding out Kirin was pregnant.

With Jack's children.

How could he have been certain they were Jack's and not his own?

And then it hit him.

There was only one way to be certain.

Kirin couldn't have still been seeing Habib before she supposedly died. At least not in the run-up to conceiving. *It was the only way she could have been certain that the children she was carrying were Jack's.*

'Mr Jack? Are you OK?'

'Sorry,' said Jack, focusing on the boy. 'I . . . er . . . just got caught up thinking.'

'I was asking what you believe is happening? Who is chasing you?'

'Cruise, I honestly don't know. Someone powerful. They have contacts in the police in England and they tracked me here. Somebody with a lot of influence.'

'Are you being caught up with these kinds of peoples back home?'

Jack thought back to his corner shop. For a moment he was rueful about leaving it behind. Burned to a heap of ashes.

Like Kirin.

Everything he had ever loved had gone up in smoke in less than a week. He was hit by a wave of homesickness. It surprised him, because Jack had never felt strongly about Bradford.

'I've done business with a few characters from the underworld,' replied Jack, thinking about his low-key contraband business, 'but nothing even close to the connections these guys have.'

Cruise was fidgeting, cogs working overtime.

'You are being caught up with government officials. Across two continents. This is really some big plot,' said Cruise. He spoke with awe but there was also fear in his words.

'This isn't a plot, Cruise – this is my life,' said Jack, with rather more bite than he intended.

'Sorry, Mr Jack. I am being – how are you saying? – insensitive. I am not meaning to be.'

'Forget it. We'll check into a hotel tomorrow. I cannot ask any more of you, Cruise. This thing is dangerous. You've done more than I could ever have asked for.'

Cruise dismissed it with another airy wave of his hand. 'Mr Jack, are you seeing all those books over there, by the table?'

Jack had indeed: reams upon reams of literature about movies, plots and script-writing. There were also DVDs of every Tom Cruise movie ever made.

'I am running taxis to see the world. I am driving all across India in very short space of time to see people. Understand people. I am knowing that one day, I am going to write something so amazing that India is finding another prodigal son, like Amitabh Bachchan. This is not chance, me picking you up – it is kismet. You are knowing this word?'

Jack looked at him impatiently. 'Cruise, I've been speaking Punjabi since before you were born. Of course I know it.'

'Well then, I am staying with you, Mr Jack, because you are needing me and I am having to know how this story ends.'

'It might end with my blood all over the streets of Delhi,' Jack told him.

'It might,' replied Cruise, 'but then it might end with such an ending that my kismet is revealed to me sooner than I thought.'

Jack was alone now, lying on the floor, once again staring up at the ceiling fan. Cruise had activated the mosquito repellent and a calming blue light shone from the device plugged in at the wall. It was midnight. The day – a trial, not a day – had finally ended.

Once again, Jack's mind pulled him back seventeen years, to that apocalyptic night where his wife had told him she was leaving.

He closed his eyes. Saw her face. Swollen from where he had hit her.

Hit her – because she was leaving him with little explanation. *Leaving with his kids.*

Kids he hadn't even known about.
But somebody else had.
Someone powerful.
Someone who wanted those children at any cost.

But why? What was so special about his children? Were they still alive?

A vital piece of the puzzle was eluding Jack, yet it felt close. One thing was certain – the level of power and influence possessed by the men tracking them down could only be with the support of someone as wealthy as Habib, with all his connections. Jack didn't know how Habib might be connected with Detective Singh but he was certain there must be a link.

As long as Jack had Aisha, he had leverage.

She was key.

And Jack would go to any lengths to get Habib to talk.

FIFTY-THREE

IT WAS LATE AFTERNOON before the three of them surfaced. Sleep hadn't come easily to anyone.

Jack woke because he was starving. The smell of chickpea curry and *paturai* – rich fried dough in the form of a chapatti – reminded him of his youth. He realized he hadn't eaten a thing yesterday and was quickly up to investigate the source of the aroma.

Cruise was in the kitchen, dressed in a traditional grey *kameez*.

'Morning,' said Jack, his mouth dry, his voice croaky.

'Ahh, Mr Jack, good morning to you,' said Cruise, full of energy. He was unpacking foil-wrapped parcels, and the water on the stove was coming to the boil.

'English tea or Indian?' he asked.

'I like the outfit,' said Aisha, entering meekly and standing beside Jack.

'Ouch! Sister, are you being all right?' asked Cruise. The

swelling on the side of Aisha's face was dark and looked sore. She looked like she'd been in a fist-fight and come off the loser.

'Are you OK?' Jack asked her.

Aisha chewed her lip, apparently considering her response.

'I'd understand if you think it's over, Aisha, and want to return home. Kirin's dead and we've nowhere else to go. I'm sorry for what happened last night. I'll help you get a flight back to England.'

Aisha shook her head. This time when she looked at Jack, something had hardened in her expression. When she spoke, her voice was calm and authoritative. Jack got the impression that she had thought long and hard about what she was going to say.

'Do you both remember that child yesterday? The one by the car when we first got in the taxi. He was holding a bloodied tooth.'

'Yes,' they both replied, unsure of where this was heading. Cruise removed the pan of boiling water from the stove.

'I dreamt about him last night. Trapped in a life where he has to use a bloodied piece of his anatomy to get me to sympathize and give him money. He spoke to me and told me that compared to what he goes through on a daily basis, I'm damn lucky. I will never know the perils or despair of that life. I am so fortunate, and in spite of everything that happened last night, I'm still in a better position than he will ever be. Yesterday, I lost a woman I have never known. I cannot mourn a mother I never had the chance to love.'

Jack and Cruise listened silently. Something had changed in Aisha. She was standing differently and fixing them both with a look they couldn't place. Resolve? Confidence? Anger? Jack wasn't sure.

'What happened afterwards was not your fault, Cruise. We'd never have got this far without you.' Aisha paused, then turned to Jack.

'And as for you,' – she pointed to his wrist, where he'd torn away the *rakhi* – 'I don't need a piece of cloth to protect me from you. It was a peace offering, that's all. A handshake is just as good.'

Jack was burning up. He felt small in her presence.

'Today is a different day. A day we either take a stand together to find out what happened to Kirin, your wife, *my mother*, or I will do it alone. I cannot spend the rest of my life not knowing. We might be up against a powerful network, but we have something they don't. They are chasing a ghost, but we are chasing the truth.'

She turned to leave the kitchen, paused, but didn't turn back to face them.

'The truth, as everyone knows, will set us free,' she said, and walked away.

The food was bursting with flavour. Coriander, garam masala, mint and just enough chilli to make the mineral water necessary. The *paturai* were dripping in oil and sliding around the plate.

With greasy hands and fiery mouths the three of them ate in silence, focusing only on their stomachs. The meal was more than just a breakfast at four p.m. It was more of a silent reckoning. When they had finished, the three of them cleaned up, Cruise joking about whether Jack or Aisha would be the first to suffer from the legendary Delhi belly.

Afterwards, Cruise brought Indian tea made with cardamom seeds through to the living room.

'Tea in a glass?' asked Aisha.

'Indian tradition. You are using mugs back home,' replied Cruise, grinning. 'My old customers are telling me about this.' He put on a terribly stiff English accent: 'I'll have tea in a mug, Arthur!'

'Arthur?' she replied.

'You know, like the king.'

'King Arthur?'

'That's the fellow.'

'Fellow?'

'You know, chap.'

'Your English needs work, Cruise.'

'So did Mr Schwarzenegger but he made it into the movies just fine. Plus, I am having the teeth,' he said, cracking a wide grin and displaying his gleaming white teeth. 'Finally, I am having many different Hindu gods to help me. He had only one. It is really being all about the math.'

Aisha grinned. 'Well, I hope your gods can send us a little more luck than we've been having lately.'

'Sister, you are alive. Mr Jack is sitting here with us. Apart from a few bumps and bruises, we are being ready to hit the mean streets of Delhi again. I am thinking Shiva, god of war, shot one of his arrows last night into the heavens. The monsoon came – tears from the sky. We are all being forced back together. God is being here, Sister.'

'Is that a passage from one of your movie scripts?' she asked.

'Just made it up,' he said. 'You like?'

Aisha smiled at him.

Jack was staring at them both, wondering if they all yet had some part to play in finding the truth. More importantly, would the three of them carry on together to see this through? Cruise was just a foolhardy kid living an adventure. He was blissfully unaware of the risk he was taking by harbouring them both.

Aisha had woken up with a steely determination. Her face displayed impressive war wounds but it hadn't dampened her spirit.

Jack thought about what was at stake here.

Twin boys. My sons.
Alive?
Dead?
It was time to find out.

It was almost seven p.m. before they finished discussing their course of action. Jack had tried desperately to convince Cruise to leave this alone. It was dangerous. What they were proposing could backfire. While the situation affected Aisha and Jack directly, Cruise had little to gain by risking his own life.

Cruise, though, wasn't having it. He insisted on finding out the truth along with them. He didn't want to spend the next thirty years wondering about the puzzling strangers from England. Plus, he needed an ending to his movie. He was, after all, just driving, so what real risk was he subject to?

Aisha reluctantly agreed but only because she *needed* answers. In a country where corruption was infectious and lives were traded like cattle, they would find the truth.

Because they were meant to.

Whether or not you believed in kismet, she insisted, it was not just chance that had brought Jack and Aisha together after decades of deceit.

'Mr Jack, I am in,' said Cruise eagerly. 'You are needing my help to see this plan through. Together, we are being able to do it.'

Jack looked at Aisha. She was in too. He could see it in her eyes. She was angry. Images of the child with the bloodied tooth, her mother bleeding to death and the attack at the slum had all left their mark. She was furious. And it made her formidable. For a moment, Jack could see his wife in her. Punjabi blood. Hot-headed, with a will as strong as iron.

'OK,' said Jack, standing up. He looked out of the window towards the sunset.

Yesterday they had been forced to take the role of victims. It was time to turn the tables and start right at the beginning, at the only real clue they had – even if it meant entering the most dangerous part of Delhi.

'We need to go to GB Road,' said Jack.

FIFTY-FOUR

GB ROAD.

Delhi's seedy red-light district. An area saturated in filth. The hell-hole that had been Kirin's prison cell for almost two decades had been listed in the file Jack had taken from Sister Catherine in Bradford. That felt like a lifetime ago.

Prostitutes were leaning from buildings with caged windows, smacking kisses to potential clients walking by below, and making lewd gestures. Some of the men looked boldly back at them. Others were nervous – walking past several times until they gathered the courage to enter.

The four-storey building listed in Kirin's file looked deformed, lopsided almost. White paint on the walls and window frames was covered in dirt and orange dust from the road. Each floor had its own tin roof which overshot on to the roof below.

The road was hard-packed dirt, breaking up unevenly along the kerb, where a makeshift gutter appeared to be blocked. Power cables dangled perilously outside the building, giving off the odd hazardous spark.

They were inside Cruise's car, parked in darkness, observing the building. There were streetlights on GB Road but none on this section. The building lay in shadow, offering the punters a cloak of secrecy.

Jack was going to walk inside like he owned the place. He knew who he needed to speak to.

Yasmina. That was who Sister Florence had said was Kirin's friend in there.

And Thakur – he was the owner; a man who had favoured Kirin. *That was who Jack was here for.*

'Are you ready?' asked Aisha. She was rubbing her hands nervously against her knees.

Jack nodded. 'Cruise – you know what you're doing?'

'Yes,' he replied and handed Jack the bottle of Bagpiper, having carefully screwed the top back on.

Jack tapped on the passenger-side window. 'Do me a favour and keep these wound up – I don't want your damn teeth giving us away.'

Cruise beamed his best Bollywood grin. 'I am flashing these babies at the right time and blinding the bad guys. Genius thinking.'

Jack squeezed his shoulder, then looked back at Aisha. 'Wait for my call and be ready.'

'We will,' said Aisha firmly. 'Go and find some answers.'

Jack took a few moments in the shadows, moving away from several malnourished dogs scavenging for food. Rickshaws zipped past him, weaving their way in and out of steadily moving traffic.

Three lorries were parked outside. They were banned in Delhi during the daytime, a policy aimed at limiting traffic and pollution. By night, though, Delhi was jammed with thousands of them. Clearly, these drivers were taking a break inside.

Jack's nerves were jangling. The darkness surrounding the brothel seemed threatening – the seediness starting before you'd even walked through the front door. He glanced up at the sex workers, who continued to beckon at passers-by from their cages above. They looked like servants. Their appeal lay in their availability, nothing more. None of them had charm or striking looks. They were merely single-use vessels.

Jack strode purposely towards the entrance and nodded at a teenager sitting outside. He was wearing a dirty white *kurta* with a black scarf wrapped around his face to shield it from the dust. He spoke to Jack in Hindi but quickly changed to English.

'Good time, sir?' he said, standing up and removing his scarf. His face was affected by a severe case of vitiligo; the white patches looked like bleach stains. He couldn't have been more than fifteen.

'I want a good time. A really good time,' said Jack.

The kid smiled. 'Guaranteed good time in here, sir. Come with me.'

The stairs were slippery and covered in rainwater. Jack followed the kid carefully; a tumble on these steps would break bones. Each concrete block seemed steeper than the last. They rounded three dark corners before reaching the third floor.

The reception was a forlorn affair, a couple of lanterns on a makeshift desk. Another kid, this one perhaps a little older, was perched on a stool. His hair was slicked tightly across his scalp and glimmered in the darkness.

'Good time, sir?' he said, like it was scripted.

'Yes,' said Jack.

'Very good, sir. You are referring to me as Don, and I am being your helper for today,' he replied, with an unpleasant smile. Jack wasn't sure which was worse – his heavily stained teeth or the silver fillings.

'How long?' asked the boy. The one who had brought Jack

upstairs disappeared back to his post. 'We are having shortest time of fifteen minutes. Then we are going to thirty minutes or one hour.'

Jack tried his best to sound confident, even though his legs were shaky. 'Depends on the woman. Let me have a look and then I'll decide.'

'Ha ha, very good, sir. You are being from England?'

'Yes. My friend told me to come here. Said a woman named Yasmina was good. That I should see her.'

There was a pause of no longer than a few seconds but in Jack's head it lasted ages.

If Yasmina's not here, you've got the wrong damn place.

'No problem, sir. Yasmina is being busy at the moment.' He leaned towards Jack across the counter. 'Very popular,' he said with a wink, and cracked another distasteful grin.

'Then I'll wait,' said Jack.

'Sir, we are having plenty of girls. Some very young,' he said emphasizing the 'very'. 'Take a look?'

Jack could think of nothing worse, but he realized he needed to act like a genuine client. 'Sure,' he said.

The kid spied the bottle of Bagpiper in Jack's hand and grinned. 'Sir, I am only allowing you to take it in if you are giving me a little taste.'

Jack gripped the bottle tightly. Shit, this was about to unravel before it even got started. He forced a smile and said, 'I don't share my whisky, but here . . .' Jack fished a 500-rupee note from his pocket and handed it over. 'Go and treat yourself, Don. You look after me and I'll look after you.'

The kid looked flabbergasted at the money.

'Take it,' said Jack. 'Have a good time,' he added, and winked.

Don led Jack to a dimly lit room which had nothing more than a few wooden chairs and a table. Jack took a seat while Don went off to get the girls. The walls of the waiting room were covered in dirty yellow paint and there was grime all over the floor. The unsanitary conditions made Jack wince. On the chair next to him were ancient dirty magazines. They all looked European, white girls with their tits out and pouting lips.

Jack didn't have to wait long for the girls. Chewing his lip nervously, he tried to appear calm and as if he belonged here. The girls were all young, no older than twenty. Indian society judged fair-skinned girls as being the most desirable. None of these girls had that quality. They were as dark as charcoal with overly white eyes that displayed little sign of life. Their skinny bodies dressed in sleazy outfits. Don lined them all up, his hands lingering on their bodies just that bit longer than necessary.

'You are having one, more than one, or all of them?' he sniggered.

Jack walked slowly along the line, looking at each girl in turn but not really seeing any of them. Despite their mask of contentment, misery was etched into their eyes. They smelled of sweat and Jack was certain not all of it was their own. He felt vile, walking along the line, pretending to be spoiled for choice.

The last girl smiled at him, but with no genuine warmth. Jack could see she was pleading with him to choose her. She looked the oldest, a little over twenty maybe. She licked her lips suggestively and Jack felt sick. He looked away and turned back to Don.

'They're a little young for me. I prefer the experienced woman,' he said. 'I'll wait for Yasmina.'

Don shrugged and told the girls to leave, giving the last one a seedy slap across the thigh and telling her that if she didn't get a punter in the next half-hour, she'd be seeing to him for free.

He laughed, winked at Jack and said, 'Sir, are you wanting to stay here or wait in one of the rooms?'

'I'll wait in the room,' said Jack.

'We are needing payment first,' said Don and gave him yet another wink.

'I'll take an hour,' replied Jack. 'I'm sure she'll be worth it.'

'Oh, she is,' said Don, grinning. 'You are taking it from me.'

The room was just a tiny cubicle – a single bed and a small wash-basin in the corner. There were bars on the window with a flimsy red sheet strung across them. The bed had a ragged brown towel, a handful of condoms and another dirty magazine on it.

Jack walked over to the window. It was a relief to see Cruise still parked across the street. The sex workers in the next room continued to call to the men below, vulgar profanities in Hindi and Punjabi. It brought home to Jack just what torture his wife's life here must have been. He felt nauseous.

Jack sent Cruise a text, telling him he was in place and wait-ing for Yasmina. He sat down on the bed and looked again around the room, plaster crumbling from the damp walls.

It was only a few minutes before there was a knock at the door and a woman entered. She was considerably older than the girls he had seen, probably in her late forties. She was heavy-set with broad hips and a stomach that sagged over the ridiculous mini-skirt she was wearing. It looked ready to split at the sides.

There was a smear of red lipstick across her teeth; she had clearly rushed her makeup. She wore a nose ring and her hair hung limp across her shoulders. There was perspiration on her brow and Jack wondered whether she had actually showered since her last punt. She was possibly the most unattractive woman Jack had ever seen. Once again, the desperation of this place hit him hard.

She sauntered over to Jack and sat down on the bed next to him, running her hand up his thigh.

'Good time, baby?' she said, and the smoke on her breath hit him like a slap.

FIFTY-FIVE

JACK CHECKED THAT THE door was closed, disappointed to see there was no lock.

'No one is coming, baby,' said Yasmina in a thick Indian accent. Jack turned to face her. She had removed her blouse, displaying fleshy oversized breasts. She juggled them clumsily in her hands. 'Englishman want to suck?' she said, smiling.

Jack stared at her large brown nipples. He couldn't remember the last time he'd seen a woman intimately. Yasmina moved towards him, almost pinning him against the door. She pressed her body into him and raised her thigh to his waist, rubbing against him.

Jack shook his head and pushed her away. 'Put your top back on,' he said.

She gave a cynical laugh. 'It is going back on now and then off in a few minutes.'

'Make yourself decent. I didn't come here for that.'

She shrugged and threw her blouse loosely around her shoulders. 'You want another girl?' she asked bluntly.

'No, I want you.'

Yasmina sat down on the bed. 'First time?'

'Yes.'

'Take off trousers.'

'Like I said, I'm not here for that.'

'Everybody here for same thing.'

'Not me. I came to talk to you.'

'Talk before. Talk after. Up to you.'

Jack sat down beside her. He removed his phone and showed her a photo he had taken of Kirin the day before. Yasmina looked at it. Then she almost snatched the phone from him and stared at it, bringing it closer to her eyes. The shock on her face told Jack he was with the right woman.

'Kirin?' she whispered, her lip quivering.

'Yes,' replied Jack, 'Kirin. Kirin Baxi. My wife.'

She turned her face slowly towards him. The earlier expression of nonchalance had vanished. 'Your wife?'

'Yes.'

'Jatinder?'

Jack was startled she knew his name. 'Yes.'

She handed the phone back to him, eyes wide and disbelieving. 'Why are you here? Kirin is alive?'

'No,' replied Jack. He didn't really know how to tell her and ended up simply blurting it out. 'She died yesterday.'

Yasmina shot up. 'You . . . you cannot be here! If they are finding out I am talking to you, they are killing us both. Please, you must leave. Please.'

Her face had twisted with fear.

Jack stood up and put his hands on her shoulders. 'No one is doing anything to us. I am not alone. I can take you away from here,' he said, dropping his voice. 'But, Yasmina, I need to know everything. I need to know how she ended up here.'

'What?' said Yasmina, shrugging his hands from her shoulders. 'You know why,' she said.

'No, I don't.'

'You are selling her to this place,' she said bitterly. 'You sold her to Thakur.'

Jack recoiled at the accusation. 'What?'

'Just like all the men who sell their wives or daughters.' She spat on the floor. 'If I tell Thakur who you are, he will hurt you. This place is where bodies are sold, not rescued.'

'Yasmina, please, hear me out. Nothing is as it seems. Just give me ten minutes and then if you still don't believe me, I'll leave.'

She stared at him, considering.

'If I had sold my wife to this place, then why would I be here now?' he said in desperation.

Yasmina took her time, looking him up and down. Jack stood there nervously, each second feeling like an hour.

'OK,' she said finally, 'tell me.'

Jack gave her a summary of what had been happening over the past few days. Yasmina listened intently without interrupting. When he was done, she crept over to the window and peered out of the corner. Cruise's car was by the side of the road. When she turned back to face Jack, he had pulled a fistful of notes from his pocket and now handed them to her.

'Ten thousand rupees. They'll never know. Keep it safe. Tell me what you know. Please. I have to find out the truth.'

Yasmina took the cash and stuffed it down her underwear. She looked solemnly at Jack. 'If what you are saying is true, then I am not understanding what is happening.'

'Kirin was your friend, right? That's what I heard. She used to talk about you. She was worried about you. You've shared secrets with each other, so only you can help me piece this together. Please, Yasmina. Help me – I'm begging you.'

She didn't immediately reply and Jack thought he'd lost her.

'It is sad story,' she said finally. 'I tell you what I know. Because for you to be here – like this? Maybe it is your fate to find out what happened, just like it is my fate to suffer like she did.'

Yasmina told Jack that Kirin had been bought by Thakur around twenty years ago. She had arrived at the same time as Yasmina. But Kirin was different to the other girls. She was fair-skinned with big green eyes and a desirable body. She had become Thakur's favourite, spending most of her time living in his quarters. The other girls had been jealous, but Yasmina was also a favourite, so together they shared the boss. They became friends, which was rare in a place where women competed with one another.

Yasmina told Jack that Kirin had been abducted from England. She had been pregnant.

'You're sure?' asked Jack.

Yasmina nodded. 'You know this,' she said accusingly.

Jack shook his head and looked despondently at the floor. Why did everyone think he had set all this in motion?

'Go on,' he whispered.

For a few months after arriving in India, Kirin was looked after. She talked of taking walks in beautiful fields. Of seeing farms as far as she could see. She was a prisoner and always under surveillance, but she was allowed many freedoms. She saw only elderly women and, while they treated her coldly, they made sure she wanted for nothing. They made sure she was strong and healthy enough to give birth.

When she delivered the twin boys, she never got to hold them. One day, she was drugged and when she woke up, she found herself here, in the brothel. She never knew where she had been kept prisoner. Like all the other women in the brothel, she had eventually accepted her fate, hoping that one day she would be released to find her boys.

'Did she ever mention anybody called Habib Iqbal?'

'No,' she said, shaking her head.

Jack was confused. 'She must have,' he said desperately, then realized his mistake. Kirin would not have known that Habib had changed his name.

'What about Asif Khan?' said Jack.

Yasmina nodded. 'I know that name. I am hearing it from her but I cannot remember why. Much time ago this is all happening.'

Habib was involved – Jack knew it.

'Were they my sons? Did she tell you that?'

Yasmina nodded. 'She told me you took them from her.'

'Why didn't she go to the police? Or the British embassy?' said Jack.

Yasmina sniggered. 'In twenty years, I go to market only once. We do not leave. We do not have access to anything except men. If we do not earn money, they throw us out. The police are our best customers. This is India. Money buys everything. Money, and this,' she said, pointing to her crotch.

'What makes you think I sold my wife into a life like this?' said Jack.

She looked at him accusingly. 'Because this is what Thakur is telling her.'

'Look, I need to talk to him. Only Thakur knows where he got Kirin from. I need to follow the trail. If you help me, I promise I'll get you out of here. I have money. You can start a new life.'

He could tell she didn't believe him. 'No second chance for women like me.'

'Well, I'm offering you one. If you take me to Thakur.'

'If he is telling you, he is also telling the people he get her from that you are coming.'

Jack nodded. 'That's a risk I'll have to take.'

Yasmina told Jack she would tell Thakur he wanted to take her for a whole night. It was seldom allowed, and only in instances where the client was already known to the brothel. But Jack was from England and had money. The request would at least get Jack an audience with Thakur.

They walked to the end of the corridor, the creak of beds and the faked moans of pleasure filling the air.

On the top floor, there were three rooms. Two were reserved for special guests: the police or well-connected locals. The last was Thakur's personal quarters.

'I don't think the boys are here,' she whispered to Jack.

'The ones outside?' he replied.

She nodded. 'They guard this place for him. They will kill for him,' she said bitterly.

He gestured for her to continue.

'Wait here. If someone comes, tell them you are waiting for Thakur,' she said, then knocked twice on his door. A voice from inside ordered her to enter and she opened the door and disappeared inside.

Jack took out his phone and hurriedly sent Cruise a text. Then he tiptoed swiftly around the top floor to get the measure of the layout. The three rooms were simple annexes, just four walls and a door. They didn't run parallel – each one was a few metres from the next.

Jack went back to the landing and waited. Yasmina had given him a lot to go on. She had confirmed that Kirin had delivered twin boys and that they were the reason for her abduction. Jack could sense the answers he sought were close.

Yasmina appeared and beckoned Jack towards her. 'He will see you. I told him you pay lot of money to take me for one night.'

She showed him inside the dimly lit room. There was an oil lantern in the corner and a row of candles on the other side. Thakur was lying on the bed, smoking a cigarette. He was only a shadow from here and waved Jack towards him.

About halfway across the floor, Jack felt a sickening blow to the back of his head. He fell to his knees, the world spinning. He tried to raise his hands but was too late. The next blow sent his body crashing unconscious to the floor.

Thakur got up slowly. 'So,' he said, walking towards Jack, 'this is the man who's come to kill me?' He snorted and prodded Jack's limp body with his toe.

'Yes,' replied Yasmina. 'I did well, Thakur, didn't I?' she said eagerly.

His lips curled in a wicked smile, causing his moustache to rub against his nose. He reached out and grabbed her face, his bony fingers squeezing her cheeks. 'Yes,' he replied, 'you did well. Now, tell the boys to go and fetch the other two from the car and bring them to me.'

'The girl as well?' replied Yasmina hesitantly, her voice distorted by his grip on her face.

Thakur's eyes narrowed.

'Oh yes. Especially the girl.'

FIFTY-SIX

WHEN JACK CAME ROUND, he was tied to a chair, his hands secured behind his back, and he was looking at the bleeding body of Cruise, secured to a second chair.

Jack glanced to his left and saw Aisha lying on the bed, restrained and crying. There was tape over her mouth and Jack could see her body shaking. There was no sign of blood but her clothes looked torn. She didn't look as bad as Cruise, whose face seemed to be swelling right as Jack was looking at him. A gag in the boy's mouth was absorbing a steady trickle of blood from his nose.

Thakur's warm breath suddenly polluted Jack's ear. He didn't say a word, just made sure Jack knew he was there behind him.

Without warning, his hand whipped round and clenched Jack's groin. The squeeze brought tears to his eyes. Thakur's fingers tightened around his balls until they felt ready to collapse. Jack groaned in agony and Thakur laughed.

'Do you know how many of these bitches are trying to escape from me, Jatinder?' said Thakur.

Jack was in no position to offer a response with a gag around his mouth.

'Six,' continued Thakur. 'Six tried and all failed. Do you know what is happening to the men who tried to help them? Some are falling in love with the women. Others are trying to save somebody they know. None of the women are escaping and none of these men are ever returning home.'

Jack saw the end of a cigarette, still lit, roll along the floor to his left. There was the strike of a match and then a whiff of fresh smoke. Thakur's footsteps were pacing back and forth behind Jack.

Jack glanced at Aisha and saw that she was looking at him, her eyes wide and terrified.

What the fuck had he done?

He was thinking desperately of a way out of this. He rocked the chair ever so slightly, feeling its fragility under his weight. One moment of brute force and the damn thing would shatter.

The dull ache persisted between Jack's legs. He felt nauseous and couldn't get enough air between the gag and his mouth.

'Yasmina is telling me your story,' said Thakur. He blew smoke steadily at the back of Jack's head, prickling the hairs on his neck. 'I knew your wife *very well*. She was my Kirin. My beautiful one. Fair skin, green eyes, Punjabi hips. Hai, hai,' he said, reminiscing on nights Jack didn't want to think about. 'I was sad when I had to let her go but she had outlived her use. Her mind was broken.'

Jack wanted to see the bastard. Having the man behind him was pissing him off. He turned his head to the side, trying to steal a glance. Immediately a brutish fist sent his head spinning the other way. Jack tasted blood. He groaned, partly with pain, mostly with anger.

'Next time, I will use my cigarette,' said Thakur. 'Do you want to know how she ended up here? With me? Before I send you to join her?'

Jack remained motionless, listening intently for an answer he had come here to find.

'She was given to me. To execute. It is what I used to do. But when I am seeing her, I am realizing I can make so much more money from her. India is having two currencies. Cash. And sex. She would bring me both. English girls always make more. But she was something special. She was having fire in her eyes. Fire in her hands. Fire where men need it to be. She was my best earner,' he said laughing.

His breath was closer now. Back at Jack's ear. Warm. Stale.

'And I wanted her. I needed to hear how she screamed,' he whispered.

Jack felt more enraged than he'd ever been.

'All the way in Punjab, we were. I was supposed to take her out to the fields and kill her. But I didn't. I told them I had, but I brought her to Delhi.'

Jack couldn't look at Aisha or Cruise. He closed his eyes.

'So who are they, Jatinder? Who wanted her dead and why?' Thakur whispered, and then paused as if thinking of his next words.

Jack wondered if he was concocting some lie, but Thakur had no need to do so. He was in complete control.

'She is telling me about the boys – but she is not knowing why she was taken or why they were taken from her,' said Thakur.

He moved across the room. Jack heard him pick something up. He braced himself for further assault and opened his eyes.

'Bagpiper whisky? This is good shit,' mumbled Thakur, spinning the bottle in his hands.

All Jack could see was the silhouette of his back as he made his way towards Aisha.

'She told me about her lovely daughter too.' Thakur sat on the bed next to her. He slid his palm over Aisha's body, up her thighs and then slipped it under her top. Jack saw her body tense and tried desperately to free his hands, but there was no give at all.

Aisha was breathing rapidly. Thakur's clammy hands felt like a slug's trail on her skin.

'Your mother struggled the first time too. And the second,' he whispered. 'I lose her, only to have you take her place. Your fate is tied to hers.'

Thakur moaned with pleasure as his hand cupped her breast. Aisha held herself completely still. She would not let him relish her fear. A furious rage she didn't know she was capable of had started to explode inside her.

She wanted to kill him.

The hatred was as real as his hand on her breast. She wanted him to suffer. Scream for mercy. She wanted him dead.

He removed his hand from her breast and ripped the tape from her mouth.

Aisha made no sound, startled by the move.

She didn't plead with him. It would be pointless. Instead, she tried to relax. *Think outside the box*. Find a solution to their situation.

'I enjoy the screams. Do not disappoint me,' he said, and got up.

Thakur, his face still camouflaged by the darkness, now focused on Cruise. He pushed Cruise's chair towards Jack until their knees were touching. Then he wrapped a length of thin rope around Cruise's neck, pulled it tight in one fluid motion and began to strangle the boy. Jack struggled violently in his chair. It took Aisha a few seconds to make out what was happening in the gloom. Then, as Thakur had expected, she started to scream.

Tears rolled down Cruise's cheeks as he struggled to breathe. Jack tried his hardest to break free of the chair.

'Stop! Please stop,' screamed Aisha. 'I'll do anything you want!

Please!' Thakur continued to drag on his cigarette, blowing smoke from the side of his mouth, the light catching it, highlighting the swirls.

Jack saw the terror in the young boy's eyes.

'Have me!' shouted Aisha desperately. 'I'll do whatever you want, just please don't kill him!'

Jack let out a cry as Cruise's eyes suddenly rolled lifelessly back in his head. Satisfied, Thakur threw the rope to the floor before turning towards Aisha.

'Jatinder dies next unless you scream like I want. Your body is mine. But your voice must be your own.'

Thakur left Jack, broken, sitting opposite Cruise, anger replaced by despair. Cruise's head lolled forward.

Thakur towered over Aisha. She still couldn't see his face. 'One move to displease me and you know what will happen,' he said quietly.

He took a knife from his pocket and cut the tape from her feet. With her legs free, Aisha curled away from him.

'Open your legs,' he said.

She didn't move. Before she could stop herself, her voice betrayed her courage. 'Please . . .' she said.

Thakur turned away and started towards Jack. 'Please . . .' he taunted.

'No!' she shouted. 'OK, OK, I'm sorry.' She had never tasted such bitterness. Pleading with this monster to come back to her was so shameful.

'Open your legs,' he said, without turning to face her.

Slowly and with every morsel of courage she had, Aisha obeyed.

Thakur turned around. The sound of his belt being unbuckled brought bile to Aisha's throat.

Thakur dragged harder on his cigarette. She heard him unfasten his zip.

The knife came towards her and slashed her clothing, leaving her legs exposed. He touched her. Sandpaper on silk.

Using all her resolve Aisha held her legs open and swallowed a scream.

Thakur dragged down her underwear.

Aisha couldn't help it and started to cry.

'So like your mother,' said Thakur, goading her.

Aisha used the last scrap of courage she had left. 'I'll do whatever you want. Scream louder than any woman you have ever fucked,' she said calmly, 'but I want one thing. After that, I will give you a show that someone like you can only dream of.'

Thakur made no reply.

'Give me one mouthful of whisky,' said Aisha.

Thakur laughed wickedly. 'Oh, this is my kind of bitch,' he said, and picked up the bottle of Bagpiper. He handed it to her and said, 'Take as much as you want and then I'll drink some from your mouth.'

Aisha asked him for a glass.

'Too good to drink from the bottle?' he sneered, but moved over to a sink in the corner of the room, where he picked up a plastic cup and threw it towards Aisha. She lifted it from the bed, opened the bottle of whisky and filled the cup to the rim with a trembling hand.

Jack stared at the scene, dumbfounded. Aisha glanced at him, her look full of rage.

At last he saw the play.

FIFTY-SEVEN

JACK WATCHED AS AISHA placed the bottle of whisky back on the side table and kept firm hold of the plastic cup.

Except it wasn't whisky in the bottle; it was petrol, something Jack had intended to use as part of his own escape plan.

Thakur came towards Aisha, cigarette still burning in his mouth. As he went to climb on top of her, Aisha threw the full cup of petrol at him. The cigarette ignited the fumes before the liquid had even touched his face and Thakur's head turned into a fireball. He fell to the floor, screaming, his hands clawing desperately at his face.

Jack didn't hesitate. He stood up and launched himself in the air, throwing his weight backwards and landing on the chair. The legs shattered on impact and the seat detached from the back. The tape came loose and Jack wasted no time in freeing his arms and legs.

He charged at Thakur, who had stumbled to the toilet in the corner of the room and plunged his head into the bowl. The flames doused, he rolled on the floor, howling. Jack gave the bastard a brutal kick in the stomach and the howling stopped. Thakur lay there, winded, his face melting.

Jack rushed over to Aisha. He grabbed Thakur's knife from the floor and cut through the last bond holding her to the bed. She snatched the knife from him and then tore across the room towards Thakur.

'No!' shouted Jack, going after her, but she got there first, raised the knife and slammed it into his shoulder. Still winded, Thakur could only moan in pain.

Jack grabbed Aisha and hauled her away. She thrashed, screaming wild profanities he never thought she knew.

'We need him to tell us what he knows,' said Jack, amazed that no one had burst into the room to investigate the commotion. 'Check on Cruise,' he urged.

Aisha bent by his chair. 'There's a pulse, Jack. It's weak but he's not dead,' she said, and started to work on him.

'Aisha, do everything you can to bring him back to us,' said Jack. Then he turned and kicked Thakur again in the stomach. Jack ripped the knife from his shoulder blade and pointed it at the man's badly burned face.

'Look at me, you son of a bitch,' said Jack.

Thakur was choking. He could barely breathe and skin was peeling from his chin. Jack saw seedy slit eyes gazing at him in desperation.

'Tell me who sold my wife to you and I'll make it quick. Otherwise, I'm going to light you up again,' said Jack. He picked up the bottle of Bagpiper.

Thakur raised his hands. 'Please . . . hospital . . .' he whimpered.

'Who was it?' Jack shouted, and began to pour petrol over Thakur's body.

'No!' the man yelled. 'I will tell you. His name is Baljit-Gill. He is being head guard at Wagah border.'

'What?' replied Jack, not believing a word of it. He splashed more petrol over Thakur's ruined face.

'I am telling you the truth,' pleaded Thakur. 'Baljit-Gill. He was supposed to kill her but instead he is asking me to do it. I told him I did.'

'Where can I find him now?' said Jack.

'He is still being head guard at Wagah. She is being somebody, Kirin – she is being somebody. This is why they are taking her.'

'Who is she?' said Jack.

'I am not knowing. Honestly, I am just low-caste criminal.'

Jack had no more use for him.

'Aisha? How's Cruise?'

She had laid him out on the floor, his head propped up, and was talking to him.

'He's coming round, Jack. He was unconscious, that's all.'

'Get him up. Quickly,' he said.

Aisha ran over to the sink, grabbed a towel and soaked it with water. She brought it back to Cruise and rubbed it gently across his face.

'Get him up,' said Jack, pressing her again.

Aisha helped him to his feet, both of them on unsteady legs. Cruise tried to speak but moaned in agony.

'Don't talk,' Aisha said to him.

'We're leaving,' said Jack.

'How?' replied Aisha. She spied Thakur quivering by the bed, shock starting to consume his body. She could smell burned flesh and hoped it was as painful as it looked.

'The same way I planned at the start,' said Jack. 'With a diversion. 'Cruise, you got the car keys?'

The boy searched his pocket and nodded.

Jack grabbed Thakur and dragged him towards the door.

'We don't have much time,' Jack said. 'This needs to be quick and chaotic. How many men took you from the car?'

'Two skinny little boys, but they were armed, Jack,' she said.

'You're both going to have to dig deep now. Just outside, the roof slopes down on to another one and then one at the bottom, and then it's a drop to the pavement. It's our only way out. Don't stop for anything,' he said forcefully. 'Whatever happens, don't look back and don't stop. Cruise, can you do this? Don't quit on me.'

The boy looked like he wanted to cry but gave Jack a weak thumbs-up.

'Aisha?' said Jack. He pointed to the windowsill in the corner of the room. She nodded, and went over to pick up a burning candle. Jack kept Thakur facing the door.

'Thakur, this is for my wife,' he said, and spat at him. He then opened the door, hurled Thakur outside and took the candle from Aisha. He tossed it at Thakur's petrol-soaked body, turning him into an immediate inferno.

Thakur's screams echoed into the night.

Moving quickly, Jack, Aisha and Cruise hurtled past his flailing body and clambered out over the shallow wall of the rooftop.

The corrugated roof beyond wasn't strong enough to take their combined weight. It buckled and collapsed into the roof below. That one held and the three of them slid on to it, careering into each other.

Jack grabbed hold of Aisha as they slid towards the edge. Cruise didn't wait. He jumped off the middle roof, to the lower level and then took a leap off that one on to the ground before running towards the car.

Jack pulled Aisha to her feet, and helped her on to the level below, just as Thakur's screams started to draw attention. Jack glanced back and saw dozens of people streaming up to the top floor. He followed Aisha and they both teetered at the edge of the lowest roof. Aisha was shaking her head and turned to Jack, panicking.

'I can't make this jump, Jack. It's too high,' she said, terrified.

Jack turned and saw the melee playing out on the rooftop. The boy, Don, was looking directly at him, pistol drawn, taking aim.

'Jump,' shouted Jack to Aisha.

'I can't, it's too high.'

A bullet cracked on to the tin roof, the ricochet causing them both to duck. There was nowhere to hide. The kid had a free shot.

'Goddammit, jump!' said Jack. He tried to push her but she slapped him away. Don stepped over the wall on to the collapsed roof.

'Aisha, you've got about five seconds before he puts a bullet in you.'

Jack swung his body over the edge of the roof, used his arms to support his weight and then jumped the final few feet.

Another shot fired.

This one didn't hit the tin. Instead there was a sickening thud. For a moment, everything slowed down. Then Aisha's body slumped over the side, teetered and fell into Jack's outstretched arms. He collapsed to the ground with her.

Cruise brought the car screeching towards them, the passenger door flung open.

Jack scrambled to his feet, holding Aisha's body like a child. He struggled into the car. Cruise didn't wait for him to close the door. He floored the accelerator and they roared away from the brothel with bullets puncturing the ground all around them.

Aisha was limp in Jack's arms.

Her eyes were closed.

Her blood, *everywhere*.

FIFTY-EIGHT

ST STEPHENS HOSPITAL WAS on GB Road, only a mile from the brothel. Jack was sitting alone, outside the emergency theatre. He had broken all the rules to get Aisha help. Used his credit card. Given their real names.

Told the truth.

Somewhere, deep in the back of his mind, he wondered who knew they were already here. How quickly the transactions were being relayed.

None of that mattered. He had Aisha's blood all over his hands. He had felt her slipping away in his arms. Her breathing slow. Strained. He had applied pressure to the bullet wound in her back but blood had continued to gush through his fingers.

Cruise was being attended to by another doctor.

What had he done?

Cruise was just a boy, and Aisha . . .

If she dies, it is because of you, Jack.

Don knew he'd hit her. The hospital was the obvious destination.

Jack was out of moves, waiting for the bastards to come and get him.

A few hospital personnel hurried past him, each one giving a concerned look at the blood, smeared all over him like paint.

Behind him, through the solid white doors, Aisha was being operated on.

Her blood was sticky on his hands. It changed the lines on his palms, smearing them into a chaotic jumble.

You need to get out, Jack.

Play this out. Follow the lead. Get to the bottom of this. Don't wait here for them.

He looked at his watch. Midnight: the end of another traumatic day.

The Wagah border.

India's most protected region. The line that separated India from its bitter rival, Pakistan. Two countries stained with each other's blood. There would be armed guards – one of whom was paramount to this puzzle.

It's a suicide mission, Jack.

He couldn't take his eyes off his hands. Rubbing them incessantly. Trying to wipe Aisha's blood from his skin.

Kirin, what did you get involved in?

What happened to my boys?

Cruise appeared at the end of the corridor. He made his way slowly towards Jack and sat down next to him. The silence remained for several minutes before Cruise broke it.

'Any news?' he croaked.

Jack shook his head. 'How's your neck?' he asked, without looking at him.

'Sore. But I am being alive. I am seeing Tom Cruise play dead in one of his movies when he was in similar situation. I was lucky Thakur stopped.'

'You need to go home. It's . . . it's . . . too much.'

Cruise leaned forward, elbows on knees, hands clasped together. 'I am not leaving you now, Mr Jack.'

'I won't have your blood on my hands too.'

'This story is not ending like this. Sister is going to be fine.'

'They'll be looking for us, Cruise. You know that. We took out their boss. They know she's hurt. Hospitals will be the first place they'll look.'

Cruise said nothing. The truth, painful as it was, could not be ignored.

'The doctor said he'd get the staff to contact the police. If what you say is true and the brothel has the police in its pocket, then you have no time to waste sitting around here.'

Cruise took Jack's hands in his own. 'You are not causing her blood on your hands. They are doing so.' He stood up. 'I am being outside in the car, Mr Jack. If I am seeing them coming, I phone you.' He handed Jack his spare phone. 'If I call, get out, Mr Jack. There is no law here that will be protecting you.'

'Thanks,' said Jack, refusing to look at him.

'I am saying a prayer for Sister. If you are seeing her, be telling her, please.'

Cruise left Jack alone, moving silently away from him.

An hour passed slowly. A tense hour. Jack kept looking to the end of the corridor, expecting to see Don, pistol in hand, back to finish the job. Jack wouldn't die quietly. But he would die without understanding what had got him here in the first place.

And that wasn't fair to Aisha or to himself.

He owed her his life. *Again.*

Jack wasn't sure how she had calculated the trick of throwing petrol all over Thakur's face, knowing the cigarette would ignite it, but she had almost certainly saved his life. She was far tougher and more clever than he'd given her credit for. Shit, he needed her to come round so he could apologize.

I've been such a bastard to her.

The doors to the operating room opened and a chunky Indian surgeon in a blue apron appeared. He looked shattered. He made his way over to Jack with his hands in his pockets. He hung his head, eyes rooted to the floor.

Jack jumped to his feet, speaking when the doctor was still a few feet away.

'Doctor – please, how is Aisha?'

'Mr Baxi, please. Sit down,' the man replied.

'Just tell me, is she all right?' said Jack.

The surgeon directed him back into the chair and took a seat next to him. Jack could smell the sweat from his labours.

'The bullet perforated her chest cavity. She lost a lot of blood, Mr Baxi, and her heart stopped beating.'

Jack stared at him numbly.

'We were unable to restart it,' the doctor said quietly.

'What? No . . .'

The surgeon put his hand on Jack's shoulder. 'I am very sorry but I am afraid Aisha passed away a few minutes ago.'

FIFTY-NINE

JACK WAS STANDING NEXT to Aisha's body.

She was so still. So pale.

A plain white sheet covering her body had left only her face exposed. Her blood-soaked clothes lay in a heap on a metal counter.

Jack could see his wife in her. Maybe it was the stillness that made it so pronounced. He was crippled with guilt. He had never thought that getting the answers he needed would prove so dangerous.

You stupid fool.

Jack felt as though he had been anaesthetized.

It was surreal, but Aisha looked asleep. Jack didn't know what he had expected. For her to look more like a corpse perhaps. And she looked anything but. Almost peaceful.

Goddammit, she was blameless in all this.

Kirin had her faults. She had cheated and lived a life of deceit. Jack had served his time in prison, always breaking the rules. They both deserved their karma.

But Aisha was innocent.

He didn't realize he was crying until the tears dripped from his jaw on to the floor, steadily landing beside his feet.

It cannot end like this.

He opened his mouth to say something but the guilt renewed its assault.

Don't you dare speak to her. This is all your fault.

You bastard, how could you let her die like this? She had her whole life to live.

You led her to her death.

Jack opened his mouth, gasping for air.

He took a few deep breaths.

Inhale the scent of her death, Jack. It will be with you for ever.

His tears quickened.

Lose control, Jack – show them you have no fear. Don't let her die without finding out the truth.

She said it herself, remember: *the truth will set us free.*

He nodded. Allowed the guilt to fizzle out. Gave the anger free rein.

'You will pay. Whoever you are, I promise you that you will pay,' he whispered.

He thought about the Wagah border. All the guards and the patrols. But it didn't matter. It didn't seem such an ordeal. Her lifeless body gave him perspective.

'I have nothing to lose,' he whispered. 'Nothing.'

Jack walked slowly to the heap of Aisha's blood-soaked clothes.

With his hands quivering, Jack took almost a minute, wavering before his fingers made contact. He tore a strip from her clothes, making sure it was stained with her blood. Then he moved back towards her.

Aisha's hands were under the sheet. It took several minutes for Jack to build up the nerve. He slipped his hand under the sheet and exposed her arm. Her skin was growing cold already.

Jack put the piece of cloth in her hand and closed her fingers around it. He waited a while and then opened her palm. Carefully he placed her hand back under the sheet.

He tied the scrap around his wrist. He knotted it twice, using his teeth, tasting her blood, metallic and bitter.

Jack cleared his throat and slipped his hand under the sheet again, grasping hers.

'Earlier on, Aisha, when I removed the *rakhi*—'

He struggled with the words, lips trembling. 'I . . . I was wrong.'

He squeezed her hand, as if he hoped it would recharge her lifeless body.

'I'm sorry, Aisha,' he whispered, and now he did break down.

Outside the hospital, Jack headed towards the car. The *rakhi* felt tight on his wrist, as if Aisha was holding on to him.

He took out his phone, scrolled through his contacts and found the one he was looking for. He didn't hesitate.

The phone was slow to grab a connection but when it did, the dial tone confirmed what Jack had suspected. Habib was in town. Jack had no qualms about calling him.

Habib was pissed off and seething with an anger Jack recognized.

'Jack – where is she?' he said.

'You're in Delhi, right?' said Jack coldly.

'You know I am.'

'St Stephens hospital, GB Road.'

'What's happened? You'd better not have hurt her.'

Even though he hated the man, Jack couldn't bear to tell him Aisha was gone.

'Ask for Dr Ajmani. He'll give you an envelope. Everything is in there.'

'You son of a bitch. What have you done to her?'

Jack hung up. He removed the SIM card from the phone,

dropped it on the floor and stamped on it before making his way over to where Cruise was parked.

'Sister?' asked Cruise.

'She's fine,' said Jack, pulling the door to alongside the passenger seat. He hated himself for lying but he had to keep Cruise focused on what needed to be done. 'I phoned her father. He's a powerful man and he's here in Delhi. He's coming to take care of her.'

'Am I being able to see her before we leave?' asked Cruise.

'No, she's asleep. She can't be disturbed until morning.'

Cruise nodded dejectedly.

'Are you tired, Cruise?' asked Jack.

The boy shook his head.

'How many hours to Wagah?'

Cruise puffed out his cheeks. 'Sir, it is taking ten, maybe twelve hours by road.'

'I'll share the driving. Let's finish this story.'

SIXTY

THE GRAND TRUNK ROAD was the longest-running major road in Asia. It spanned one thousand six hundred miles, running from Bangladesh through northern India to Pakistan. It would lead Jack from Delhi through the heart of the Punjab to the Wagah border.

Leaving Delhi had taken them almost an hour: the night brought thousands of lorries on to the road, each of them belching out thick clouds of choking fumes, some large enough to envelop Cruise's car.

Cruise was going to drive to Karnal. From there Jack would take over, allowing Cruise to sleep.

Jack's seat was reclined and his eyes closed. He drifted into a semi-conscious state where he was aware of the radio playing quietly and Cruise clearing his throat every few minutes, still feeling the effects of his ordeal at the brothel. Jack was running through the last few days in his head.

Habib might have reached the hospital by now. He wouldn't understand. How could he? Jack had scribbled a note to him, briefly explaining what had happened and where he was headed. He had finally come to the realization that Habib wasn't involved in this.

Kirin – she is being somebody.

Thakur's words kept replaying in his mind.

Just who the hell *had* his wife been?

Kirin had clearly been caught up in something far larger than any of them realized. Perhaps larger than she'd even realized. Jack thought of the cash they had been clearing in the 1990s, the underworld connections they had made. Yet Kirin had never been at the forefront of any of that. No, there was some other treachery involved here. He had never thought it possible she'd be capable of having an affair, never mind with someone as vile as Habib. And then harbouring a secret child and conspiring to leave him, taking his own kids with her?

Kirin – she is being somebody.

Jack thought back to his wedding, the pomp and ceremony. There had been a large delegation of religious men from India – Sikh elders whom Jack had been told he needed to treat as father figures. An intimidating group, they had nonetheless treated Kirin with praise and reverence.

A phrase from the father-of-the-bride's speech came into his mind:

It was written this way. This union was forged in blood decades ago . . .

Jack had always remembered those words because at the time, it had felt as if his marriage to Kirin was more than just a matrimonial affair. The phrase needled Jack now. En route into the heart of the Sikh holy land, a new picture was emerging, still hazy – one he didn't yet understand.

It was three a.m. before Cruise tapped him lightly on the shoulder.

'Mr Jack, we are being at Karnal. If you are wanting to give me a break, this is being fine.'

Jack opened his eyes. A blanket had been pulled over him.

'It was for your comfort,' said Cruise.

'Thanks,' replied Jack. He was surprised he'd fallen asleep.

They switched places quickly.

'Jesus, it's cold out there,' said Jack.

'You are seeing only daytime temperatures in Delhi,' said Cruise softly, massaging his throat.

'How is it?' asked Jack.

Cruise took a swig of some syrup he'd been given at the hospital. 'It is being painful,' he said, grimacing as he swallowed. His eyes were bloodshot and the skin around his neck was purple and inflamed.

'Try and get some sleep, Cruise. So I just stay on GT Road?'

Cruise nodded. 'It is being signposted well for Ambala and Ludhiana. If you are being stuck, just be waking me.'

Jack drove with the window ajar. The cool breeze on the side of his face kept him alert. A potent smell of rubber came from the endless wheels of all the trucks he overtook.

They passed a KFC and a McDonald's, which made Jack think of home. He thought about the last time he had eaten. It had been with Aisha and Cruise almost ten hours ago. His stomach rumbling, Jack pulled the car off the road towards the outlets.

Having eaten and with a large strawberry milkshake in his lap, Jack felt a tad better. The sugar rush was just what he needed. He hadn't woken Cruise – the boy was out cold, snoring loudly, and Jack had made the decision that sleep was more important. He'd bought the boy some food for when he woke up, not knowing when the next stop would arise.

They hit Kurukshetra and Jack pulled over to take another break. He was tired and with a stomach full of food he was fighting the urge to fall asleep. With a bitter cold caressing his skin, Jack stood by the side of the road, staring up at a poster advertising a nearby monument to the most famous battle in Indian history, the Mahabharata. This had been when Lord Krishna had revealed to the prince Arjuna the sacred text of the Hindu holy book, the Bhagavad Gita.

Shivering all over, and his focus on the towering statue in the photo, Jack realized he had seen it before. It came to him in a rush of memories.

He had done this same journey from Delhi to Amritsar as a child with his father. And they had stopped off to visit the monument, where Jack had been told of its significance and how the pilgrimage they were taking was also steeped in Indian history.

A phrase came back to Jack now, something his father had said to him.

Remember, Jatinder, your life is not about you. It is about service. It is about being a symbol and an icon of what it means to be a Sikh.

His father had pointed to the statue. *Like that, yours is also the blood of warriors. Of legend. And one day you will realize that you, my son, are no ordinary little boy.*

Jack fell to his knees, his breath shallow and rapid.

'Christ, what's happening to me?' he whispered. He staggered to his feet, unable to take the cold any more, and returned to the car. Jack drove away, feeling as if the eyes of the monument were on him as he left the place behind.

And for the very first time he realized that, perhaps, this was not about his wife.

This was about him.

SIXTY-ONE

THEY WERE SIX KILOMETRES outside Amritsar, the last city before the infamous Wagah border, when they came across the first sign for the Golden Temple. Jack had woken Cruise at six a.m. and let the boy take over.

Punjab was vastly different to Delhi. The air was cleaner and the constant black smog of the Delhi skyline thankfully absent. Agriculture was the dominant industry out here, with fields and pastures as far as he could see. The terrain was flat, mostly green, but broken up every so often with yellow fields of wheat.

Amritsar was the holiest city in the world for Sikhs and the location of the Harmandir Sahib, or, as the Western world knew it, the Golden Temple. It was where the original copy of the sacred text of the Guru Granth Sahib was kept. The book was a collection of *shabda* that described the qualities of God.

It was every Sikh's obligation to make a pilgrimage to the temple at least once in their lifetime. His father had brought Jack here when he was a child, a trip he didn't remember with any real clarity, although seeing the words 'Golden Temple' stirred up distant memories of being read sections from the religious text. If his father hadn't died so young, Jack's life might have taken a different turn.

'Tell me, Cruise, how many times have you been to this city?' Jack asked.

'Oh, many times. Maybe twenty? People are thinking that Taj Mahal is busiest tourist destination. But they are being wrong. Golden Temple is attracting more than one hundred thousand people during the week. And, sir, it is my opinion – you can be disagreeing, but Taj is nothing compared to Harmandir Sahib.'

'My father brought me here when I was just a boy,' replied Jack, 'but I have little memory of it.'

Cruise whistled. 'Really?'

'Yes. Funnily enough, I was born in Punjab.'

'You are being born here?' said Cruise in shock.

Jack nodded. 'We moved to England when I was two.'

'May I ask why?'

'My dad thought we'd have a better quality of life in England. There were jobs, opportunities in the textile mills in Bradford. I was supposed to come back here when I got married, take my wedding blessings at the Golden Temple, but for some reason it never quite materialized. Kismet perhaps.'

'Sir, before we are going to Wagah, I am advising you to visit the temple. It is giving you strength.'

'You really believe that, Cruise?'

'Of course.'

'It's a building, just like any other. And if there were a God, he wouldn't have put me through this ordeal.'

Cruise whistled patronizingly. 'Life is being about ordeals. It is the ordeals that are making us all different. Sir, I was thinking about Sister, being in the hospital. Are you, please, phoning them to see how she is?'

In the holiest city for Sikhs, Jack felt guilty as the lie left his lips. 'I'm sure she's recovering fine, Cruise. Her father will be there by now, but yes, I'll phone when I can.'

Cruise nodded, looking troubled. Jack looked away out of the window, pushing thoughts of Aisha's body on the hospital bed from his mind. His hand went involuntarily to the blood-soaked *rakhi* round his wrist.

Now they were off the highway, the traffic started to build. Motorcycles vastly outnumbered cars. Almost every man was wearing a turban: blue, pink, yellow – a multitude of colours and designs. Women wore Punjabi suits with their hair respectfully covered. While it was nothing like the chaos of Delhi, it was peaceful. Entering Amritsar, however, all notion of serenity vanished. Orange dust once again covered the roads and the din of car horns returned.

'The Wagah ceremony of the closing of the gates is being at half past five,' said Cruise. 'We are having five hours. Are you knowing what you are going to do?'

Jack had an idea, but it didn't sit well. In fact, Jack didn't want to go at all. He had a feeling it might be a journey he wouldn't return from.

'I'm shattered, Cruise. Find me a hotel. The best one there is. I want a shower and to sleep for a few hours to get my head right. Then I'll tell you what we're going to do.'

'This I can help you with, sir. Hotel, no problem.'

Next to the Alpha One shopping complex in Amritsar was the Hyatt Regency Hotel, a plush five-star resort with armed security guards at the entrance. Burly Sikh men in blue turbans and carrying rifles, they acknowledged Jack's arrival with a nod.

Jack handed over his passport at reception and opted for a deluxe room with a view over the pool. He booked a room for Cruise as well and had to repeat himself to the receptionist, who looked amazed at the gesture. The boy needed a rest just as much as Jack did. He paid with his Mastercard, having run short of cash. It didn't bother him. He knew this was the end of his journey. He would either get the answers he needed or end up in the ground. Either way, his location being compromised was of little significance now.

The room was everything his journey had not been.

Luxury.

There was a king-size bed, a plasma TV and floor-to-ceiling windows that afforded a view across Amritsar.

The en suite had a large walk-in shower that Jack wasted no time in using. He spent almost thirty minutes sitting on the tiled floor, allowing the steaming jets of water to massage his scalp.

Tucking his white bathrobe around him, Jack sat down on the armchair facing the window. He massaged his feet on the thick carpet and poured two of the miniature whiskies from the mini-bar into a glass.

With the taste of whisky on his lips and his body refreshed, Jack felt almost elated. Sitting on the top floor of the hotel, his mind turned for a moment to the possibility of just leaving.

'Passport, money, no ties,' he whispered, looking out over the bustle of Amritsar in the midday heat. 'Book a ticket and disappear.'

It was a nice thought. But he had to see this through – for Aisha.

He downed the rest of the whisky and glanced at his watch: noon. Four hours until the border closed, the crowds dispersed and he'd have the best chance of tracking down the man responsible for handing his wife over to Thakur.

Four hours until he found out the truth.

SIXTY-TWO

HABIB IQBAL WAS STANDING beside the cold metal table on which his daughter lay, still and peaceful. Her body was covered by a simple white sheet. She looked to be asleep, not . . .

Habib couldn't even bring himself to think the word.

Sara was standing by the window, her hands resting on the ledge, staring out into a darkness that also seemed to fill the room.

His head bowed, Habib again read the rushed note Jack had written, droplets of smeared blood spoiling the page.

How had it come to this?

He wanted to reach out and touch Aisha's face but he was afraid. He closed his eyes and thought of all the times he had sat by her bed and watched her sleep as a child. There had been something peaceful and beautiful in it. Habib could remember vividly Aisha turning her bedtime into a game, trying her hardest to stay awake, talking to him for as long as she could. She had never been able to manage more than a couple of minutes before her eyelids began to droop and the inevitable sleep overcame her. She would fall asleep smiling, and no matter how stressful Habib's day had been, those moments had brought much-needed balance.

'Open your eyes, Aisha. We can have all the late-night talks you want, my child,' he said, his voice nothing more than a whisper.

This time, though, Aisha would not open her eyes. That cheeky smile was consigned to Habib's memories and no matter how hard he tried, he could not bring himself to reach out and touch her face.

It was more than the fear of what she might feel like.

It was . . . guilt.

While he still could not understand why any of this had happened – why it was still happening – deep down, he felt as though this was just punishment for his life of dishonesty.

He had been ruthless in business, ruthless in his relationships – whether with Jack, Kirin or even Sara. He glanced over at her silhouette by the window. She remained absolutely still, continuing to stare into a night far darker than any of them could ever have predicted.

Was this karma?

It certainly felt like it.

Yet why did his daughter have to be here, like this, to punish the sins of the father?

That wasn't fair.

That was far from fucking OK.

Habib crumpled Jack's note in his hand and dropped it to the floor.

Finally, he put his hands to Aisha's face, felt how cold she was and started to cry.

Sara remained standing by the window. Her eyes were steely as she observed an ambulance pulling away from the hospital on to the road. Its blue lights began to flash and as quickly as it had appeared it was gone.

Behind her, she could hear the sounds of Habib's misery: deep, painful sobs. She clenched her jaw, the coldness from the room feeling like it was now infecting her insides. She closed her eyes and balled her hands into fists, digging her nails into her skin.

It was always the women who suffered.

First Kirin, then Sara and now Aisha.

And all because of Habib and Jack – embroiled in this chaos, continuing to hurt not only themselves but the innocents around them. Without Jack Baxi, none of this would ever have happened.

Sara opened her eyes, everything suddenly clear to her. With Aisha's cold body lying there and Habib's wailing echoing through the room, she turned to face him. She watched him cry, his arms wrapped around his daughter's body.

Sara was angry. Bitter. And now . . . vengeful.

She moved towards Habib and picked up Jack's note from the floor. She read it, her eyes wide and disbelieving.

Amritsar. That was where they were now headed – for a resolution that as yet no one could understand.

Sara put the note in her pocket.

No longer would she be a simple bystander in all of this.

For the first time, she knew exactly how this saga was going to end.

SIXTY-THREE

IT WAS EARLY AFTERNOON when Jack surfaced from the hotel and made his way to the car. Cruise looked refreshed in a change of clothes and had taken advantage of the hotel's buffet.

They drove in silence, both clearly nervous. The Wagah border had the tightest security in India, with hundreds of military guards. Cruise eventually broke the silence.

'Mr Jack, are you knowing what you are going to do when you are arriving at Wagah?'

Jack said nothing and continued staring abjectly out of the window, into a sunshine so bright he had to avert his eyes. The reality was that he had no idea what he was going to do at the border, only that this journey had to be made.

The opening and closing of the border gates and the famed ceremonial lowering of the Indian flag was high on the tourist agenda, renowned all over the world for its pomp and history. Cruise had visited many times, but this was the first time he made a mental note of the Namita Hospital as he drove by.

Cruise started talking to break the troubling silence.

'Today is being the festival of Dussehra,' he said quietly. He pointed to an open area on his left, where an enormous statue of the evil king Ravana stood.

'Are you knowing this festival, Mr Jack?'

Again there was no reply.

'It is from Hindu folklore, celebrating when Lord Rama rescued his wife Sita from the evil Sri Lankan king Ravana in the *Ramayana*. This statue is packed with fireworks and tonight it will be blown up. There will be a huge fair on this ground. We should be coming to see it,' he said, trying to be optimistic.

'It's a fitting day for this festival,' said Jack. He watched the fifty-foot effigy vanish from view. 'Does that make me Rama, and I'm off to slay Ravana?' he said, turning to face Cruise.

'When you are putting it like this, then yes, Mr Jack, it does. Good is always overcoming evil.'

'Does it?'

'Yes. It is karma.'

'You believe in that shit?'

'Of course. Look, sir,' said Cruise, clearly pleased they were talking, 'are you knowing Albert Einstein's law of the conservation of energy?'

'What?' said Jack, thinking he'd heard it wrong. Cruise was delighted to explain it.

'Let me tell you – it is being that energy cannot be created or destroyed, only converted from one form to another. It is being the only law you are needing in life. The energy of the universe is always being one. It cannot ever be less than this or more than this. One person dies; another is born. One animal dies; another is taking its place. When we die, our energy is being released into the ground or the atmosphere, but it is still keeping the energy of the universe at one. Karma, reincarnation, is simply that the energy lost from your living body when you die is transferred into the atmosphere and somewhere used to help the universe create another life. Karma – very simple really,' said Cruise.

Jack kept his silence but Cruise felt he was digesting what he had said.

A few kilometres down the road, they passed an intimidating-looking military compound. Dozens of tanks were stationary in the field. The base stretched as far back as Jack could see, sealed off by a barbed-wire fence. Otherwise the landscape was covered by waterlogged fields on each side of the road, mostly green with the odd blemish of yellow. They passed the Dreamland resort and the Sun Star Palace. Both appeared to be luxury affairs; both had signs saying 'No vacancy'.

'It is going to be busy there today,' said Cruise.

The road narrowed into two lanes as they passed a monstrous-looking power plant; a terrible eyesore amid the serenity of the farmlands. They reached a toll and Cruise paid the fee. The sign by the side of the road said 'Wagah Border, 12 kilometres'.

Passing an impressive-looking house, Jack noticed a defiant green flag of Pakistan flapping from its roof.

'Strange to see that, isn't it?' said Jack.

Cruise shook his head. 'Mr Jack, past this point, everything is becoming about identity and making sure you are displaying it proudly. You will be seeing this when we arrive at Wagah.'

The road now split into a dual carriageway and they slowed down as the lanes narrowed. On the left, dozens of lorries were parked, one behind another, awaiting inspection.

'What's the deal with them?' asked Jack.

'Border checks. India and Pakistan are trading. Plenty of trade business,' said Cruise. 'Mostly it is India exporting to them,' he added. 'These trucks are awaiting inspection by customs officials.'

Cruise switched to the wrong side of the road when their route became blocked by traffic.

'Easy now,' said Jack, gripping his seat.

The oncoming traffic simply moved to another lane. About a quarter of a mile on, a guard in a brown police uniform waved Cruise towards a parking area but Cruise ignored him, switched back on to the correct side of the road and continued.

'We are here, Mr Jack,' said Cruise, pointing to a red building by the side of the road. 'I am having to park here. Nobody can get any closer in a car.'

He turned on to a congested dirt track and inched his way along, bumper to bumper with the car in front. The car park was littered with puddles, in which vehicles parked more or less haphazardly, from what Jack could make out. In the middle, several men and a few guards were trying to free a minibus stuck in a ditch.

Cruise parked near the front, navigating his way around a treacherous-looking hole. He turned the ignition off and took a moment before turning to Jack.

'We are here,' he said, with no enthusiasm to his voice.

Jack nodded. When he spoke, his voice was shaky and uncertain.

'Here, take this,' he said, handing a piece of paper to Cruise.

'What is it?'

'Internet banking passwords. Sort code, account numbers and PIN to my accounts. If the guy I'm looking for is here, there's a good chance I might not be coming back from this.'

In order to get Baljit to speak the truth of what had happened with Kirin, Jack was prepared to put his life on the line.

'I only have one chance to get the answers I need. Even if he does tell me, my way out might be impossible.'

'But, Mr Jack, this is not the way to do this,' said Cruise, pushing Jack's outstretched hand away.

'Listen,' snapped Jack, 'I have to know the truth. There is no other way. And I don't care any more, Cruise. If the bastard's here and I get a chance, I'll do whatever I have to.'

Jack pointed to a group of guards ahead of them. 'There is no return from this. I'm just a simple guy searching for the truth.'

'But, sir . . .'

Jack raised his hand. He could see the pain in the boy's face. 'You've been a real friend to me, Cruise. You've risked your life, and this money will set you up. You can do whatever you want – make your movies, go to university – whatever. At least I'll have done something good . . .' He trailed off and opened the passenger door.

Cruise grabbed his arm. He picked up one of the small Hindu deities from his dashboard and handed it to Jack. 'On a day where the whole country will celebrate Dussehra and good overcoming evil, please, take this statue of Lord Rama. He will protect you.'

Jack took the statue from him and twirled it in his hand. Then he reattached it to the dash and shook his head at Cruise. He pushed the piece of paper he had tried to give Cruise earlier back into the boy's hand, then once more tried to leave the car. Again he felt Cruise's hand on his arm.

'Mr Jack, when you approach the border, on the left-hand side is a VIP area. Show them your British passport and they will be allowing you through. And, Mr Jack, I am waiting here until nightfall – until they force me to leave. Be careful.'

Jack nodded and Cruise let go of his arm.

SIXTY-FOUR

JACK WAS STANDING ON the main road by a sign that said that since 15 August 1947, the Wagah border had been referred to as the 'Berlin Wall of Asia'. He read another one that gave some history.

Wagah was a small village located in Pakistan, a kilometre from the boundary. The first flag-hoisting ceremony occurred on 11 October 1947 and from then on had continued daily. The only time it had stopped was between 1965 and 1971 when India and Pakistan were at war over the disputed territory of Kashmir.

There were military offices on both sides of the road, and stalls selling Indian flags, which were being snapped up by the thousands of zealous tourists making their way towards the border. Jack was surprised to see that the majority were Indian nationals, judging by their dress, and not Europeans. Among them were just a few Western tourists with cameras dangling from their necks.

On any other day, the sight would have been mesmerizing – immense trees in full blossom on both sides of the route, branches heavy with leaves, and everywhere Jack looked, the

Hindu religious symbol Om. Everything here was about patriotism and identity – Indian flags, orange T-shirts and the national anthem being played in the distance.

The temperature was in the low twenties but Jack was sweating, wondering how the next couple of hours would play out. He was descended upon by a gang of kids trying to sell him DVDs of the flag ceremony. It reminded him of the toothless child who had shocked Aisha on their arrival. He touched the *rakhi* around his wrist and handed them a few rupees. The kids moved on to another tourist, hunting in packs like wolves.

Halfway down the road the crowd came to a stop at a clumsily orchestrated checkpoint. There was no official queue – Indians seemed incapable of forming one. The crowd jostled, shouting up at the guards, who were on military horses.

Women were told to move to a separate area on the other side. The crowd of men kept inching their way forward, even though the soldiers' horses were blocking their path. There was no barrier that Jack could see. To his left was a barbed-wire fence that flirted dangerously with the crowd.

There was no order. No system. It boded well for Jack. He hoped security would be this sloppy further on. He edged forwards with the crowd towards the checkpoint. The smell of horse manure was rife.

Walking through the airport-style body scanner, Jack noticed wires strewn carelessly to the side; it didn't appear to be plugged in.

He moved towards a colossal gate. On either side were steps leading up to the bleachers from where the crowd could sit to watch the ceremony. The top row was manned by two Sikh security guards, both carrying machine guns. If they had looked carefully at Jack, they'd have seen that his hands were shaking and his face was lathered in sweat.

The VIP entrance gave way on to a path running behind the base of the staircase. Jack showed a guard his British passport and was nodded through. The path led him up to an elevated seating area where he was now less than fifty metres from the imposing metal gate marking the border. The ceremony was still ninety minutes away so only half the seats were occupied.

Jack made his way back down the steps and on to the main road, surprised he was able to get this close to security. Children were dancing wildly in front of him as a booming PA system kicked into life. With just over an hour to go, the festivities were starting to warm up.

Jack was only a short distance now from the border gates leading into Pakistan. Forming either side of the gateway stood the twin towers of the 'Border Security Force', with armed guards on top of each one, also packing hefty machine guns. On the arch between them hung a large image of Mahatma Gandhi, alongside the word 'INDIA' in bold white letters. Jack glanced towards Pakistan. At their gates stood equally impressive barbicans and the picture of President Jinnah, the man responsible for the creation of Pakistan.

Members of the public were walking around freely, mingling with the armed guards. Jack made his way over to the security building. There was a relaxed, jovial feel to the whole event – this was a bold, vibrant celebration of India's identity.

The entrance wasn't secure, just a flimsy rope across it. A guard in a brown uniform and ceremonial red hat came over to Jack and asked if he needed any help.

'Sure,' said Jack, trying to sound as relaxed as possible. He showed the guard his British passport. 'I'm from England. Is Baljit-Gill on duty today?'

The guard took his passport and gave it a cursory once-over. 'Who are you?' he asked.

'A friend. From England. I met him many years ago. Just wondered if he still worked here.'

The music behind them was cranked up to a deafening level.

The guard handed the passport back to Jack and pointed into the security building. He grabbed Jack's arm to take him inside. Jack wasn't ready for this and stopped him, pointing to his watch.

'After,' he shouted. 'I'll meet him after. OK?'

The guard let go of him, nodded and walked away.

At five thirty the ceremony of the lowering of the flag started, with over two thousand people sitting on the stairs, the road, even each other's laps. The Indian national anthem boomed from the speakers and children were dancing crazily on the road, egged on by the master of ceremonies. He had a microphone which he used to whip the crowd up.

They shouted *'Jai Hind!'* and *'India Zindabaad!'* – 'Hail India' and 'Long live India' – whenever there was opposition singing from the Pakistani side, which had filled somewhat but was still almost half empty.

Just when it seemed the frenzy couldn't get any louder, a man with a huge *dhol* drum round his neck began hammering at it with his wooden beaters. This took the crowd to a whole new level of excitement. The steady rhythm of the *dhol* was intoxicating and Jack felt his adrenaline levels surge. It was impossible not to get caught up in the fever.

A procession of guards in ceremonial costume, two at a time, made their way down the road. They raised their legs like ballerinas, high into the air, then brought them crashing down, hammering their shoes into the road. They marched with pomp and intent towards the closed border gates, staring half-mockingly, half-murderously at their Pakistani counterparts on the other side. The show was clearly orchestrated in common, with its elaborate outfits and theatrical elements, but very much served to underline the simmering hostility between the two parties.

The Indian crowd went crazy – the blood coursing through their veins was Indian and if they could have spilled it to show

how much they loved their country, they would have. Jack had never experienced an atmosphere like it. It was passionate, aggressive, and gave him chills.

The final guard opened the gates and both parties lowered their respective flags. They were folded carefully, all the time handled like the most precious of silks.

With the border open, the opposing guards, enemies to one other, finally faced each other. They shared a stern robotic handshake before spinning on their heels and marching away, heads held high, to the rousing cheers of their respective fans.

With the gates open and the flags lowered, the crowd dispersed.

Jack made his way back towards the security building. The road was heaving with tourists vying to have their pictures taken with the guards, who seemed more than happy to oblige.

Jack walked brazenly towards the entrance of the building, where a guard was having a cigarette on the sly. He approached him, passport in hand, and tapped him on the shoulder. He asked him confidently for Baljit-Gill's whereabouts, and pointed to the guard he had asked earlier, saying that he had told Jack to come into the building to find his friend.

Jack looked the guard in the eye, his heart thundering against his chest. He slipped the guard a thousand-rupee note and told him he wanted to surprise his friend.

Money changed all the rules.

The guard took the money, despatched his cigarette and allowed Jack into the building.

With everyone outside mingling with the public, the patrol building was empty.

It was easier than Jack had imagined and getting this far lifted his spirits.

The guard halted outside an office. He was about to knock when Jack stopped him.

'Surprise – remember? Let me knock and go in. Please?'

The guard shrugged and stepped aside, but didn't leave.

Jack took a deep breath, knocked on the door and entered.

An elderly man was sat behind a desk, flanked by three armed guards. They had their guns locked on Jack.

Nobody spoke.

Nobody moved.

Jack's legs were wobbling. He wasn't sure how long he could remain standing. His mouth was parched and his bladder felt heavy.

'Jatinder Baxi?' asked the old man, his voice rasping with age.

Jack was dumbfounded.

The man nodded. 'You must be. Only a Baxi would have the courage to enter this building unarmed, looking for trouble.'

Jack found his voice. 'Baljit-Gill?' he whispered.

The old man rose slowly to his feet. 'Yes,' he replied.

'How do you know who I am?'

There was no response.

'Are you going to kill me?' asked Jack.

'That depends,' replied the man.

'On what?'

'On whether you came here to die.'

SIXTY-FIVE

JACK WAS SITTING OPPOSITE Baljit-Gill in his cramped office. A guard stood to either side of him, guns lowered but not in their holsters.

The old man had a long untrimmed beard and was wearing a red turban matching those worn by the military. He was glaring at Jack with disdain.

A naked lightbulb over Jack's head lit the room with a pitiful glow. On the wall behind the man hung a withered Indian flag with a signature in the bottom left-hand corner.

'Gandhi,' said Baljit, noting Jack's interest.

'How do you know who I am?' repeated Jack.

Baljit picked up a tattered folder and threw it into Jack's lap. 'Open it. Take your time to digest its contents and then you may ask your questions.'

With shaky hands, Jack opened the folder. His jaw dropped. He was looking at an old colour photo of Baljit standing proudly next to Jack's father, arms around each other. Jack lifted it closer to his face.

There were several other photos, all of them demonstrating a friendly warmth between the two men. Jack turned one over. It was dated: 2 June 1984.

Jack read it out loud.

'Does that date mean anything to you?' said the old man.

Jack shook his head. 'Should it?' he said. The look of disgust on Baljit's face made him immediately regret his words.

'Operation Blue Star,' said Baljit.

Jack scratched his stubble. It rang a bell . . .

Baljit cursed under his breath and one of the Sikh guards at his side spat at Jack, who recoiled, afraid and confused.

Baljit asked Jack if he had a phone and when Jack said he had, Baljit asked him to look up Operation Blue Star. Jack did so and realized his foolishness.

'Oh,' he said simply.

Baljit stood and drew his *kirpan* from his waist. In one frighteningly fluid motion, the blade of it was at Jack's neck.

Jack didn't move, pinned to the chair.

'Nothing would give me more pleasure, and yet I would mourn your death as if it had been my own child,' said Baljit.

Jack held his breath. He had no idea what to say.

'Operation Blue Star – tell me what you know of it,' said Baljit, still with the sword to Jack's throat.

'There . . . there . . . was a conflict at the Golden Temple. The Prime Minister, Indira Gandhi, sent the military in to remove a religious leader she considered to be an extremist – Jarnail Singh Bindranwale.'

'And what of your father's role in this?' said Baljit.

Jack wanted to shake his head but couldn't – the blade would have sliced into his skin.

'My father?'

Baljit spoke in Punjabi to one of the guards, bitching about Jack's ignorance.

'Your father came to Amritsar to join the resistance. He helped to repel the Indian army until they stormed the Golden Temple – he lost his life in that fight. Your father was one of the greatest Khalsa warriors we have seen. Yours is the bloodline—'

He stopped talking abruptly, as if he'd said too much. Instead he lowered his sword. This time when he spoke, he was altogether calmer. 'Indira Gandhi – do you know what happened to her?'

Jack heard the question but his mind was on his father's death. *Another lie he had been told all his life.*

'What happened to Indira Gandhi?' repeated Baljit, this time with more force.

Jack spoke quietly, feeling lost and deflated. 'She was assassinated.'

'By whom?'

'Her bodyguards, I think.'

'Her Sikh bodyguards. They put their life on the line for her as bodyguards, but when she herself crossed the line, they did not hesitate.'

Jack nodded but he still didn't see what all this had to do with him.

'You still do not understand, do you, Jatinder?'

Jack was tired of the riddles. 'Why don't you do us all a favour and get to whatever it is you're building up to?'

'That job is for somebody else. You came here to find out about your wife and all I can tell you is that it was my job to end her life, and one I foolishly did not carry out. It meant she ended up in a terrible existence. For that I am truly sorry because, while her life was lived immorally, her death should have been shrouded in honour, a result of *my* sword.'

Jack shot forward in the chair. The guards either side of him pinned their guns into his chest, forcing him back.

'You'd better shoot me or tell me what the hell is going on,' said Jack, swatting the guns away angrily.

'Where is Kirin?' asked Baljit.

'Dead,' replied Jack.

'She is in no danger any more, Jatinder. Tell me where she is.'

Jack told him what had happened to Kirin, of her cremation and of the altercation with Thakur, but he didn't mention Aisha, seeing no reason to do so. Baljit told him he was pleased that Thakur was probably dead as it was one less thing to take care of.

'In order to understand the truth and why all of these things happened, you need to realize *who* you are, Jatinder,' said Baljit. His tone changed now and he became irate, waving his sword again at Jack. 'You are a disgrace,' he said, shaking his head. 'Having the name Baxi means nothing to you. You want the truth? You want to see your sons?'

'My sons are alive?' said Jack, grabbing the table. The folder he was holding fell on the ground, spilling photos of his father across the floor. 'So it is true – they are here? In Amritsar?'

The look of disgust on Baljit's face got Jack to his feet. He was immediately restrained by two guards, one of whom drew his own sword and put it to Jack's throat.

Baljit laboured to a stand and rested his hands on the table as if he needed its support.

'I have one final task to carry out, Jatinder. Then we shall see what your kismet holds.'

Baljit nodded to one of the guards and Jack felt a sudden almighty blow to the back of his head.

He slumped to the floor, everything fading to black.

SIXTY-SIX

JACK REGAINED CONSCIOUSNESS IN the back of a large SUV. For a second, he thought he was in Cruise's vehicle but then recalled his last moments with Baljit. On either side of him sat two guards from the Wagah border, both armed and wearing their military turbans. Jack glanced to the front and saw Baljit sitting next to the driver, also a Wagah guard.

Jack hadn't been restrained. He touched the back of his head and winced at the swelling. The guards glanced at him, no emotion on their faces.

Jack glanced at his watch. It was roughly thirty minutes since he'd been knocked out, so they couldn't be far from the border.

'Where are we going?' asked Jack, to nobody in particular.

When he got no reply, he fell silent.

He was certain of one thing. If they wanted him dead, they'd have done it at Wagah.

There was something else going on here.

Baljit had confirmed that Jack's sons were alive. He wondered if

300

he was going to see them. Something told him that was not the case.

The car slowed and passed a checkpoint. They were allowed past by several Sikh guards, the Khalsa, resplendent in their long blue robes with matching turbans and orange scarves draped around their necks. They were known as the protectors of the Golden Temple and were ready to sacrifice their lives for its protection.

Jack's father's voice filtered into his mind.

One day, Jatinder, you too will become one of the Khalsa.

They continued a short while longer into the midst of what Jack could only describe as a ghost town. The driver parked in the middle of the road, turned off the engine and had a short exchange with Baljit. The driver was refusing to exit the vehicle.

Baljit's tone was sympathetic. He asked the guards beside Jack if they wanted to stay or accompany him and Jack.

They too decided to stay.

Something about this place appeared to unsettle them.

Baljit got out of the car and opened the back door. 'Out,' he said sternly to Jack.

Jack did as asked, stepping out on to a dirt track. A suffocating humidity wrapped itself around his body. His breathing became heavy and laboured.

'Do I need to draw my weapon?' asked Baljit, putting his hand on his sword.

Jack glanced around at the desolation of the area. Empty buildings sat here and there on vast expanses of dead earth with no touch of greenery to be seen. The only sign of life appeared to be the proud flapping of giant flags in the Khalsa orange in every direction.

'What is this place?' asked Jack.

Baljit's hand was still on his sword. Jack nodded towards it.

'If I'm not in any danger, then neither are you.'

Baljit thought for a moment, then let his hand fall. 'This is where your kismet is revealed to you, Jatinder Baxi.'

He emphasized the name 'Baxi', and pointed to a plot of land adjacent to a large decaying building. 'Over there.'

Baljit waited until Jack started moving and kept a few paces behind him.

Jack went through an open gate into a graveyard. He paused. There were roughly a hundred graves.

A sense of déjà vu hit him, like he was reliving a dream.

In the centre, by the largest grave, was a small figure in a wheelchair. Beside him stood the unmistakable figure of Detective Singh, dressed in the blue uniform of the Khalsa and wearing an orange turban. He drew his sword from his waist and it glimmered in the darkness.

Baljit shoved Jack forward. 'Over there.'

Jack's mouth was parched and his head felt heavy, as if he'd received another blow. He kept moving but his footsteps were shorter, heavier. The graves he passed were all those of women, the name 'Kaur' on every one.

More déjà vu.

Kaur was a middle name given to Sikh girls when they were born, just as Singh was to males.

Jack stopped short of Detective Singh and the wheelchair-bound figure, who was cloaked from head to toe in orange fabric printed all over with the emblem of the Khalsa. Jack felt no danger, just an overwhelming sense of loss and a feeling of some sort of history he was yet to understand.

'Look,' said the figure in the wheelchair to Jack.

Jack looked at the gravestone and read the inscription.

'Tanveer Singh Baxi, died 15 August 1947. Founder of the Shere-Punjab and protector of our women.'

And now everything came screaming back to Jack.

He had been here before.

The visions hit him hard and he doubled over, dropping to one knee.

Standing here with his father, Jack only a child, and placing a bunch of orange flowers on the grave. His father weeping. Whispers of prayer and promises to continue a legacy.

For the first time since meeting Detective Singh, Jack knew exactly why he was here.

SIXTY-SEVEN

THEY HAD ARRIVED IN a large decaying hall next to the grave-yard. Rows of dusty, rotten pews lay before a grand staging area.

Once again, the orange flags of the Khalsa were scattered around the space.

Jack slumped on to a pew and put his head in his hands. The man in the electric wheelchair came to rest at his side. Detective Singh stood a little distance away, while Baljit appeared to have returned to his vehicle.

'My name is Sahib. I am the person you have been seeking.'

His voice was gravelly and had a shakiness to it, and while he had a strong Indian accent, his English was enunciated perfectly. Jack couldn't see his face, hidden by his orange cloak. With gloves on his hands, he was an unnerving sight, with not an inch of his skin on show.

'You are in no danger in this place, Jatinder. It is important you know this.'

'Who are you?' said Jack.

'I am the head of the Shere-Punjab. You must have heard of us?'

Jack now recalled his father mentioning the organization.

'They're a myth,' he replied.

'Hmm. When you consider all that has happened to you and listen to what I have to say, I am certain you will change your mind.'

'Even if they exist and you are their leader, what business is that of mine? I'm not part of your group,' said Jack bitterly.

'That is where the first problem arose. You were supposed to inherit your grandfather's legacy, passed down to your father Sandeep. The grave outside says it all. This is your bloodline.'

Jack nodded. Visions of seeing that grave with his father once more flickered across his mind.

'Tanveer Singh Baxi was your grandfather. When you were a child, your father told you the story but perhaps not in its entirety.'

'I know the name but have no memory of the story behind it,' Jack said.

'Listen carefully and you will understand.'

India was partitioned in 1947. Sahib spoke bitterly of the process – of how the British had left with a single day's notice, without having any idea of how partition would be handled. It was left in the hands of the Indians and those who became the Pakistanis. Fear was rife. As soon as the precise location of the border was known, the largest migration of people took place that the world had ever seen. Fifteen million people crossed the border, trying to find safety in a land they thought would accommodate them. Muslims fled to Pakistan, Hindus and Sikhs to India.

'At that time, most of Punjab had Muslim majorities, except for Amritsar, which was predominantly Sikh,' said Sahib. 'We had argued for years for an independent state of Khalistan but the British did not listen. India refused to acknowledge a separate Khalsa state.'

'I know all this,' replied Jack. 'What does this have to do with me?'

'You never did have any patience – your father used to tell me.'

Jack didn't like how familiarly Sahib spoke about his father, as if he had known him better than Jack had.

'On the fifteenth of August, when Pakistan was created, your grandfather and I were living here, in this village. We are on the border, Jatinder, very close to Wagah. You could say that we are now standing in a land which officially belongs to Pakistan but, after what happened in this hall, was never claimed. This is no-man's-land now, but for us it is sacred, which is why we guard it heavily. Back in 1947, we had hoped to keep our land and live peacefully with the Pakistanis.'

Sahib paused. The silence stretched out for almost a minute.

'While your grandfather died in this hall, my own fate was less kind.'

Sahib slowly drew back the veil from across his face.

Jack stopped breathing, momentarily stunned and afraid.

'Sahib, you do not need to show him,' said Detective Singh, his voice pained.

'I do,' replied Sahib quietly.

Jack found it impossible to guess his age but Sahib was old and decaying. His face was missing – that was the only way Jack could describe it. The skin was horrifically scarred.

Sahib replaced the veil.

'On the day when blood flowed through this hall deep enough to bathe in, I was spared my life. The Muslims who—'

He was cut short by Detective Singh, who firmly but kindly told Sahib that he did not need to tell Jack a history he did not respect. Sahib dismissed the objection and continued.

'I was covered in petrol and set on fire. Not to die, but as a reminder of these times – a warning that would be spoken of for decades. After several minutes of my skin melting from my body, they rolled me in blankets to put out the flames and then ensured I made it to hospital. I often wonder if I should have died but perhaps God had greater plans for me. The Muslims who did this to me wanted me to live as a reminder of the true horrors partition resulted in. I left hospital almost one year after being admitted. And that day, I became a symbol – an icon if you will – for the Shere-Punjab. Never will we allow those times and those deaths to be repeated or forgotten.

'Your father was six months old. His mother, your grand-mother, managed to escape the massacre and was smuggled into India, where he was raised by the Khalsa.'

Detective Singh came across to Sahib, removed a bottle of water from his pocket, inserted a straw into it and handed it to Sahib. From underneath the cloak, the old man took the water. He took his time drinking. Singh turned to Jack, irritation across his face.

'The fact that he showed you his face is an honour. Under-stand that.'

Sahib handed the water back, composed himself and con-tinued.

'It is important to understand, as I do now, Jatinder, that Hindus and Sikhs murdered Muslims just as the Muslims mur-dered us. Panic took hold of people. Neighbours turned their swords on each other. Hysteria and violence scattered so much blood on our land.' Sahib was clearly struggling. 'This is not easy, Jatinder. Please, I need a moment.'

A voice from the shadows took over. A female voice, speaking in Punjabi. 'I will tell the next part,' she said.

Jack recognized it instantly and the hairs on his neck stood on end.

It couldn't be.

Sahib remained motionless as the woman emerged from the shadows and came to rest in front of Jack. He wanted to stand up but didn't trust his legs not to buckle.

Jack was looking at a woman he hadn't seen in twenty years. *His mother.*

SIXTY-EIGHT

JACK'S MOTHER OFFERED HIM no comfort.

There was no maternal instinct to embrace him. Her eyes were frozen, mere cubes of ice where once there had been life. She had aged badly and was painfully thin with thick wrinkles across her face.

She took a seat on a bench opposite Jack, her hair covered with an orange Khalsa veil.

She spoke to him, heartlessly, abruptly, in Punjabi.

'I may be your mother, but first and foremost, I am a Khalsa wife. Listen. Try and understand – if you are able.'

Jack recalled their last meeting, the arguments about Jack's immoral ways of living and how he had disgraced her, forcing her to move back to the land of her birth. Now it appeared there had been an altogether different reason. It all slotted into place now – the timing of her departure so soon after Kirin's death.

She looked him straight in the eye and continued Sahib's story.

When the border line was drawn, a huge part of Punjab became

Pakistani territory. Sikh women were the worst to suffer. The Muslims came for them – to rape the ones they desired, convert others and murder the ones they could not turn.

'Your grandfather, Tanveer Singh Baxi, gathered all the women of this village into this very hall we are now inside, while the men tried to defend their land. But our men were heavily outnumbered and every man in the village died.'

She pointed at Jack angrily, her face flushing. 'Your grandfather, Tanveer, had no choice!' She paused, gathered herself and said, 'He killed all the women before the Muslims broke in.'

Another pause.

'And he started with his eleven-year-old daughter.'

Jack's mother leaned forward and dropped a knife on the floor. It clanged on the concrete.

'Look at me, Jatinder.' She pointed to the knife. 'Pick it up and cut off my head. Can you do it?'

Jack didn't reply.

'When Tanveer's daughter was dead, do you know what the women in this room did?'

Jack was shaking. He wasn't sure if it was with anger or in shock.

'They started to scream – not out of fear but to go next! To die honourably at the hands of their brother.'

'Stop,' whispered Jack.

'You find this painful?' she said mockingly. 'Eighty-six women died at the hands of a Khalsa sword and it was their privilege! And you? Grandson of one of the most revered Sikh warriors of our time. Which path do you take? Brokering black market deals with Muslims. Taking them as your brothers! *Losing your wife to them.* Serving time in prison – protecting the very filth your grandfather died fighting. You shatter his memory and that of your father.'

Jack opened his mouth to speak but she silenced him with her hand.

She continued, almost spitting her words out. 'Do you think the blood stopped in 1947? For twenty years the Khalsa lost their brothers. We protected this sacred land. Honoured our heritage. Your father was one of the greatest Khalsa that has ever stepped foot in the Golden Temple. He died defending it.

'He wanted the same commitment from you. He taught you everything you needed to surpass him. But you lost yourself in the West, with women, alcohol and money. I am glad he never saw what you became. You have failed your heritage. Your bloodline. *Yourself.*'

Each brutal blow took Jack further into a pit of shame. He felt the air thin and gasped for breath.

Sahib manoeuvred his wheelchair to Jack's side. Detective Singh followed quietly.

Sahib handed Jack an old black-and-white photograph. 'Remember?' The image was of Jack and his father, outside the Golden Temple. Jack had been only six.

'That is me, in the wheelchair next to you,' continued Sahib.

Jack handed it back to Sahib before it could be ruined by his tears. He shook his head.

'It becomes harder the more you listen. Shall I continue?' said Sahib.

Jack nodded but kept his head bowed.

'Kirin came to your mother the night before she vanished. She was lost, broken and needed counsel. She told her she was pregnant with your children but that she had also become embroiled in a complex relationship with the Muslims you saw as your friends. She was afraid. She told your mother of a child she had conceived while you were in prison. We tried hard to get Kirin to move to India with your mother when you went to jail, and on reflection we should have forced the issue, but none of us could have foreseen what choices she would make.'

Sahib paused for breath.

Jack's head was spinning; he felt more alone than ever before.

Sahib finished by telling Jack that his mother had heard Kirin book a taxi and then call for Habib to collect her by the canal. Seeing their chance, his mother had organized for Detective Singh to intercept Kirin.

The rest Jack now knew.

'Why didn't you tell me?' he whispered, drained of all energy. 'She was my *wife*.'

'You were lost to an existence of money and deceit, long ago disregarding the Khalsa way of life. Kirin was mother to a daughter she had left behind – trying to lead a dual life with you. We were forced to realign the fate of your sons.'

'What if they weren't actually my sons?' asked Jack. 'She was having an affair.'

'We tested their blood when they were born. We too had this fear. But they are your sons. Good strong Khalsa boys. They will continue a legacy you could not.'

Jack raised his head and stared out into the dark void where Sahib's face should have been. 'How could you do all this?'

'The Shere-Punjab has no boundaries. In every country in the world there are Khalsa working quietly in the shadows. When we require their help, it is given without question. Banks, border security, immigration, hospitals, crematoriums. *Every-where.*'

'I don't believe you're that powerful,' said Jack.

'There is nowhere the Shere-Punjab cannot reach.'

'But Kirin – me – we meant nothing to you?'

'This is where you fail yourself. Your grandfather brought great power to our cause. He made the ultimate sacrifice. He led by example. The bravest of the brave.'

'In Bradford. You tried to kill me?' said Jack, glancing at the silhouette of Singh by his side.

Sahib's breathing became heavy. He didn't answer.

'I told them to do it,' said his mother.

This hurt Jack so deeply he felt the air being knocked out of his lungs.

'But you're my mother,' he whispered.

'I died for you many years ago, as you did for me. I didn't want you to know the truth and make trouble for the Khalsa.'

'Trouble?' said Jack.

Sahib cleared his throat. 'Kirin should have died after giving birth. But one of our men – the one who brought you here, Baljit – could not bring himself to kill her. Kirin was also from a proud bloodline, but like you, or perhaps because of you, she too became embroiled in the ways of the West and sacrificed her heritage. Baljit knew her family well. He was weak and out-sourced it to this parasite Thakur, a man we knew, who betrayed us. It is a scar we have to live with but it was never intended this way. She should have died cleanly at the sword of a Khalsa.'

'You people are unbelievable. You talk about death like it's a matter of course.'

Sahib was unrepentant. 'Look around you. If you dig the soil of our land deeply enough it will be red with blood. We do what is necessary to protect our legacy. Nothing more. Every religion has its protectors. The Shere-Punjab are whispers in the night. We do not scream and shout from the rooftops like many other religious organizations. We take care of our business covertly.'

'And what about Benedict Cave?'

'Every war has its casualties. He would not let it go.'

'And Aisha? She was just a girl,' said Jack, his voice pained.

Sahib didn't reply. The room suffered an uncomfortable silence.

'What now?' said Jack.

'That is your choice,' replied Sahib.

'Meaning?'

'It was your kismet to arrive here. Your grandfather died in this very hall. Your father died close by in our sacred temple. It is not by chance that you are sitting before us, broken and bitter. Do you know what Amrit Sanskar is?'

Jack nodded.

'Listen to me, my son,' said Sahib, putting a gloved hand on Jack's knee, 'the Amrit Sanskar ceremony is not beyond you. Your blood is that which lions have shared. To lose oneself in life is common – but to *find* oneself again is rare. Amrit Sanskar is the first step for men to one day become Khalsa. Go to the Golden Temple and enter the sacred pool. Wash yourself. Rid your body and mind of their sins. When you emerge, you will be a newly baptized Sikh. You will be able to join your sons as they learn how to absorb the Khalsa into their lives.'

'I cannot live with you people,' said Jack.

' "I" is not what is important. "I" is nothing. We are a community in which there is no "I". Enter the pool. Listen to the Granthis. Visit the Guru Granth Sahib,' said Sahib.

'And if I don't?'

'You can return to England whenever you choose.'

'I want my sons with me.'

'That is not possible.'

'I could force your hand,' said Jack. 'Go to the Home Office.'

Sahib sighed. 'You are not listening, Jatinder. There is no organization we do not influence – especially in India. You would not make it very far.'

'Do my sons know I'm alive?'

'No,' replied Sahib. 'They know nothing. And they cannot know. They are trained, dedicated disciples of the Golden Temple. They know nothing except the way of the Khalsa.'

Jack got to his feet. 'I give you my word. Let me look at them once before I leave. After all I've been through, it is my right to see my sons once before I decide what my future holds,' he said.

Sahib's silence was broken by Detective Singh.

'Sahib? If I may?'

The old man nodded.

'Let him see them. If it does not persuade him to start a new life, then nothing will.'

Jack was surprised. He looked in puzzlement at Singh.

Sahib's voice was gentle and measured. 'Jallianwala Bagh, next to the Golden Temple – you are familiar with its history?'

Jack nodded. In 1919, the Jallianwala Bagh massacre had taken place when Acting Brigadier-General Reginald Dyer, now known as the Butcher of Amritsar, had ordered troops of the British Indian Army to fire their weapons into a crowd of unarmed Indian civilians. Almost four hundred people had died and many more had been grievously wounded.

'They are closing up the gardens there. We will take you to them, Jatinder, but only after you cleanse yourself and enter the sacred pool of our Golden Temple.'

The doors to the hall flung open and Baljit entered, dragging someone behind him.

Baljit threw the boy on to the floor near Jack and pointed the tip of his sword at him. Cruise appeared unharmed, if terrified. He raised his hands and turned to Jack in desperation.

'Mr Jack, sir! I am just following to see that you are being OK,' he said.

SIXTY-NINE

CRUISE WAS DRIVING JACK to the Golden Temple. Sahib and the others had remained in the ghost town and arranged to meet Jack in a couple of hours once he had immersed himself in the sacred pool. It was an act he felt forced to undertake, yet deep down, some part of him welcomed the opportunity to potentially start over. His bitterness at what had transpired with Kirin, his mother and the Shere-Punjab was in no way diminished, but Jack had to put his mind in a place where there was hope and an opportunity to live the rest of his life with his sons.

What else did he have?

Cruise had not spoken since they had set off.

Jack could tell there was something troubling him. There were so many questions to which Cruise would need an answer. Yet when he pulled over into a layby, turned off the ignition and broke the silence, he floored Jack with the one piece of information Jack had concealed from him.

'I am phoning Sister's hospital, Mr Jack. I am knowing that you lied to me.'

Jack couldn't look the boy in the eye. The shame was crippling.

'I didn't want you to find out like this,' said Jack quietly.

'Why you are not telling me?'

'I didn't want you to be hurt.'

'You are meaning you are needing me to keep driving?'

Jack looked at him in alarm. 'No, you must know that is not the reason.'

'I am taking you to the Golden Temple. Then I am leaving. This is not for me any more.'

'Cruise, look—'

The boy restarted the engine, turned the radio on loud and pulled the four-by-four aggressively back on to the road. The statues of the Hindu gods again fell to the floor. This time, Cruise left them where they were.

The route to the Golden Temple took them past Gandhi Gate, a towering red stone arch with a clock on top of it. Jack glanced at the time.

Almost eight p.m.

The temple was open twenty-four hours a day but busiest during evening worship.

As they grew closer, the roads became even more densely clogged, with traffic travelling bumper to bumper. Crowds surged alongside, drawn towards the temple by the mesmerizing chant of prayers, relayed far and wide by loudspeakers.

Orange flags on the top of every building fluttered in the blustering wind, bearing the Sikh religious symbol of a circle and three swords. They were the flags of Khalistan, a movement that called for Sikhs to have their own land, independent of India or Pakistan.

Cruise parked carelessly on the street and they now went on foot. The sky was dark and the wind whipped through the streets. Heavy rain was on the way; you could feel the moisture in the atmosphere. Cruise was a few metres ahead and stuck an arm out to indicate a sign on his left: Jallianwala Bagh, the site of the massacre Sahib had spoken of and, unbeknownst to Cruise, the place Jack's sons were. Jack felt pulled towards it, desperate to see them, but resisted the temptation. For now, he had to obey the rules Sahib had set.

The Golden Temple rose to their right, its magnificent domes dominating the skyline, with orange Khalistan flags flapping in the wind. It was a mesmerizing sight – a white marble building constructed around four sides of a vast square. The increase in security here was immediately apparent, with armed guards patrolling the area.

Jack followed Cruise up a flight of steps to an outbuilding that stored visitors' shoes, which had to be removed prior to entering the holy site.

They walked on a withered brown carpet up to the entrance of the temple. On either side stood blue corrugated sheets of metal, acting as barriers.

A brilliant blaze of lightning lit up the skyline and the first droplets began to fall.

The entrance to the temple now lay directly in front of Jack. He rolled up his trousers and waded through a shallow pool of water, which cleansed worshippers' feet before they entered the outer quadrant of the temple.

Jack walked down a flight of steps, with images of himself as a child following this exact route now flashing into his mind. Thick marble pillars to each side were covered with plaques, commemorating Sikhs who had donated money to the temple or sacrificed themselves in wartime. Jack stopped dead when he saw a large central panel in the centre of the wall. It bore his father's name and the year of his death in 1984 – during Operation Blue Star. Jack swallowed a lump in his throat. He ran his hand over the panel, and then moved hurriedly away to enter the main square of the temple.

The central building, the golden sanctum, lay at the centre of a large lake. The only access to it was by a single marble path along which worshippers were queueing to pay their respects to the Sikh holy book, the Guru Granth Sahib.

Sikh guards, the Khalsa, marched past Jack, displaying their swords at their waists.

His father's voice rang out in Jack's head:

One day, Jatinder, you too will become one of the Khalsa.

A gigantic plasma screen in the far corner of the complex displayed a bold message:

There is but one God. True is His Name. By the True Guru's favour, he is attained.

There was a compelling sense of peace inside the complex with the continual chanting of the holy scripture by the Granthis. A sweet scent of halva, a rich dessert made from ghee butter, sugar, almonds and sultanas which was offered to all worshippers, made Jack's mouth water.

Cruise joined Jack by the edge of the sacred pool.

'It is hypnotic, isn't it, Mr Jack?' he whispered. 'The sound of the *shabda*. You are knowing what this word means?'

'Cruise, I was born into this religion. These hymns are the soundtrack of my youth.'

Jack was surprised that Cruise had come over to speak with him now that he knew about Aisha. For a moment the two of them just looked at one another.

'In this sacred place, Mr Jack, there can be no tension between us.'

Jack smiled and looked around the temple, feeling an unfamiliar sense of peace.

*

The enchanting sound of the prayers filled their silence. Jack watched as men stripped down to their underwear and entered the pool, many of them crying, overwhelmed at undertaking the sacred Amrit Sanskar.

'About Aisha—' started Jack.

'Leave it, Mr Jack. Please.'

Jack put his hand on the boy's shoulder. 'I am sorry. I need to say that.'

'Sister was not deserving this,' whispered Cruise.

'I know.'

'I am not being able to pay my final respects. This is what is upsetting me, Mr Jack. You were being able to say goodbye.'

'I'm so sorry about that, Cruise. But Aisha wanted the truth and that is what we are here for.'

'Did you arrange someone to collect her body?'

Jack thought of his call to Habib and how that all had turned out. 'Of course. I would never have left her alone like that. *Never.*'

'I am entering the temple, Mr Jack. I will pray for her soul when we are inside.'

'Of course.'

'You will be joining me?'

Jack touched the *rakhi* on his arm. Then he looked at the pool. 'We'll see,' he replied, and watched his friend leave.

Jack closed his eyes and for a while simply listened to the Granthis chanting. He imagined his father standing where he was and felt a deep sense of loss and disappointment that he had not followed a path set for him so many years before.

His sons were close by and Sahib had been insistent that he would not allow Jack to meet them without cleansing himself in the sacred pool.

Jack opened his eyes, slowly stripped to his underwear and then, like so many before him, entered the pool and immersed his entire body.

SEVENTY

HAVING DRIED OFF AND put his clothes back on, Jack saw Sahib and Singh waiting for him at the far corner of the complex. People were getting down on their hands and knees and seemed to be worshipping Sahib.

Cruise made his way over to Jack, eating halva, and offered him some.

'No thanks,' said Jack, continuing to observe the hysteria around Sahib. Cruise noticed it too and finally asked the one question of Jack that still remained.

'Who are these people and what is this all about, Mr Jack?'

Jack thought and then finally said, 'Have you heard of the Shere-Punjab?'

Cruise nodded. 'Lions of the Punjab. They are being a legend – urban myth.'

Jack looked at Cruise and with the sound of the Granthis echoing around the temple, the two men held each other's gaze until Cruise's jaw dropped.

'This is being the work of the Shere-Punjab?' whispered Cruise.

Jack nodded. 'Nothing mythical about them.'

'And you are not being in any more danger?'

'Only if I put myself in it.'

'Meaning?'

'We are going to see my sons. They are closing up Jallianwala Bagh.'

'This is being miraculous development,' said Cruise, and stuffed the rest of the halva into his mouth.

'You can leave now, Cruise. You've done enough for me.'

'No, Mr Jack, I am going upstairs and having langar.'

Langar was the food the temple distributed to worshippers free of charge every evening.

'I am taking my meal and you are meeting me back here when you are finishing?' said Cruise.

Jack nodded.

'Are you being OK, Mr Jack?'

'I can't think straight, Cruise. I'm about to meet my sons off the back of so much death. I should be excited and yet I feel lost inside.'

Cruise pointed towards the temple. 'When I am inside, saying a prayer for Sister, I am realizing one thing' – he stared solemnly at Jack – 'you must end this bloodshed tonight, Mr Jack. No more can be spilled.'

Detective Singh walked by the side of Sahib's wheelchair, with Jack a few paces in front. They exited the Golden Temple and waited for Jack to retrieve his shoes.

Jack felt dirty, being escorted by the men inadvertently responsible for Aisha's death. He was also deeply bitter at his mother's betrayal, at how easily she had disowned him when his life had taken, as she had put it, an immoral path. It seemed that unconditional love was not something Jack's mother believed in.

En route to the Bagh, Jack thought about his ancestry.

Steeped in honour.

An honour he had not adhered to.

Was he ultimately to blame for all of this?

His head was pounding at the accusations swirling through his mind and he found himself fidgeting with the *rakhi* around his wrist, still stiff with Aisha's blood.

They paused outside Jallianwala Bagh. A row of shops ran parallel to the entrance. The closest one, Chocolate Planet, was still open and a few tourists were enjoying a late evening snack.

Detective Singh turned towards Jack. 'In Bradford,' he said, taking Jack by the arm and leading him forcefully away from Sahib, 'what I did at your shop – that was my job.'

'Do you enjoy all your "jobs" this much?' said Jack, shrugging his arm free. The bastard had tried to kill him and Jack wasn't in a forgiving mood.

'I don't entertain the luxury of conscience,' replied Singh. 'I am given orders. I follow them.'

'Your point being?' said Jack.

'When we step inside, I ask you not to force my hand.'

'Meaning?'

Singh just looked at him.

'They are *my* sons. Not yours,' said Jack.

'We are all Khalsa sons. First and foremost.'

'Do you have children?'

Singh nodded.

'Put yourself in my shoes.'

'I cannot. It is abhorrent to me how you have lived your life, especially with such revered ancestry.'

'I just want to see my sons,' said Jack, tired of all of this. Something was bothering him but he couldn't put his finger on it.

'And you will see them,' replied Singh. 'But let me be clear:

this is our land, our way of life. If you cause trouble here, in this sacred land – there will be no second chances.' He tapped his sword.

'Are you finished?' said Jack.

Singh nodded.

'I'm ready to see my sons.'

The courtyard outside the entrance had a sign written in Punjabi and English. Jallianwala Bagh was a massacre involving the unlawful killing of local men and women. Two thousand of them had gathered in the beautiful grounds to demonstrate peacefully against the British Raj. A plaque described how one thousand six hundred and fifty rounds of ammunition had been fired by General Dyer and his men, lasting almost twenty minutes. The official death toll was 379, with over 1,200 injured, but the real number was thought to be much higher. The Brigadier-General had been acting under orders, with the British wanting to stamp their authority across the region during a period of unrest and send a message that they were not to be crossed. Ultimately, however, the event turned public opinion against the British and may have helped lead towards Indian independence.

Sahib turned off the power to his wheelchair. He stood up slowly, arthritically. Singh handed him a walking stick. They would be on foot from here on.

The darkening sky threatened more rain, the atmosphere heavy with moisture. Behind them continued the sound of the Granthis, booming the Guru Granth Sahib around Amritsar.

They walked slowly through the doors of the Bagh, down a narrow path. A sign said 'Historical Lane'. It was where people had fled when the firing began. Bullet holes were still visible in the walls. Jack felt a lump in his throat.

The end of the path led through to an exquisite garden, deserted except for a few birds pecking for food. Powerful spotlights lit up a central path with colourful flowers in full bloom to either side.

In the middle of the gardens was a large well, the Martyrs Well, where one hundred and twenty people had died, throwing themselves in to escape the bullets.

Jack walked slowly behind Sahib, scouring the area for any sign of his sons. Unease was spreading through his body.

He had seen something outside.

When Singh had been talking to him.

Jack hadn't registered it at the time. But now, in the serenity of the gardens, the hazy image started to clear.

'There,' said Singh suddenly, pointing towards the end of the path.

Jack stopped dead.

Two broad-shouldered boys, dressed in the blue and orange outfits of the Khalsa, were walking slowly towards them, their swords shimmering on their waists in the darkness.

'You're to say nothing to them about who you are,' said Singh, turning to Jack with a threatening stare. 'Please,' he added, trying to defuse the hostility. 'This is not the time or place for confrontations, especially on these sacred grounds.'

Jack heard the words but wasn't really listening.

How had he missed it?

Those tourists in Chocolate Planet – one of them had looked strangely familiar.

Sara.

Jack spun round to see the menacing approach of Habib Iqbal, with Sara a few steps behind.

Habib raised his arm, pointing a gun directly at Jack.

SEVENTY-ONE

SINGH DREW HIS SWORD and Jack's sons came charging down the path towards them. The heavens, expectant with rain, finally surrendered. Heavy drops of water began thudding at their feet.

'Who are you?' said Singh, pointing his blade at the hostile visitors.

'Put your swords down,' said Habib, waving his gun at them. He was accompanied by another man, who was unarmed. Jack remembered him from his awkward visit to Habib's home with Aisha – he was Habib's chief bodyguard. Sara was standing behind both men, looking coldly at Jack.

'That is not possible,' replied Sahib calmly, 'not while you are armed.'

'Jallianwala Bagh. You couldn't have picked a better place to end your life, Jack,' spat Habib angrily. 'She was just a child. Twenty-one – and you took her from me, you bastard!'

His hand was shaking with anger.

'Who are you?' asked Sahib.

Singh was sizing up the men. Jack's sons hadn't spoken, just

326

surrounded Sahib protectively, their swords primed, waiting for someone to move. Jack could see them out of the corner of his eye but lacked the courage to turn round and face them. It seemed easier to focus on Habib.

And the gun.

'My name is Habib Iqbal. And I am here to kill this man,' he said, pointing the gun at Jack.

He doesn't realize they're my sons.

'Habib Iqbal,' replied Sahib slowly. 'The girl's father?'

He nodded. 'Are these the guys, Jack? The ones responsible?'

'Habib – put the gun down. I can explain,' Jack replied.

'Losing Aisha is something I will have to live with,' said Habib. 'Allowing you to live is a different matter. The only question is: do I take these other bastards with me?'

'That won't be possible,' said Sahib. 'You have but one pistol. There are three soldiers here with swords. While you might kill one of us, perhaps two, the third one will cut off your head.'

'Baxi,' hissed Habib, 'he's the one I came for. The rest of you can leave.'

'This man is working towards a new way of life. His family is tied to this city. We will not allow what you propose.'

Habib's bodyguard looked nervous, as if he hadn't signed up for this. He looked far from competent to deal with the situation.

Sara was stony-faced. She looked ghostly, shrouded in a black headscarf. Jack tried to catch her eye but she refused to look at him.

Habib retreated a few paces, out of reach of the swords. Singh wasn't stupid. He moved with him, keeping him in range.

'Don't,' said Habib.

'If you shoot, it'll be the only bullet you fire,' said Singh. Jack's sons moved from his periphery to stand side by side with Singh. They moved as a trio towards Habib. Closing off the space.

'Stop!' said Habib, panic in his voice. He fired a shot in the air, over Singh's head. 'The next one will kill you,' he threatened.

Sahib stepped forward, his whole body, as ever, covered by an orange veil. 'I know who you are,' he said softly.

'Then you know why I'm here. This man killed my daughter. I will not rest until his blood is pooling at my feet.'

'You blame this man for your loss?' asked Sahib.

Habib nodded and turned the gun back on Jack. His finger was tense on the trigger.

'You are standing in the land of warriors,' replied Sahib. 'We do not interfere with fair combat. You have a grievance. It will be settled.' Sahib now stepped in front of Jack.

'I offer you both a sword. Settle your dispute, man to man. Anyone can pull a trigger,' he said, almost goading Habib.

'I don't believe you.'

Sahib stepped closer still. Jack could tell Singh didn't like it. The old man was at Habib's mercy but didn't seem at all concerned. 'Give your wife this weapon, as insurance. In a fair fight there will be no interference. It is not our way. You have my *kasam*,' said Sahib.

'He's too afraid,' said Jack, seeing an opportunity to remove the power from Habib. Whether Sara could ever pull the trigger was an unknown. Habib, though, would have no problem in doing so.

Habib's eyes sharpened. His ego began to stir.

'If you pull that trigger, you will most certainly die,' continued Sahib. 'When you fire, the bullet will kill Jack but there are three armed Khalsa here and before your finger can pull the trigger again, your head will be on the ground. This fact is undeniable. This way, the better man will emerge victorious and should that be you, it is something we shall have to make our peace with. We do not retaliate if the combat is fair.'

'Throw down one of the swords,' said Habib.

Sahib spoke softly to one of Jack's sons.

'No,' said Singh. 'Take mine.'

He waited for Habib to hand the gun to Sara, then lowered his sword, turned it round and held it out by the handle to Habib.

One of Jack's sons turned to Jack and offered his sword. As Jack took it from him, for the first time, he came face to face with his own bloodline.

Please do not spoil this sacred place.

That was the request on the sign hanging from one of the trees.

Ironic, thought Jack, as he moved cautiously towards Habib, his sword pointing at his head.

The two camps were standing on opposite sides of the grass. Sara was holding the gun, pointing it at Jack.

He thought about what Sahib had said – about his father and his grandfather.

About his heritage.

His bloodline.

Shere-Punjab.

Lions of the Punjab.

Jack's eyes narrowed and he gripped the sword confidently. He'd been taught how to use it as a child and, while he hadn't held one for decades, it didn't feel alien in his hands.

He glanced at the *rakhi* on his wrist and thought of Aisha.

Was he really about to make amends for her death by trying to take her father's life?

'Do you remember back in Bradford, Habib, how I told you the next time I got my hands on you, I'd kill you?' Jack said.

'I remember,' said Habib, twisting the sword nervously in his hand.

'I meant it, and yet now, after all I've been through, and with your daughter's voice firmly in my mind, I don't wish for your blood also to be on my hands.'

Jack lowered his sword.

Singh and Sahib were standing a few feet away, watching as Jack let his arm fall.

'What is he doing?' whispered Singh.

Sahib took a moment and then said, 'It is not our fight any more.'

'We cannot allow a Baxi's blood to be spilled in this Bagh – and by a Muslim, no less,' hissed Singh.

Sahib turned his head towards Singh. Rainwater dripped steadily from his hood on to the ground.

'Have faith: on this land, at this hour, he will not lose this fight. Trust me. Something tells me there is a hand yet to be played.'

With his sword by his side, Jack took the heat out of his voice. 'One hundred years ago, nearly four hundred people died in these grounds when an egotistical prick let the power go to his head. And now here we stand, about to add to that list? For what – revenge? Honour?'

'All that and more,' said Habib.

Jack pointed his blade at Habib. 'You want to know who's to blame? Maybe it's you, Habib, for taking to bed a woman you said you'd look after like a sister. Maybe we start there, with that.'

Jack saw that his comment had hit home. Habib's gaze dropped.

'Or maybe I'm to blame for letting all that money we were making go to our heads. For embracing an impure way of life rather than taking a better road. We both knew what we were doing back then. So, is this our penance? I've lost my wife and everything I own and now, with nothing to lose, I stand here before you, ready to defend the only thing I have left, my life.'

'You . . . you took my daughter from me,' said Habib.

Jack shook his head. 'I did not kill Aisha. She needed to know the truth about Kirin. I tried to get her to leave. There was nothing I could do to stop her. You must know that stubborn will of hers.'

His eyes were drawn once again to the *rakhi* on his wrist. He threw down his sword.

Habib looked at him, perplexed.

'Enough death for now.' Jack glanced again around the gardens. 'I won't defile this place with *our* dirty history. Your daughter, a girl who tied a *rakhi* on my wrist,' said Jack, raising his arm, 'would not want us to end it like this. No matter whose sword strikes the fatal blow, Habib, we are both losers in this story.'

Jack's words seemed to have struck a chord with Habib. He lowered his own sword and now, instead of the pure bitterness on his face, Jack saw pain and suffering – a father mourning for his lost child.

Habib threw his sword to the ground.

No sooner had he done so, then Sara stepped to the side of the two men and raised her weapon.

Without warning, she aimed and pulled the trigger.

SEVENTY-TWO

TIME SEEMED TO FREEZE as Habib's body thudded to the ground. Sara had shot him in the chest.

No one moved.

Jack stared at her, stunned. Sara fired another shot at Habib, this time in the back.

The man accompanying Sara came to her side, seeming as shocked as Jack. Then he took the gun from her, before taking her into his arms.

And only now did Jack understand what was happening.

History, it seemed, had returned to Habib, although this time he was on the receiving end of deceit.

'Sahib?' said Singh, aghast at the development. 'What new evil is this?'

Sahib spoke softly, but as if he had perhaps seen this coming. 'It would appear that Habib's kismet is darker than any of us realized.'

*

Sara walked towards Jack and motioned for him to stand aside.

Jack did so, unable to take his eyes off her. Gone was the submissive woman he had once known.

Sara stood in front of Habib, her face without expression or emotion.

Habib was gasping, dying in front of their eyes, his blood blossoming around his enormous body.

'This all started with your affair with Kirin, Habib. Tonight, it ends with my affair with your most trusted guard, Rehaan,' she said, nodding towards him. 'I'm done with your infidelity and powermongering. And in a country five thousand miles from home, there will be no one to uncover what happened here tonight.'

Habib's breathing became erratic. Bright red mouthfuls of blood spurted from his lips.

Finally he lay there in silence, his blood seeping into the soil.

Sara turned to Jack, her face icy in contrast to the darkness behind her. 'I was never a wife to him, Jack. I endured his presence and got used to living in wealth. When I saw you, it made me realize what I had become.' She pointed towards Habib. 'And now I can be whoever I want to be. The old Sara. Or a new one? I'm free of him at last.'

Jack had taken Sara to the building at the end of Jallianwala Bagh. The information centre was closed but the covered foyer sheltered them from the rain lashing the gardens.

Sara's voice was tired. Jack wasn't sure she realized yet the full extent of what she had done.

'How do we move forward from this?' said Jack.

'I'll go back to England,' she replied. She nodded towards the Sikh men dealing with Habib's body. 'I assume they'll take care of matters here?'

Jack nodded. 'I'll see to it.'

'I killed him. I finally did it,' she whispered. She said it almost nonchalantly but Jack saw that she had thought about it many times before.

'I . . . I'm sorry, Jack,' she said. Sara looked ghostly in the darkness and Jack wondered just how much she'd had to put up with as Habib's wife.

'Why did you stay with him?' he asked. 'We were friends – you could have come to me for help.'

She shook her head. 'I was afraid. Everyone was afraid of him. Tonight I . . . I saw my opportunity and I took it. No longer do I have to pretend I don't know of his affairs, and tolerate the way he sees people as nothing more than slaves to make him money. The world is a better place without Habib.'

'And now?' said Jack.

'I'm rich,' she said, looking at him. 'A widow who commands an empire worth millions. And I intend to spend the rest of my life living, instead of just existing.'

Jack watched his sons, obediently helping Singh to move Habib's body. He still hadn't met them properly, but observing them deal with the trauma so efficiently made him feel strangely proud. They possessed remarkable strength and character.

'Will you return to England?' she asked him hesitantly. Sara didn't want him to. Jack heard it in her voice. They needed to be as far from each other as possible. The distance would act like a sponge, soaking up the truth of what they had done.

'No,' he replied. 'There is nothing for me in Bradford any more. Seems my roots are here. Those are my sons,' he said, nodding towards the boys. 'I don't know if I can salvage anything but I have to try. I guess there's no better place to start over than here in the land I was born in.'

Sara put her hand on his arm. 'I hope you can start afresh, Jack, I really do.' She paused and added, 'You were always good to me.'

'What about Aisha?' he said. He touched the bloodstained *rakhi* on his wrist.

Sara sighed heavily. 'Her body's still at the hospital.'

'We need to organize a burial,' he replied.

She nodded.

'I'll help you with it.'

'I can manage—'

'No, I insist,' he said. 'Please. I need to make it right with her.'

'Do you think they can help us?' she said, nodding towards Sahib.

'I'm sure they will. Aisha deserves an honourable burial.'

'I need a driver, Jack. Someone trustworthy to get me back to her.'

Jack managed a tired smile. 'You're in luck. I just so happen to have the best driver in India nearby. Kind of crazy, but in a good way.'

'Are you sure I can trust him?'

'With your life,' he replied.

'Can you ever forgive what we did to you?' she asked him.

'I am far from blame-free, Sara. But tomorrow I will wake up without all these lies burdening me. I've heard so many secrets these past few days that I don't feel like my life has been my own.'

'I know how you feel,' she replied. 'When I saw you again after all these years, I wondered how this could all come so full circle.'

Jack took a moment to reply. He looked at Sahib, then at his sons. And with the soundtrack of the Granthis from the Golden Temple all around them, he simply said:

'It was our kismet, Sara. It was written to be this way.'

ACKNOWLEDGEMENTS

Thank you to my editor, Natasha Barsby, and to the incredible team at Transworld for continuing to support me. These thrillers are so tough to write and it's amazing to have such a talented team on my side.

To my agent, Simon Trewin, for always being on the end of a phone when I need him.

To my friends and relatives in India who were so helpful in making this book possible, especially Sandeep and Rajeev for guiding me through the complexities of Sadar Bazaar. They allowed me to creep into spaces I never knew existed and (somehow) emerge alive and with a notebook full of ideas!

To the Red Hot Chilli Writers – Ayisha Malik, Abir Mukherjee, Imran Mahmood, Vaseem Khan and Alex Khan. You're the most talented bunch of people I know and you all continue to motivate (and teach) me. I promise that one day, I will learn how to spell . . .

Many thanks to the brilliant team who work alongside me at the pharmacy, notably Gemma, who keeps me sane . . .

somehow . . . anyhow. To quote your favourite movie, *Rocky*: 'one more round . . .' And I keep telling you that, Gemma!

To my family. Gosh, I know I'm such a pain to be around when I'm writing – always absent and lost in my own little world. To my twin sister and my best friend: thank you for being there when I needed you the most – all the time, anytime. I doubt two other people could burn away as many hours as we do, often talking aimlessly to each other when it started off as a 'five-minute chat'.

Final thanks, as *always*, for my wife, Sam. I couldn't do this without you. I'm not sure how we ended up here with all these books, but I'm certain that you are the reason I keep sitting in the chair. You're my first reader – the one I write for, the one who always believes in everything I do. So I'll finish with the same words I use at the end of every book: keep doing what you do, it makes me do what I do.

ABOUT THE AUTHOR

A. A. Dhand was raised in Bradford and spent his youth observing the city from behind the counter of a small convenience store. After qualifying as a pharmacist, he worked in London and travelled extensively before returning to Bradford to start his own business and begin writing. The history, diversity and darkness of the city have inspired his critically acclaimed Harry Virdee novels. *The Blood Divide* is his first standalone thriller.

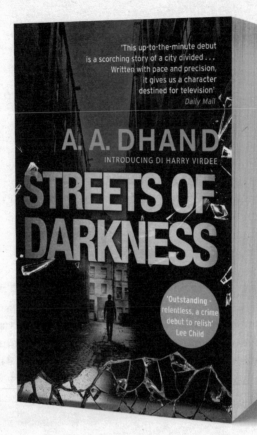

Enjoyed *The Blood Divide*?

Read *Streets of Darkness*, the first book
in the explosive Harry Virdee series

'Outstanding'
Lee Child

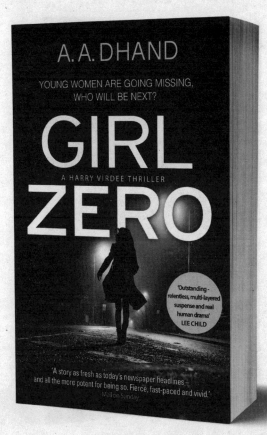

A. A. DHAND

YOUNG WOMEN ARE GOING MISSING,
WHO WILL BE NEXT?

GIRL
ZERO

A HARRY VIRDEE THRILLER

'Outstanding –
relentless, multi-layered
suspense and real
human drama'
LEE CHILD

'A story as fresh as today's newspaper headlines –
and all the more potent for being so. Fierce, fast-paced and vivid.'
Mail on Sunday

The second book in the gripping
Harry Virdee series

'Dhand is a fearless writer'
Sunday Times

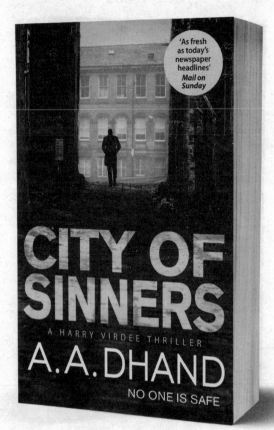

'As fresh as today's newspaper headlines'
Mail on Sunday

The third thriller in the action-packed
Harry Virdee series

**'As fresh as today's newspaper
headlines'**
Mail on Sunday

A.A.DHAND

A HARRY VIRDEE THRILLER

ONE
WAY
OUT

Read the fourth book in the high-stakes
Harry Virdee series

Shortlisted for the CWA Steel Dagger